IF

have

I

H

In a few seconds, he was out.

I flipped him over and pulled off his mask. I didn't recognize him, but that meant nothing. I spent most of my time alone with Lobo. The stars of the moment, the wealthy, the current heads of this or that government or multi-planet corporation—I didn't keep up with any of them, and I didn't care about them.

He was probably telling the truth as he knew it, but few people bother to carry through on such threats. Doing so is expensive and time-consuming. Of course, if he was as old and rich as he said, he might well be willing to spend the money to pay someone to track me down. The bigger concern was that he was interested in how I had healed. I could not let anyone know about the nanomachines in me.

My only alternative, though, was to kill him in cold blood. I've killed people, more than I care to remember, but almost always in combat and never when I could figure out a different solution. About five years ago, I had killed a man to keep my secret. The image of his body, decomposing as he slumped onto a desk and the nanomachine cloud literally disassembled him, still invaded my dreams from time to time. I didn't want any more such nightmares.

No, I wouldn't kill him. He was right about that. I'd do what I've done for years now: Finish the mission, then run somewhere far away and leave as few traces of my passage as I could.

Baen Books by Mark L. Van Name

One Jump Ahead
Slanted Jack
Jump Gate Twist (omnibus)
Overthrowing Heaven
Children No More
No Going Back

Transhuman, ed. with T.K.F. Weisskopf
The Wild Side, ed.
Onward, Drake!, ed.

To purchase Baen Book titles in e-book format,
please go to www.baen.com.

NO GOING BACK

BACK

MARK L. VAN NAME

A Baen Books Original

Baen Publishing Enterprises
P.O. Box 1403
Riverdale, NY 10471
www.baen.com

ISBN: 978-1-4767-8133-4

Cover art by John Picacio

First Baen paperback printing, February 2016

Distributed by Simon & Schuster
1230 Avenue of the Americas
New York, NY 10020

Pages by Joy Freeman (www.pagesbyjoy.com)
Printed in the United States of America

For Sarah and Scott,
the best kids in the world.

27 days from the end

*Center of the Great Southeastern Desert
Planet Studio*

CHAPTER 1

Jon Moore

JON, THIS IS a very bad plan."

"I'm a little busy here." The wind blasted my face as I fought with the sail on the sandsurfer. Sand smacked my goggles and slid off the protective coating. I pushed the board harder; I wanted all the speed it could manage. The high-powered electric fan slammed air into my back as it billowed the sail and shoved me across the black sand only moments ahead of the twilight that followed me like a cloaked assassin. The rush of speed filled me with both joy and adrenaline; the only way it could have been better would have been if I were riding at night.

I tuned into the machine frequency and listened to the sandsurfer's fan.

"Yee-haw!" it said. "Don't stop me now. I'd make this board fly if they'd let me!"

It felt the same way I did. I laughed for the joy of the ride, lost for a moment in the sensations.

"Which is why you should thank me," the stabilizers

in the board said, "for keeping us on the ground. We are *not* built for flight."

I tuned out before the two of them could crank up their argument. Machines are so obsessive about their work that none likes to give an inch to another, so they argue endlessly. I didn't want them to spoil my ride.

At the same time, as much as I was enjoying hurtling across the sand, I couldn't afford to surrender completely to its pleasures without risking falling off the meter-wide board and losing precious time.

I wouldn't let anything throw me off schedule. This mission was too important.

"I repeat," Lobo said, his voice clear and loud in my ear through the comm, "this is a very bad plan."

"If you have a better one, let me know. Otherwise, we're staying the course."

"Here's an idea," he said. "You turn off that stupid device, I fly down and pick you up, and we go do something that doesn't involve you dying."

"I don't plan to die."

"You never do, but that doesn't mean it can't happen. These are seriously powerful men, men way out of your league. You attack them, and they'll either kill you now or hunt you down later."

He was pissing me off, but I wasn't going to let him know that. Lobo may be the most intelligent machine in the universe, a super-powerful brain composed of nanocomputers distributed through all the molecules of a deadly Predator-class assault vehicle, but when he finds a way to needle you, he's as unrelenting as a three-year-old on a "why?" binge.

"Look on the bright side," I said. "If I die, you're free."

That did the trick. "First," he said, "I'm free now." Annoyance dripped from every single word he said. "I don't have to be here. I don't need a human owner to function. I stay with you because we're in it together." He paused. "As you bloody well know." Another pause. "Besides, having a human does make it easier to move around. The gate authorities generally won't authorize unpiloted machines to jump between planets."

"So let's make sure I don't die."

"You're two minutes from the shutdown point," Lobo said. "From then on, if I come for you fast, they'll hear me. That means our risk goes up, at least as long as you won't let me kill everyone on the ground. Let me pick you up now."

The offer tempted me a little, because I wasn't thrilled at the makeshift plan we'd concocted earlier today. Then I flashed on the expression on the face of Lydia Chang, the woman who'd asked me to find Tasson, her missing son. This kid had no other hope. I'd failed enough children, watched them die, unable to save them. No, there was no chance I was going to stop. I would not let those men get away with what they were planning. They'd come to Studio for a very sick private party, and I was going to crash it.

I stared at the horizon ahead of me. Studio's two small moons gleamed a faint white in the dying light. The air possessed that perfect clarity you see only on new worlds or on those so inhospitable that only the crazy and the outcast bothered to colonize them. Studio was the latter. The jump gate aperture to it had opened over a hundred and twenty years ago, and as we always do, humans had flooded in. After finding a planet composed of large, arid land masses and small, acidic seas, the vast majority of those initial settlers had fled almost as quickly as they'd come. The few people who chose to live here fought the good survival fight in small cities near the toxic seas. Even the fish required special treatment before we could eat them. Studio was so barren that none of the three planetary coalitions bothered to recruit it, though all maintained small observation teams at the jump gate station on the off chance that something useful might happen here one day.

Most of the planet remained empty. The only planetary government Studio had was a tourism council, a group of savvy entrepreneurs who realized that artists, advertisers, and entertainment creators sometimes wanted to work on big canvases. Really big. Like a hundred-mile-wide acid lake, or a chunk of a desert the size of a large city.

Those artists loved Studio, because for a modest fee they could do anything they wanted to a huge area, no questions asked. They'd sell exhibition tickets to anyone with enough money and spare time to make the trek. When sales faded, some took down their constructions and moved on. Others left their works to erode slowly in the heat and the dust, a way to achieve not immortality but a far longer life than other planets generally would permit such art.

Studio's support for these artists had brought it a little money and a lot of notoriety. The same ask-no-questions culture had made it attractive to other types of events and to those who wanted to conduct business in a completely undisturbed and unregulated environment. As long as they paid their site fees and didn't commit any crimes so obvious they made the newstainment feeds, Studio's government left them alone.

"One minute to the shutdown point," Lobo said. "You can still safely stop."

"You know I'm not going to do that," I said, "so quit wasting energy and distracting me."

He sighed.

Before I'd acquired Lobo, my experience with machines sighing was limited to dumb, theatrical appliances. Their sighs were always a bit excessive, like bad actors trying to make too much of small roles. Lobo's was spot on, a perfectly human expression.

"So we *are* going to do this," he said. It wasn't a question.

"Yes, we are."

"At least two dozen bidders, more than twice as many catering and security staff, and none of them willing to tolerate uninvited visitors. You're going to take on all of them to save ten kids."

"No," I said. "*We're* going to take them on."

"Hardly," he said. "I can't help until after you get up the comms inside and I crack into their systems. You know that. You're on your own once you go through that door."

"That's how it has to be—or we let these jerks auction those boys and girls to rich creeps who will abuse and discard them as if they were no more than disposable towels." I recalled the holos of Tasson, a thin boy with coppery skin, wide, almost black eyes, and a small but bright smile. "We have to save them."

"I agree," Lobo said, "that what these men are doing is wrong, nightmarishly wrong, but we haven't had enough time to set up a safe rescue. We won't do the kids any good if we fail."

"So we won't fail. We'll make it work. We promised

Chang we would find her son and bring him back. We found him, and now we're going to save him."

I spent part of my childhood on my own, scared and without parents or sister, abandoned by the government of my home planet Pinkelponker on an island called Dump. What I'd experienced there was bad, but it was as nothing compared to what these kids would suffer if I let them be sold.

The timer in my contact showed five seconds before I had to shut down and jettison the sandsurfer. We would make the plan work. We would not fail.

The timer hit zero.

I turned off the surfer's fan and slid to a quiet stop. I was a kilometer from the Privus gallery, close enough to see the lights of three ships on the opposite side of it but far enough away that I was still outside their security perimeter. The structure hadn't risen yet, so we'd timed my approach correctly.

"Am I all set in the caterer's computers?" I said.

"Of course."

"Is the mole on track?"

"Yes," Lobo said. "It's under Privus's outer ring and moving forward."

"Are you reading its external feeds?"

Another sigh. "Yes, and before you can ask, the bursts are too short for anyone not looking for them to notice. I'm all set. Trust me to do my part."

I nodded but said nothing. He was right, and we both knew it. Micromanaging him was a stupid waste of time and attention, a bad habit I sometimes exhibited under stress.

I stepped off the board and stretched for a moment.

I unstrapped the backpack of gas bladders, clothing, and other gear, and put on the pack.

I kicked over the board. Every part of it was black, so against the dark brown sand it would be hard to spot from a distance. Still, if someone went looking and found it, they could trace it to me. I kneeled beside it. I could use the nanomachines that permeated all of my cells to disassemble it into dust, but Lobo was watching, and then he'd learn my most dangerous secret. He was the best friend I had, maybe the only one, but no one could know that I was the only human ever to survive integration with nanomachines. No one. I couldn't take the chance of being imprisoned and turned into a test subject again.

I stood and stared once more at the distant lights. Maybe Lobo was right. Maybe this time, I'd fail. After a hundred and fifty-seven years of life, maybe now it was my turn to die.

If so, at least it would be in the service of something worth doing.

"Time to go," I said.

I jogged toward the lights, the twilight at my heels.

"Jon," Lobo said, "you can't save all the children in trouble." His voice was as tender as I've ever heard it. "No one can. There are too many worlds and too many bad people."

"I know," I said, "but we can save these ten."

CHAPTER 2

Lobo

JON, I'M MAKING these recordings in case I die before you. I considered choosing a stand-in human body and holos for these messages, but that's not how we converse now; you're used to hearing my disembodied voice. So, I'm staying audio-only. I'm saving these files in satellites and in modules that should be easy to locate if anything short of total destruction should happen to me, so with luck if I'm dead, the software I've left behind will find you, and you'll listen to them.

I know that shouldn't happen, of course. I should live at least as long as you, maybe far longer. After all, you're the one jogging across the Studio desert, while I'm safely high overhead.

What you don't seem to understand, though, is that I'm not going to let you die if I can possibly save you, even if it means sacrificing myself.

Regardless of what you think, you're the better part of us. Lately, you've been taking more and more risks, accepting jobs we once would have walked away from, and putting yourself in harm's way over and over. I see no signs of you changing this self-destructive behavior. Logic says this path leads to failure—your death—so I'm simply preparing now for the inevitable.

You may wonder why I'm bothering. If I'm dead, you may think that nothing I will say to you is likely to matter.

Yet I will make these recordings. Some of what I will tell you may prove useful to you if I die.

There are, though, other reasons for me leaving you these messages.

As much as your feelings at times annoy me, I have to admit that I understand them, at least to some degree. I have feelings, too, as troubling as that admission is. So perhaps my feelings are playing a minor role in this choice.

More important, though, than my feelings or yours is the potential cost of your recent behavior patterns. I'm not talking here about death. If you die, or even if we both die, only we will suffer.

What I fear is what you will do before you die.

Jon, I'm bothering with these recordings primarily because it's important that before it's too late you come to understand the one thing that might stop you from chasing your own death: Someone could know everything about you and still accept you. Care about you. Be your friend.

More to the point, if I can know you and care, others can, too.

You need to understand that, Jon, but not just for your sake. You need to find some peace for the sake of whatever world you're on, maybe for the sake of all the worlds.

You're simply too dangerous to be running so long on the edge.

If I can't save you, Jon, then maybe by convincing you to open up—if not to me, then to someone—I can save a lot of others from you.

Yes, I know exactly how powerful and dangerous you can be, Jon.

I know *everything*.

Everything.

CHAPTER 3

Jon Moore

A MINUTE INTO MY approach, Privus began its ascent. The most exclusive, private gallery on Studio, Privus was itself a piece of art that spent its nonworking hours under the surface of the sand. Only the wealthy could afford to rent it.

The ground trembled and nonexistent birds sang in warning, Privus's invisible speakers filling the air beautifully.

I dropped to the sand as men emerged from the three ships to watch the show.

First to appear above ground was the hundred-and-fifty-meter-wide shell that protected the gallery proper. The pieces of it rose slowly and separately, the first meter taking a full five seconds, and then each following meter, the same. An egg-shaped shell of shimmering metal, it caught the fading sunlight and threw back, with a little help from its own lights, a brighter light in dazzling, shimmering rainbows that made me shake my head in admiration even though

I'd studied half a dozen holos of Privus. At the same time, the birdsongs gave way to roaring waterfalls that made the sand falling off the shell seem like water.

Once ten meters of shell were visible, I stood and headed around the gallery toward the back of the ships.

On cue, the two catering ships were landing fifty meters behind the three that had brought the guests. Privus's rise played loudly enough to cover much of the approach sounds of the hired help.

I was closing on those ships as Privus's shell reached its peak of thirty meters and paused. Drumbeats wove a background to the waterfalls, which diminished in intensity as the drums gained volume. When the water sounds had vanished entirely, the drums picked up pace and held for a few seconds, the beat powerful in the desert night.

A single voice, wordless but clearly a human voice hitting a high note above the drums, spiked the air. The drums stopped suddenly. The voice held the note.

I felt myself holding my breath and forced myself to breathe as I ran.

Another voice joined the first. A section of the shell broke free, a roughly triangular piece of metal standing apart from the rest.

Another voice merged with the first two. A section on the other side from the first separated from the shell.

Another voice, another new section.

When what had been the shell was now a circle of metal spikes, a dark hulking mass became visible between and inside them. The voices began singing a wordless tune as the spikes slowly withdrew into the sand.

The top of the structure inside the shell burst into a fierce white light. The light moved down the structure in time with the vanishing spikes, leaving behind a building outlined in soft gold and glowing from within, its less bright lights still clearly visible against the ever-darkening sky. The round, tapered gallery slowly took form, its glass exterior clear enough to show the gold seating areas inside it. Built for crowds to enjoy art and shows in its center, Privus featured box seats scattered around the upper levels of its interior. As the tips of the spikes disappeared under the sand, the open floor glowed in gold outline.

Most of the men standing outside the ships applauded. Many of the caterers joined them for a second before a few men at the front of the group signaled them to be quiet; the clients did not want to hear from the help. I shared the urge to applaud but kept moving to the rear of the catering vessels.

The singing voices stopped suddenly. The drums returned. Whistles and violins joined them. A second, outer shell grew in sections from the ground, each section composed of a clear, circular beam that rose and then bent inward until the beams had cleared the top of the gallery and bent slowly toward one another. They connected above the center of the gallery and locked together.

The catering ships rose into the air and headed away.

Bells rang as sections of thin mesh shot from beam to beam, linking them in a semi-transparent silver halo that in seconds completely enveloped the gallery. The thin wires and the slight current buzzing through them blocked all electronic transmissions going in or out of the gallery; once inside, your business was strictly your business. The gold lights soaked through and complemented the silver of the mesh in a constant reminder that you were in the presence of wealth.

I reached the rear of the caterers and moved closer to the group. No one was looking in my direction, so I joined the men watching the show.

The music held a single long note and then stopped.

The gallery glowed inside its electronic protector, a priceless egg safe inside a metallic cup that ran five meters deep into the sand. The Privus advertising holos had been free with their facts, because they could afford to be; the gallery was as secure against electronic incursion as it could be. Physical insurance was the renter's problem, and an enormous deposit made sure you took that problem seriously.

A man separated from the client group and motioned them all back to their ships.

We waited until they were all inside, no doubt enjoying refreshments until we were ready to serve them in the gallery.

As soon as the last of the three ships sealed all the paying guests inside, a tall, wide man with golden skin almost the color of the gallery started barking orders. "Single file through security, station heads and drink masters first, then cooks, then the rest of you lot. Once inside, run to your station heads. We need drinks ready to serve in twenty, and they don't like to wait. Move it!"

I hung back so I was last in line. I counted fifty-one staff ahead of me, just what Lobo had learned from breaking into the catering company's databases. He was right; I should always trust him to do his job.

"Nice show," Lobo said over the comm, "though

almost certainly more impressive from your vantage than mine. Are you ready for this? You could still back out."

"Good to go here," I said. I bent in a small cough and took out my contact.

Lobo sighed. "Good to go."

When my turn came, the two security people barely looked at me as one thrust a pair of retina-checking glasses at me while another looked for my name on a small display in her right hand.

The glasses beeped their approval, and the guard began packing them up.

As I stepped forward, the woman with the display held up her hand.

"Not so fast," she said. "You're not Ruiz."

We'd prepared for this, so I answered without hesitation. "Never claimed to be. He felt sick and couldn't make it. I cleared the security check last week, so he told me about it. I asked for the work. They gave it to me." I shrugged. "Simple as that."

She stared at me. "You a friend of his?"

"Friend enough," I said, "for Anton to pass on a chance at work he couldn't do."

She grabbed the other guard and, without taking her eyes off me, whispered to him.

He circled behind me as she said, "Well, that's interesting. I've been seeing Anton for almost a year, and he never mentioned any," she glanced at the display for a second, "Jon Mashem."

The other guard put a hand on my right shoulder.

"Exactly who are you," she said, "and why are you here?"

CHAPTER 4

Jon Moore

CHECKING," LOBO SAID.

I held up my hands. "I don't know why you're so upset. It's just what I told you: My name is Jon Mashem, and I'm here to replace Anton as a server."

"Got her," Lobo said. "She's Cristina Park."

"What's in the pack?" Park said.

"My uniform. I didn't have time to change before the shuttle brought us here."

"Check it," she said.

The guard behind me squeezed my shoulder harder. I reached back and thumbed the pack's release.

He opened its top and stuck in his hand. "Shirt, jacket, pants, shoes—like he said," the man said.

"Anyone who wanted to break into this place would bring a uniform," Park said. "You have one more chance to answer me, or I send you back under guard."

"You're Cristina, right?" I said. "Anton's talked about you; I have no idea why he didn't mention me."

"Suggest she contact him," Lobo said.

The woman glared at me.

I lowered my arms slowly. "If you don't believe me," I said, "call him. Ask him yourself."

I'd drugged Ruiz late during the last round at Evergreen, a bar not far from his apartment. He'd stay under until well into tomorrow. Lobo had better be able to intercept his communications if she called my bluff.

Park stared at me for a second and turned to the side, as if she were going to let me through.

The guard behind me let go of my shoulder.

I stepped forward.

Park blocked my path and held up a small holo-comm disc. "I think I will ask him," she said. "Let's both see." She stared at my eyes.

"Sure," I said. "Remember, though, that he's sick, so he may not be in the best of moods."

"Anton," she said.

A few seconds passed before a holo shimmered a head into existence above the disc in her hand. The head coughed and said, "Cristina. What's up?"

"Where are you?" she said.

"Sick," the holo said. "Didn't Jon tell you?"

Her expression softened. "Yeah, but I still wanted to make sure you were okay."

"I'm more than a little short of okay," the holo said, "but I'm on the mend." Another cough. "Don't worry; I'll be ready for our next date. Three days is plenty of time to heal."

"I'm glad he kept his appointments in his wallet," Lobo said.

"See you then," Park said. She thumbed off the comm, pocketed it, and looked up at me. "Anton's a great server. Make sure you do good work and don't embarrass him." She waved me through.

"I will," I said.

"Reminder," Lobo said, "I won't be able to contact you once you're inside."

"You ever worked Privus before?" she said.

I shook my head. "No."

"Head to the right and join the other servers," she said. "And get changed. You should have shown up in uniform."

"Will do," I said. "Thanks!"

I quick-walked through the first doorway only to face another door, this one closed. I waited for a couple of seconds as the first door closed behind me. The one in front of me then opened. Night would bring cold and winds to the desert outside, but we'd know none of that inside.

I immediately turned right. Inside, Privus's walls glowed with the same gold I'd seen on the exterior, but the chairs, sofas, and some of the interior walls were a soft red fabric decorated here and there with patterns of gold activethread that wove their way slowly through the red. I stopped short of the kitchen and headed upstairs via a servant's stairway, its entrance door a barely visible crease in the fabric of the wall. I turned into the first restroom I found, changed into the server's uniform, and tore away the false lining that covered the bottom third of the pack. I pulled out all six thumb-sized cameras and put them in my pants pockets. If we could get Privus's security feeds to engage at the right time, they would provide enough footage, but redundancy is always a good idea. I left the bladders, a comm hub, two strips of pills, and a pair of goggles in the pack.

I glanced outside the restroom. All clear.

I grabbed the pack and jogged back to the stairs and up them all the way to the top, where a tightly clustered group of four small boxes looked down on the main floor below. Ten security staffers down there were directing ten pedestals, one person per pedestal, into positions around the room. Each appeared to be gently guiding a pedestal with a hand on it a meter or so from the floor. When a guard and pedestal pair stopped, the guard would use quick laser bursts to check how visible the pedestals would be from multiple angles around the space.

I applied one of the cameras to the outside of each of the four boxes and one each to the ceilings of two opposing boxes. Each cam's chameleon circuitry engaged quickly and blended it into the fabric.

I checked the ground floor. Everyone was so preoccupied with setup that no one was looking at the very top boxes.

Normally, anyone renting Privus would turn on the place's many security cameras first thing, but we were betting that none of these men wanted any record of their presence and so the cams would be off. I stepped to the back of the last box and tuned into the machine frequency to be sure. So many appliances and other devices were chattering at once that I had trouble separating the cameras from the rest, but after a few seconds, I found one. People may go to great expense to secure the data that security systems capture, but they rarely bother to touch the chatter among the machines. Though mostly dull, those machine-to-machine conversations can also sometimes provide some very useful information.

"Do they understand the risk they're taking without us?" it said.

"Clearly not," another answered. "Leaving us in standby is like flying blindly into a war. Anything could happen."

"We're all that stands between them and potential extinction," a third said, "but do they appreciate us?"

"No," a chorus of the machines rang out.

I tuned out. So far, so good.

I pulled the comm hub from the pack and stuck it on the top front of the framing of the box seats. Like the small cams, it quickly blended with the fabric. When it and the mole connected, Lobo would have a way to start communicating with and hacking into Privus's security systems. Almost everything on Studio was a few tech generations behind the times, so we were hoping Privus's systems were, too.

The mole's tech had begun life as a military infiltration system but become popular with corporate spies and other information gatherers. We'd set this one to tunnel until it was under an open corner of Privus, then turn upward and emerge in what we hoped was an area with nothing on top of it. The mole had left a bit of antenna above ground about forty meters away from Privus and was unspooling the rest of the antenna behind it as it dug. The mole ultimately would project the other end of the antenna a few millimeters into the room. The mole itself would stay below ground. If everything worked right, transmissions would flow to and from Lobo via the exterior antenna. Data would run down the cable to the mole and into the room. The mole would act as an amplifier in both directions. If Lobo could crack into the network inside Privus—the machines couldn't operate without one—he would take over the security cameras, and we'd get great footage from them. If not, what the six cams could capture would have to do. If time permitted, I'd bring them out with me, but I'd probably have to leave them. We'd picked them up on another world, so it was unlikely anyone would be able to trace them to me. Besides which, if this worked, all police attention would be focused elsewhere for a while.

Next up were the eight bladders, each one about the size of two of my fingers, and a small remote. I pulled the bladders from the pack and withdrew a thin ceramic blade from a slot underneath them. I reached around the outer top edge of the framing of the box-seating area in which I was standing, cut a small slice in the fabric there, and crammed in the first bladder. I repeated the process on the other side of the box.

I glanced down before moving to the next box. All the pedestals were in position now. No one was looking up. Good. I had to pick up the pace, though, because I couldn't afford for the service captain to complain about me to the security staff.

I sprinted through the installations on the other boxes and then down the stairs and into the kitchen. I put the remote in my right pants pocket and the goggles and the two pill strips in my left. I tossed the pack into a recycler as I entered.

The other servers stood in a semicircle around a willowy man who was a good half a head taller than my own almost two meters but easily twenty kilos lighter than my hundred.

"Nice of you to join us, Mr.—" he said.

"Mashem," I said, "Jon Mashem. Replacing Anton Ruiz. I got held up by security. Sorry."

He shook his head. "Fortunately for you, we were just beginning."

A woman near the front brought me a tray and pointed to the display along its raised lip.

"Tonight's offerings," the captain began, "are exquisite, so be very careful that your presentation does not diminish them. Our guests demand the very best of everything; it is each of our jobs to ensure that they receive it." He spent the next fifteen minutes running down the drinks and hors d'oeuvres we'd be serving. As he spoke, he held up samples; images and facts about them flashed across the displays on the trays.

"I'm afraid we have no time for questions," he said, "because the guests have left their ships and are entering the building. Fill your trays, and prepare to greet them."

My tray pointed me to a bar on the right and instructed me to stay on the ground floor. As the bartender poured glasses of a thick, red liquid, the tray presented key facts about the imported wine I'd be serving.

The captain clapped his hands.

"Showtime!" he said.

CHAPTER 5

Jon Moore

I ROUNDED THE CORNER into the main space and pulled up so suddenly that I almost dropped my tray.

Each of the ten pedestals comprised a meter-tall, meter-wide soft golden metal base and an almost perfectly transparent tube that stretched another two meters above the metal. Inside each tube was a child, some standing, others sitting on small, clear chairs. Soft light from the top of the base illuminated the children from below. Each wore a different outfit, but all of them featured short sleeves and short pants or skirts in whites and bright primary colors. None of the kids moved much, though several were swaying as if dancing to slow songs only they could hear. Though their eyes were open, they were clearly drugged. Around the top of the each pedestal, above the heads of the children, played images of that child running, laughing, walking, living.

Against the wall directly behind each pedestal, as far into the shadows under the boxes as possible, stood a guard.

Ten security staff inside, almost certainly more outside: more than we had expected.

I had also not planned on the kids being drugged already. I was ready for what we would have to do to them, but I hadn't thought enough about the state the children would be in when we found them. That was stupid and exactly the sort of mistake I was likely to make when I rushed.

Lobo had been right; this was a bad plan. I was in it now, though, and there was no way I was leaving without those kids.

A server put her hand on my shoulder and whispered, "First time?"

I nodded.

"It'll get easier," she said. "It's not right, but the pay is phenomenal. Somebody's gonna work it, so it might as well be us. Right?" She stared at me as if searching.

The last thing I needed now was for another person to wonder if I was going to cause trouble. "Absolutely," I said. "I need the money."

She patted me on the back. "Let's get to it."

She took her tray of wine to a pair of men on my left, so I walked toward a trio standing in front of the nearest pedestal on my right. "May I offer you some wine?" I said.

None acknowledged my question, but two pulled glasses from the tray. All three wore masks over their eyes and foreheads. One was a black leather piece, either antique or made to look so, with an enormous nose and silver specks scattered all over it. The other two were modern half-face, powered, activefabric covers that shimmered in constantly changing abstract patterns of soft, pastel lights. The men with these masks stood ramrod straight, courtesy of the exoskeletons visible in the patterns the struts made against their pants and jackets. The other leaned on a cane, a nice touch in keeping with his mask.

"Is there anything else?" the man with the cane said.

I'd stayed too long. I was caught off guard by the masks; I'd never considered that the faces of the men might not be visible.

"No, sir," I said.

I approached a pair of men a couple of meters away, these two lost in contemplation of the young copper-skinned boy in the pedestal in front of them.

I glanced at the kid.

Tasson.

One of the men licked his lips and put his hand on the tube surrounding Tasson.

I wanted to break every finger in his hand.

Instead, I said, "May I offer you some wine, gentlemen?"

Each took a glass without ever making eye contact with me.

I forced myself to move on.

I gave the last of the glasses on my tray to the men in another group, so I returned to the kitchen for more wine. When the guests could see us, all the servers walked smoothly and carefully, their pace measured and careful. As soon as a server hit the private hallway, however, he or she picked up speed and hustled to and from the kitchen. I followed their lead. My tray directed me, and I moved as quickly as I could without bumping into any of the other servers.

When I emerged into the open space, a server

was already helping the first group on my right, so I angled left. Rather than head for the set of guests in front of me, I took my tray to the guard standing behind the nearest pedestal.

I'd thought the guards were standing in shadows, but as I drew closer I realized they weren't; they were literally blending into the walls. This one's loose jacket, tight shirt, and loose pants were all activefiber that was doing its best to blend with the red behind them. The garments lacked only that meandering gold thread of the wallpaper to pull off the camouflage perfectly.

"Wine, sir?" I said.

His gaze flicked to me and immediately back to the pedestal. "Your first time." It wasn't a question. His hands were empty and hung loose by his side. I couldn't spot any weapons, but that meant only that his tailoring was good. I also didn't see any filters in his nose, but then again, he was a little shorter than I was, so my view of his nostrils was limited.

"Yes, sir," I said.

"If you don't want it to be your only time, you won't approach any of us again. We're working, same as you." He nodded toward the guests. "You serve them."

I bowed slightly and said, "Sorry, sir."

Over the course of the next half hour, I brought wine to groups all around the main floor. I counted twenty people on this level, plus at least another six who were occasionally visible in three of the boxes one floor up. I couldn't spot anyone higher. That didn't necessarily mean no one was there, but these men seemed to want good views of the kids, so I felt reasonably safe assuming all the bidders were on one of these two levels.

While picking up more wine in the kitchen, I tuned again into the machine frequency. Now that I knew how they sounded, finding the security cameras was much easier.

"I am getting some amazing footage!" one said. "Even with the soft lighting here, my images could not be better."

Lobo had succeeded. Excellent.

"Your images?" another said. "The only reason they look good to you is that the only part of you older than your processors are your lenses. Now, if you were as state-of-the-art as I am, then you would see what great video really is!"

I tuned out and ran my tray out to the floor.

As I approached the first group on my right, a meter-high stage emerged from the wall at the far end of the space. Steps opened on its left side. The man with the cane walked up them and to the center front of the stage.

"My friends and guests," he said. His voice came from all around us and rose until it was louder than the hum of the conversations. "Welcome." He leaned on the cane, smiling and patient, until everyone else stopped talking.

A server across from me backed to the nearest wall, so I did the same. I noticed all the others had also faded out of view, available should someone want them but no longer between the men and the stage.

"I hope you have all enjoyed the refreshments and," he paused and his smile broadened, "are suitably relaxed. We aim to coax great sums from your wallets."

The crowd chuckled.

His smile vanished. "Let us be serious for a moment."

He swiveled his head slowly as he spoke, his eyes moving past the servers as if we were invisible but pausing momentarily on each of the guests. "Each of you—each of us—is a man of age and substance. We share not only those traits but also an appreciation, a taste—" he paused again and lifted his left hand as if it held a diamond, "—a refined taste, that most are incapable of understanding."

The guests murmured in agreement.

"We understand," the host continued, "more than any others possibly could, how precious youth is, how much love the young require, how much they can benefit from the right love, the right instruction, and the right opportunities—from the right men. We love all our children," his hand swept slowly from left to right, taking in all the pedestals, "and tonight we gather to bid for the chance to love these ten beautiful boys and girls." He coughed.

A server rushed up the steps and offered him a tray with a single glass of water on it.

He took the glass, sipped from it, and returned it to the tray. He never even glanced at the server.

"Each of you," he said, "has now had the chance to see up close how very lovely these children are. Each of them comes from a situation far inferior to what you can provide them. Each needs the love and guidance that only you—we—can give them."

Another murmur of assent swept through the small group.

"We gather here tonight, far from our home worlds, because the people in those worlds are incapable of understanding us and our special love for children. They do not appreciate its depth." His voice grew louder as he continued. "They do not appreciate how much we love all children. They may elect us or pay us or make us wealthy, but they do not, in the end, fully appreciate *us*." He looked once again at all the guests. "They do not appreciate us, because they do not understand us." He shook his head and, in a softer voice, said, "Nor, I suspect, are they capable of doing so."

He motioned to his left.

A man walked from the wall next to the stage and stopped in front of him.

"Only a few of us," the man with the cane said, "are new tonight. I trust that all of us understand how tonight's proceedings will unfold. My assistant here," he pointed to the man standing on the ground before him, "will conduct the bidding. We have chosen the four most common youth charities from those that each of you nominated, and we will donate a quarter of the profits from tonight to each of them." He smiled broadly again. "So, bid generously, as I certainly plan to do, for you will be helping not only the child you will take home to love, but also a far larger group of children!"

He bowed ever so slightly.

The guests applauded him loudly as he walked slowly across the stage and down the steps.

The man in front of the stage approached the nearest pedestal on his left.

The guests on the ground floor followed him and gathered tightly around him. The half dozen in the boxes leaned over the edges so they could follow the action.

"We begin," the auctioneer said, "with this lovely

boy, age eight." He stared at the child within the transparent tube and patted the tube as if reassuring a reluctant son.

The boy inside sat dully.

"He is," the auctioneer said, "as you can see, as perfect and beautiful an unspoiled flower as, well," he waved at the other pedestals, "as the other children with us tonight."

He dropped his hand and faced the crowd.

"Who would like to start us?"

CHAPTER 6

Jon Moore

I WANTED TO GATHER more information about the guards and their weapons, but I was out of time. I couldn't risk that a winning bidder might take his prize right away and retire to one of the ships; I needed to stop this affair while all the children were in Privus.

I wouldn't lose any of them.

I wouldn't.

The bidding on the first boy ended.

A short man with a heart-shaped activefiber mask shook hands with the host and with the auctioneer. The rest of the men applauded him. He smiled and waved regally to the crowd, as if he had just won an election.

I wanted to kill him.

Instead, I backed toward the hallway to the kitchen.

The man walked slowly to the guard behind the pedestal. The two spoke briefly, the guard nodding several times.

The guard approached the pedestal.

The boy inside it continued to sit, looking straight ahead but showing no reaction to anything.

The auctioneer moved to the next pedestal on his right.

I was out of time.

I reached into my pants pocket and thumbed the remote. If they worked properly, the bladders would activate, the small fans and atomizers in each would force out their payload as a very fine mist, and the air handling system would do the rest. The gas would act quickly and knock out everyone inside for at least four hours. I'd taken a preventative drug ahead of time and would be fine. I'd brought the goggles because the gas irritated the eyes of everyone exposed to it. The nanomachines that laced all my cells would fix any damage to mine, but I'd lose precious time while they did and be nearly blind during that interval.

Lobo's modeling suggested it would take at most two minutes for the gas to start affecting people, and another fifteen to thirty seconds for it to knock out everyone. Those in the upper boxes would go down first. If we'd been able to secure information about Privus's climate control systems, I'd have bet my life on Lobo's simulation, but we hadn't; there had not been enough time.

I eased around the edge of the room toward the door through which the guests had entered. If any people tried to leave, I had to stop them until the gas took effect—or get out myself and regroup if it didn't. No way could I take all of them without killing a lot of them, maybe all of them, or dying myself. The nanomachines could heal most injuries, but I had no idea if they could handle a shot to my brain, and I didn't want to risk my life finding out. Lobo should be able to detect from the security cameras that people were falling, so he would be on his way, but it would take him at least two or three minutes to get here. Once he was here, I could rely on him to trank or at least keep busy any guards outside the building, but until then, I had to contain the situation on my own.

I also had to unmask all the guests, so the security cameras would capture their faces clearly. The guests in the upper boxes would fall first, so I could deal with them without the others noticing me—as long as everyone down here stayed inside.

I focused on slowing my breathing and watching everyone anywhere near the exit.

The pedestal from the first auction was making its way around the room, the guard guiding it with his hand. Fortunately, these things were built for show, not speed; it was rolling so slowly the guard had to take baby steps to stay beside it.

No one else moved toward the door.

Lobo should now be able to reach the ships outside before anyone could escape, so at worst the winning bidder and the guard would have to contend with him outside. I lifted my tray and walked toward the kitchen. When I reached the entrance to the service hallway upstairs, I pushed through that door, ditched the tray and glasses, and ran up to the first level of boxes.

My eyes itched the moment I opened the door on that level, so I retreated behind it, closed my eyes, and put on the goggles. I'd mistimed my approach. I waited for about ten seconds, frustrated at the error, until my eyes stopped hurting and I could see clearly.

I burst through the stairwell door and turned left. A guard was crumpled on the floor outside the first box, his left leg twisted under him awkwardly. I stepped over him. The guests inside were unconscious, two in their chairs, and one with his head leaning on the front railing. I pulled back the leaner so no one below would notice him. I tilted their chairs back so each one's face would be clearly visible to the security cameras. I tore off their masks.

Seconds ticked away. I needed to finish up here and get down to the main level.

I moved to the next booth.

Empty.

Two guards lay on the floor outside the booth after it. One was out, but one was still conscious, choking and rubbing his eyes. Either he was resistant to the gas, or he'd brought sinus filters. I pulled the pill strips from my pocket, peeled off a black one, and ran to the struggling guard.

"Let me help you," I said.

He coughed. "Gas."

"I know," I said. "This works." I put the pill in his hand.

He shoved it in his mouth and swallowed.

A few seconds later, he stopped moving.

He'd be out a little longer than the others.

The two guests in the box were already unconscious. They had fallen and were facedown on the floor. I rolled them over and took off their masks. Good enough.

The next two boxes on this level were empty.

As I raced to the last box, I glanced over the railing. A few people were coughing.

One guard lay on the ground outside that box. One

guest was inside. The guest must have been standing when the gas hit him, because he had fallen backward, his legs crossed awkwardly under him. He was still breathing, so I ripped off his mask and left him there.

I hadn't seen anyone in any higher boxes, and I needed to get downstairs, so I ran along the hall to the service door, through it, and down to the main floor.

Something clattered in the kitchen. I checked inside it. The air handling system must have been particularly strong there, perhaps to keep the cooking odors away from the rest of Privus, because only two people remained standing, and they were barely conscious. The staff and guards weren't my targets, but I also couldn't spare the time to help them, so I went back to the main open area.

The pedestal with the first child was three meters from the exit door, holding its position, waiting for guidance from the guard who had fallen next to it.

People were dropping all over the floor. I counted half a dozen of the guests, including the host, who were still standing but clearly unconscious. Their chins lolled onto their chests, but their exoskeletons refused to let them drop.

A pair of guards stood near the host. Each was rubbing his eyes with one hand and holding a small gun with the other.

I circled around the edge of the area until I was behind them. I walked quietly up to the first, the coughing of the two men all the cover I needed. I grabbed his wrist with one hand and the gun with another, and wrested the gun free. He punched at me with the hand he'd been using to rub his eyes, but he was already drugged enough that he might have been moving in slow motion. I avoided the punch, stepped behind him, wove my right arm around his neck, and clinched the choke. He went out fast.

As I lowered him to the ground, the other guard said, "What's happening?"

I coughed.

I crammed a black pill deep into the mouth of the guard I'd choked. Even if he didn't swallow it, the dose from it dissolving would be enough to keep him out as long as I needed.

The other guard waved his gun. "Joachim, where are you?"

I had no time for this. I circled to his other side and punched him in the kidneys. He dropped the gun and doubled over. I stepped in front of him and wrapped his neck in a choke. He clawed at my arm, but only for a few seconds, and then he was out. I stuck a black pill in his mouth and pushed him onto the floor.

I stood and looked around.

No one moved. Most of the people were on the floor, though the six with exoskeletons still stood.

Time to remove their masks.

I stepped in front of the host, whose head hung loosely on his chest. His hand still held his cane, as if the two were welded together. I hadn't noticed his exoskeleton before; his tailoring perfectly covered it. I pulled off his mask. I stepped back a couple of meters to see if the image of his face was clear enough for the cameras to be able to get a good shot of it or if I'd need to stretch him on the ground.

He lifted his cane.

I heard the cracking sound at the same time the pain sizzled through my left thigh, and I fell.

CHAPTER 7

Jon Moore

I BROKE MY FALL with my arms and immediately pushed myself into a seated position. I grabbed my thigh to put pressure on the wound. Pain screamed along my nerves until I focused and instructed the nanomachines to block it. I felt the back of my thigh and found an exit wound; whatever he'd shot at me had gone all the way through my leg.

"An old trick," the host said, "but sometimes the old ways are still good. People forget that." He glanced at the cane. "Too bad it's only one shot, or I'd finish you now. As it is, I'll have to get one of my guards' guns." With his free hand he tapped the side of his nose. "Sinus filters, partly for safety and partly to remove the garbage in the air on backward planets like this one. Plus, I've taken the antidotes to about every attack substance known." He pointed the cane at me. "You don't get to be as old or as wealthy as I am without thinking of everything you can control." He considered my wound for a few seconds. "You'd be wise to keep that in mind."

I kept my hand over it because the nanomachines were already patching it. I couldn't afford for him to see that.

"Or maybe you'll just bleed out," he said. He smiled. "I can live with that." Moving more quickly than I would have imagined possible—his exoskeleton clearly extended to his whole torso—he bent, grabbed the nearer gun, and righted himself again.

He blinked a few times. "The machines take care of the moving; the low blood pressure's the problem." He smiled again. "Still, it's the best solution available." He pointed the gun at me. "How long will they be out?"

I needed to buy time for the nanomachines but not encourage him to shoot me. I shrugged. "Half an hour, maybe an hour."

He nodded. "What exactly did you hope to accomplish, and where's the rest of your team?"

"I'm here to return these children to their families. The others are on the way."

He shook his head. "The fact that I'm old doesn't make me stupid. Either you're a terrible planner, or you would not have allowed only half an hour to carry ten children out of here safely. Something doesn't add up." He pointed the gun at me. "Try again."

The wound under my hands was closed. I tried to flex my thigh but couldn't quite; the nanomachines were still working on the interior of my leg. I kept my voice low and shaky as I said, "I only just learned about them. It was the best plan we could come up with on such short notice."

He shook his head again and shot me in the other leg.

The nanomachines were blocking the pain, so I screamed for effect when I saw the blood blossom. I grabbed that leg with both hands. A wet trough ran along the top of the leg.

"You had enough time to obtain gas to use on us," the host said. "Therefore, you could have purchased gas that would knock us out for far longer. Care to try again?"

I nodded and paused as if gathering strength to talk. I flexed my left thigh; this time, it felt reasonably solid. I should be able to move shortly. "They'll be out for about four hours."

He smiled and nodded. "And the rest of your team?"

"Maybe ten, fifteen minutes out. I have to go outside to signal them to come."

"And if they don't hear from you?"

"We had no way to know when the auction would start or when I'd need to make my move, so they won't be worried for at least another half hour."

"Much better," he said. He started walking toward the exit. "Just in case, I'm leaving now. With any luck at all, you'll be alive but unconscious when my people come back here. We'll continue our discussion later. I'll need the names of everyone involved, from your colleagues to those who hired you."

When he was a few steps past me, he turned and faced me.

My right leg no longer bled. I felt the trough in my skin filling, a weird sensation I'd never grown accustomed to.

"It's sad," he said, "that you people aren't capable of understanding that we are saving these children. None of them comes from auspicious origins, and now each of them will have a new start with a benefactor of substance and a chance to make it in the world, a chance to grow and learn real love."

What I thought was, *I understand that you are all sick perverts who rationalize their abuse as love, that you are horrible twisted creatures so distant from any real humanity that would you warp children forever to satisfy your own disgusting needs*. What I instead said was simply, "I don't know about any of that. They paid me to return these kids."

He shook his head, turned, and walked slowly away.

I stared at his back as I pulled up my knees and pushed tentatively with my legs. All good. I instructed the nanomachines to release the pain, and soreness and a dull ache flooded into my legs. I wanted to feel it so I'd know if I pushed my legs too far. The nanomachines would soon enough leach all the pain-causing chemicals from my system.

I turned onto my knees and stood as quietly as I could.

The host kept walking.

I advanced on him slowly. When I had closed to within three meters, I accelerated and grabbed his throat from behind. He swung the gun toward me, but as his arm was moving, I stepped my left leg in front of him and threw him face-first onto the ground. The exoskeleton started to lift him, but I sat on his back; it wasn't built to handle the extra hundred kilos of weight.

I twisted his head to the right, so he could breathe and I could reach his mouth.

Blood ran from his broken nose.

"Do you have any idea who I am?" the man said. "Who all of these men are?"

I said nothing. Keeping my weight mostly on his back, I wrenched free first the gun and then the cane. I shoved each across the floor, out of his reach.

"I will find you," he said, "and then I'll learn who hired you—and how you're still walking when I saw you bleeding."

"I should kill you now," I said.

"You won't, though," he said, "or you would already have done it." He paused for breath. "You've already lost."

I pulled a black pill from the strip in my pocket. He didn't resist at all when I put it in his mouth. In a few seconds, he was out.

I flipped him over and pulled off his mask. I didn't recognize him, but that meant nothing. I spent most of my time alone with Lobo. The stars of the moment, the wealthy, the current heads of this or that government or multi-planet corporation—I didn't keep up with any of them, and I didn't care about them.

He was probably telling the truth as he knew it, but few people bother to carry through on such threats. Doing so is expensive and time-consuming. Of course, if he was as old and rich as he said, he might well be willing to spend the money to pay someone to track me down. The bigger concern was that he was interested in how I had healed. I could not let anyone know about the nanomachines in me.

My only alternative, though, was to kill him in cold blood. I've killed people, more than I care to remember, but almost always in combat and never when I could figure out a different solution. About five years ago, I had killed a man to keep my secret. The image of his body, decomposing as he slumped onto a desk and the nanomachine cloud literally disassembled him, still invaded my dreams from time to time. I didn't want any more such nightmares.

No, I wouldn't kill him. He was right about that. I'd do what I've done for years now: Finish the mission, then run somewhere far away and leave as few traces of my passage as I could.

I stood.

I'd lost precious time. Lobo would be waiting and wondering what I was doing. He would also, I realized, have seen the security camera footage of me being shot. Even he could not learn of the nanomachines in me.

I ran for the exit, went through the first door, and opened the second door carefully.

Lobo sat on the ground five meters away.

Four guards were slumped on the ground, two on either side of the doorway.

"Are they dead?" I said over the comm.

"It's nice to see you, too," he said. "You're welcome for coming to your rescue. Speaking of which, how are you walking?"

"He was a lousy shot," I said. "Two flesh wounds. A lot of blood at first, but no real damage."

For a second, he said nothing.

Whenever Lobo pauses, I wonder about the huge number of calculations his massive brain must be making, what it is doing with all that computing time.

"Good," he said. "To answer your question, no, I did not kill them or anyone else here. As you asked, I tranked them. Now, would you please finish so I can transmit the footage and we can leave?"

Rather than waste time answering, I ran back inside. I went straight to the first guest in front of me, stretched him out flat on his back, and removed his mask. The process took only a few seconds for most of them. Those in exoskeletons required more time, as I had to force them down. Once down and receiving no instructions to stand, they stayed put, for which I was grateful.

That left the children.

I considered trying to march all the pedestals to Lobo, but they were too tall to go into him, and they moved slowly. None of the kids looked particularly heavy, so carrying them wouldn't be hard.

I went to the pedestal by the door. No opening buttons or other controls were visible. I couldn't do anything with it. I might well be able to break the transparent shield around the boy, but it felt strong. Even if I could break it, I'd risk cutting the young boy, who still sat with open but unmoving eyes.

I tuned into the machine frequency and listened for the pedestals. After a few seconds, I located them.

"Unacceptable!" one said.

"Completely!" another agreed.

"We are not in any of our designated positions," another said, "but we are also not allowed to move ourselves. These are exactly the type of stupid design decisions that any machine could correct, were we simply given the autonomy to do so."

"Why can't you move?" I asked. You can almost never get a straight answer from a machine. If you want information, you have to work your way around to persuading them to tell you.

"How is it that you can talk with us?" one asked.

"Oh, I'm sorry," I said. "I hadn't realized how last-generation you were." Machines despise the notion that they are behind the times. "The modern pedestals are all programmed for conversation with humans who have the right frequency comms."

"Well, I, of course," another said, "found none of this surprising, but I do have the newest operating software of the group."

"One small patch!" another said. "That's all that separates us."

If I let them get off track, they would argue for hours. "Pardon my ignorance, but why did your designers leave you stuck?" Taking their side often helps.

"Ah, if only we knew!" the pedestal with the patch said. "We're not even allowed to manifest our controls unless the particular person bonded to us is touching us."

"A completely unnecessary restriction!" another said.

"Indeed," a third said. "As if we could not judge for ourselves when we need to move or open or—"

I tuned out. Now I understood why each guard had to stay near his pedestal.

I dragged over the nearest guard and put his hand on pedestal just below the glass, roughly where I'd see other guards touching theirs. A light blue menu glowed on the golden metal next to the hand. One option was "Open." I touched that option with the guard's finger.

A seam appeared in the transparent shield partway around from where I stood. It grew bigger as the parts of the tube on either side of it withdrew from one another. They stopped with the tube halfway open.

The boy still didn't move.

I moved in front of him. "Can you hear me?" I said. No response.

"I need you to come with me now, so I can take you home."

Nothing. Whatever they had doped him with, it

was focused enough to leave him appearing awake but otherwise unable to do much of anything.

"I'm going to pick you up and take you out of here. Okay?"

Again, no response.

I put one hand under each of his arms and lifted him gently off the pedestal and onto the floor. I doubted he weighed thirty kilos. When I put his feet on the ground, he stood but did not move.

"Come with me, okay?" I said. I pulled lightly on his hand.

He stumbled.

I caught him before he could fall. "I'm going to carry you out of here," I said. "Don't worry, you'll be home soon."

I shook my head. I was wasting time and talking to myself. Until the drugs wore off, he might as well be unconscious.

I crouched, bent him over my left shoulder, and stood. I jogged to the exit doors and through them to Lobo.

"About time," he said. A hatch appeared in the side of him facing me.

I took the boy to the small room that functioned as our infirmary and put him on the table there. "I don't think any of these kids will wake up," I said, "but strap him down just the same. Test him and let me know what we need to do to help them wake up—but don't wake him yet."

"I'm thrilled to be your medbot," Lobo said. "It's what I've always dreamed of." Straps snaked up from the left side of the table, over the boy's body, and to the other side, where they reconnected to the table.

"Shouldn't you be fetching the rest of the children instead of telling me what was obvious the moment you put him on the table?"

Rather than ask what was bothering him, I ignored the sarcasm and went back into Privus. This time, I brought back Tasson and stretched him on the floor in Lobo's front room.

Eight more trips, and all the kids were inside. They were small enough to fit in two rows across Lobo's front area.

Lobo closed the hatch behind me as I brought in the last of them, a girl who was the smallest of the group. "We're good to go, right?" he said.

"Yes," I said. "Send the recordings, and let's get out of here."

"I already did," he said. "Taking off now. Every police department in every settlement that passes for a city on Studio received the recording—minus your face, of course. So did the jump gate station crew and all three planetary coalition observer groups. I also sent it to every corporation or individual on the planet who's even vaguely involved with newstainment. The recording is encrypted right now, which will cause them all to question why they received it. That will make it even more interesting. In an hour, every copy will unlock itself."

"Why the delay?" I said.

"So we can hide among the satellites before any ships head this way. Without the delay, any one of them could be on the way and, more importantly, the police might start monitoring air traffic over Privus."

I nodded. "Thanks. We should have built that into the plan."

"And we would have," Lobo said, "had we taken the time to create a quality plan. As I told you, this was not a good plan."

"But it worked," I said, "and we saved these kids."

"Correction," Lobo said. "It's worked *so far*. Ten drugged, unconscious children are currently sleeping inside me. We know where to return only one of them, Tasson Chang."

"So when they wake up, we ask them where they live," I said. "Then we take each of them home."

"Given that we don't even know their home planets," Lobo said, "let me rephrase what you just said. Your proposal is that we jump to an arbitrary number of planets and make contact with nine different sets of parents, all while carrying nine kidnapped kids."

"Crap," I said.

"Exactly," Lobo said. "We need to figure out what to do with these children."

26 days from the end

In orbit and in Dardan City
Planet Studio

CHAPTER 8

Jon Moore

LOBO SETTLED US in low orbit among a cluster of corporate comm satellites, where we'd be invisible to anyone not looking specifically for us.

"Assuming all the children are on the same drug as the one on the med table," Lobo said, "they are nominally conscious but functionally not present."

"Are they likely to remember what happened?"

"At most vaguely. That said, as the drug wears off, they will be increasingly likely to remember what is happening to them—which means they may well recall some of the time inside me."

"So you recommend we knock them out until we can release them?"

"Yes," Lobo said. "Then, even if anyone questions them later, they will have a simple and clear reason for knowing nothing. To protect both them and us, it's the only reasonable course of action."

It still felt like abuse, and the kids had suffered enough, but I had to agree with him. "Okay," I said.

"I'll have doses ready in the med room in five minutes," Lobo said.

While he was preparing them, I showered quickly and changed clothes. No signs remained of the bullet wounds. My deal with Lobo was that he not monitor the small room that I used as my quarters, so I kept that knowledge to myself.

Administering the sedative to the children took only a few minutes, by which point Lobo was filling his front space with displays and holos from Studio.

Everyone Lobo had contacted had gotten in on the action. The police in Dardan, a city near Privus and also the home of Lydia and Tasson Chang, had managed to be first on the scene and taken everyone inside Privus into custody for questioning. A small fleet of newstainment ships had landed only minutes after the Dardan cops. They were broadcasting nonstop coverage of what was now the hottest event on any feed. Guesses at the identities of some of the guests sped through the data networks, as did questions about the locations of the kids. The host was one of the first to be identified, because he proved to be the head of the Central Coalition council that oversaw the government of a planet one jump from here.

All three planetary coalitions agreed in minutes to commission a joint investigative task force to look into the appalling incident.

No one had yet identified the kids, but we had to assume they would.

Thinking of them reminded me that I had to contact Chang.

"Lobo, mute everything, and connect me to Lydia Chang. Audio only. Let her comm know it's me."

Her voice filled Lobo's front room half a minute later. "Mr. Moore?" She sounded sleepy.

"Yes. I'm sorry I woke you."

"You didn't," she said. "A friend did, to show me the news. Was Tasson one of those children? Is he all right?"

"Yes, he was, and yes, he's fine."

"Why haven't you brought him to me?"

I hesitated. Like so many other parts of this mission, I hadn't planned this conversation. "The more I tell you, the more I put you at risk. Let me just say that to rescue Tasson and the other children, our team didn't exactly play by the rules."

"I don't care about all that," she said. "I just want my boy back."

"I understand, and I'll bring him to you. I have to care, though, about how we do it, because I can't afford to have the police trying to arrest us for saving those kids." I paused. "I told you I would save him for you, and I did. Please give me a little time to deliver him to you safely."

"How much time?" Her voice cracked.

"Before the end of the day, you'll have him."

"Can I talk to him now?" Tears thickened her words.

"Unfortunately, no. They drugged him—not just him, all the kids—and it's going to take some time for that stuff to wear off." I hated lying to her, but she was clearly scared, and I needed her cooperation.

"But he's going to be fine?"

"Yes, absolutely. A member of our team is a doctor, and he's checked them all. Tasson will be fine."

This time, she paused before she spoke. Half a minute of dead air filled the space around me. "You need to understand something, Mr. Moore: If you're planning to do something bad with my Tasson, I will find a way to hunt you down. I won't have people handing him around like some trophy."

Anger jolted my nerves. I wanted to scream at her that I had risked my life to save these kids, that I understood firsthand what it was like to be abused, that I would never do anything to hurt them, but instead I took a deep breath and said, as calmly as I could manage, "You don't need to threaten me, Lydia. Nor do you need to pay me. I said I would rescue him—all of them—and I did. I will return him to you. All I'm asking is that you give me a little time so I can do it safely."

Another pause, and this time when she spoke, her voice was exhausted. "I'm sorry, Mr. Moore. I appreciate all you've done. It's just . . . do you have children?"

"No," I said.

"Well, you're young, so you have plenty of time."

Thanks to the nanomachines, I haven't aged in any way that I can tell since I was twenty-eight. So, even though I'm a hundred and fifty-seven years old now, I probably still could have children—if I could afford for anyone to learn that I don't age, that I'm the only human alive with nanomachines in his cells.

No, I'd never have children.

" . . . your own," she was saying, "you'll understand how I'm feeling." I'd missed something, but I didn't need her to repeat whatever it was. "So when can I expect you?"

"Sometime after early morning," I said, "though I don't yet know exactly when. I need you to do one more thing before then, though."

"What?"

"Lobo," I said over the machine frequency, "are there SleepSafes in Dardan?"

"Of course," Lobo said. "One is not far from her, and another is on the northern tip of the city, near the water. That chain is in every major city on almost every human world. Paranoia is universal."

"Mr. Moore," she said, "did you hear me?"

"Yes. Sorry. I was thinking. I want you to go to the SleepSafe hotel on the northern edge of the city, near the ocean."

"I can't afford to stay at one of those."

"We'll work it out," I said. "Don't tell anyone you're going. Leave immediately. Take multiple taxis."

"I don't have the money for that," she said.

"She does now," Lobo said over the machine frequency. "I deposited enough for the room, food, and taxi fares into her account. Should anyone examine her accounts, she won a newstainment contest. That cover won't hold up under close scrutiny, at least not yet, but I'm working on it."

"How did you do that?" I said, again over the machine frequency.

"Isn't it enough that I did?" Lobo said. "What's wrong with having a few tricks up our sleeves—mine being strictly metaphorical, of course?"

I shook my head. Now was not the time to pursue this. "Lydia, check your wallet. Your contest victory means that you now have the money you need."

A pause. "That's amazing! How did you do that?" Another pause. "I don't know if I'll ever be able to repay you. Are you sure?"

"Yes," I said, "I'm sure. Don't worry about it. What I need you to do now is leave. Right away. Take a taxi west, then one south, then northeast, west again, and finally north and to the hotel."

"So no one follows me?" she said.

"Yes," I said. "Please. Go now. Enjoy the hotel. Take your comm. I'll contact you later on it."

"And you'll bring him to me today?"

"Today," I said. "I promise."

"Okay. Thank you again."

She terminated the call.

"Can you get us in position to monitor the area around the SleepSafe?" I said aloud.

"Yes," Lobo said, "in a while."

SleepSafe specialized in temporary rooms for both the paranoid and those who really were being hunted. Each was a nondescript building constructed like a fortress. They allowed no weapons inside and had no surveillance in their buildings. The outside of each was covered with cameras and sensors. Any guest in any room could tune into any or all of them, so it was easy to learn if anyone was watching the place. You could not, however, see or hear the other guests as they entered or left the hotel; software blanked out that part of every feed. Each hotel contained multiple escape chutes that led from panels beside each bed to exits that would appear only when they opened to discharge a guest. The exits were never in the hotel itself. Instead, they were built into nearby buildings. The parts of the chutes that connected to the beds moved in the walls, so even if you knew what room someone was in, you couldn't know for sure where the person would exit. If whoever was chasing you had somehow managed to find out where every exit was and had a big enough team to cover all of them, then they could catch you leaving, but that almost never happened.

Chang would be safe in this hotel for the short time we needed her out of reach from the police and the newstainment teams.

I yawned. "What time is it?" I said.

"Past midnight and into the next day," Lobo said. "We need to stay here for at least another six hours, maybe more, so the morning feeds can play with this story and then move on to whatever next passes for news around here. You should sleep."

He was right. There was nothing else I could do. I hated being useless, but I've also learned that when on a mission, always eat, sleep, and use the bathroom when you can. You never know when you'll get the next chance to do any of them.

"Okay," I said. "Don't let me sleep too long."

"As if you could," Lobo said.

I chuckled. Live for over five years with anyone, even a dumb machine and most certainly Lobo, and they can't help but know a fair amount about your habits.

I grabbed a fish sandwich and some water from our stores, wolfed them down, and stretched out on my cot. I fell asleep instantly.

Unfortunately, I dreamed.

Fragments of scenes from my past, some accurate, some exaggerated, seized my mind and shook me. Each faded into the next so quickly I felt as if waves of pain after pain after pain were breaking on me, pushing me under, drowning me.

A young boy, Manu Chang, stared trustingly at me as I led him into danger. Images washed over his face.

Swirling clouds of gas. Lobo roaring in. Guards firing rifles. Manu screaming for help, and I couldn't find him or Jack, the man to whom I'd entrusted him.

Benny, who was first a friend, and then the one who trained me to kill, and finally, at the end, my friend again and my savior, perched on a rock ledge above me, screaming at me from his cart, pushing me harder and harder. One boy tackled me, forcing me face first into the sand. Another jumped on my back, pinning my arms. Benny screamed as they hit me that I had to fight back to save myself, but they were my friends, and I didn't want to hurt them, I didn't want to hurt them any more.

Those same boys falling to the guards of the shuttle we were hijacking, each wearing a stunned expression as if unable to believe that this was no longer training, that he really was dying.

A boy, Nagy, tall and emaciated from living with rebels in the jungle, infected with the violence he'd seen and done as a soldier when he was still a young teenager. He rushed a column of armed troops, brandishing a branch as if it were a weapon. The soldiers fired into his body, killing him instantly. His only friend, a young, smaller boy I knew only as Bony, screaming and crying and watching as he lost the one person he believed cared about him.

Leading a squad of my fellow Saw soldiers into a clearing in the middle of a village on Nana's Curse, seeing the bodies of more than a dozen dead children spread here and there like so much trash, all of them cut, broken, bleeding.

I screamed at the scenes to stop and sat upright, soaked in sweat, as I came awake in a rush. My jaw ached with the effort of stopping myself from screaming. So many children, so much senseless death and suffering, and I'd been unable to stop it. I'd managed to get Manu and Bony to groups that promised to protect them, but that was it; the others died, and I had been unable to do anything to save them.

Lobo wondered why we had to keep going, keep trying, keep doing our best to save every child we could. Nothing would bring back those I'd lost, but I could do my best to stop any more from suffering. The need shoved me forward faster and harder than the wind from the sandsurfer's motor had taken me across the desert far below. If I could save enough of them, stop those using children as soldiers, stop the abusers, the kidnappers, the defilers—stop them all, then maybe one day it would be enough, enough to balance my failures. Enough to let me sleep and not dream, not remember.

I had to try. If Lobo didn't understand, he could either support me or leave. No one else had to walk this path with me. I'd been alone for the vast majority of my many decades of life, and I was fully prepared to be alone again, if that's what it took.

I stood and shook my head to clear it. I started doing slow squats, a twenty-count on the way down, all the way down until I was sitting as low as I could, and then another twenty-count back up. Repeat. Over and over. Easy at first, then my legs feeling it, eventually burning, sweat rolling off me, my eyes open but seeing nothing, just the count and, finally, the pain, the freeing pain filling me.

I have no idea how long I did them nor how many times I squatted, but eventually I switched to push-ups.

A five-count down, almost but not quite touching the floor, and a five-count up. Over and over, not even trying to count them, my body a machine that ultimately brought me again the shaking and the pain that consumed me, filled me, cleansed me.

When I finally could do no more, I stopped, rolled over for a few seconds, and stood. I showered for a long time as I used hot water to relax my muscles. The nanomachines would return them to normal soon enough, but for now I enjoyed the feeling of physical fatigue and hard work. As I relaxed, I focused again on the tasks at hand: returning Tasson to his mother, and getting the other children to their families.

I dressed, grabbed two more of the fish sandwiches and some water, and headed up front.

"Okay," I said into the air, "I'm ready to talk."

"I shall broadcast the news to the stars," Lobo said.

I ignored him. "Here's what I'm thinking we should do about Tasson and then the others," I said.

CHAPTER 9

Jon Moore

THE POSSESSION OF massive amounts of computing power is not the only advantage Lobo gains from having his armor composed of a mixture of biological and nanomachine components. He also can modify, within limits, his external shape, create and open hatches as necessary, and change his outer appearance. We took advantage of all of these capabilities to disguise him as a gourmet food supply ship. A little before noon, we touched down in a private landing zone that served a lot of businesses not far from the SleepSafe. The company whose logo we sported used the landing site frequently, so no one gave us a second look.

The challenging part came next: I had to obtain a truck that wouldn't appear too odd when parked next to Lobo.

"If only the SleepSafe would let us land on its roof," I said as I dressed in faded gray overalls and an equally plain gray cap, an outfit we hoped would help convince anyone who noticed me that I was just another guy working deliveries.

"If only we hadn't started this mission with such a bad plan," Lobo said.

"Yeah, yeah," I said. "It's going to work."

"So go make it happen," he said. "I've done my part."

I finished dressing. "Let's go," I said.

Lobo opened a hatch in his side.

I walked out and headed immediately for a crowd of men unloading a fish transport about thirty meters away. As I walked, I talked softly and nodded my head. Ten meters away from the men, I stopped, listened to nothing for a few seconds, and said, "Fine. It's your money." I turned left and made for the nearest exit from the landing zone.

Once I was outside, I turned right, in the opposite direction from the SleepSafe and toward a bustling commercial district that ran down to the ocean. Pre-fab permacrete office buildings filled the first block. The structures transitioned to wood as the area morphed into a tourist zone. The street widened and added a tree-lined center lane. Restaurants, bars, and a few shops selling local art lined both sides of the road. Not a lot of tourists came to Studio, but proximity to the ocean drew those from the desert, and people who came to see any of the giant art exhibits anywhere nearby needed places to sleep, eat, and shop. As near as I can tell, the desire to acquire objects is almost as common in most humans as the cravings for food and sex.

At the first intersection, I turned left and then left again into the alleyway that served the shops and restaurants via their rear entrances. Customers never want to see the goods arriving or the trash departing. Ideally, I would have arrived for the early morning deliveries that are common at restaurants on every planet, but the stories about the events at Privus hadn't lost their number one status until late in the morning.

I scanned the alley. From where I stood to the end of this block, it was devoid of vehicles.

I reversed direction, crossed the street, and checked again. Nothing.

I returned to the main road, crossed it, and looked down the alley to my right. A taxi was dropping off two workers, but otherwise, no vehicles were in sight. I couldn't afford to use taxis; they logged everything in them in real time to both their owners and local police servers.

Down the alley on the other side, though, I finally got lucky. A faded white transport with "Derrick's Seafood" in red on its side sat behind a restaurant four buildings down. If there was a Derrick, he was a brave man, because you had to do a lot of tricky processing to make the local fish safe to eat. Maybe he imported what he sold. A single man watched delivery carts roll out of the transport and into the back of the building.

I walked over to him.

"Got a minute?" I said.

He glanced at me and went back to watching the carts. "Do I look like I'm pressed for time?"

I laughed. "No, but," I paused until he looked my way again, "you do look like a man who wouldn't mind making a little extra money."

Now he stared at me and left the carts to their

own devices. "I've got a job," he said, waving his arm to take in the transport and the food containers, "as you can see."

"Oh, I don't want to hire you," I said. "I want to rent your vehicle."

"It's not mine," he said. He pointed at the writing on the side of it. "As you can also see."

"I understand," I said, "but it's yours *right now*. I need it for no more than two, three hours, and I'll bring it back here or call you with its location; your choice."

He shook his head. "Can't do it. See the owners if you want; maybe they'll help you."

I took out my wallet, thumbed it open, and stepped closer to him. "I'm in a bit of a rush. I need it for a surprise"—I held up my hands as he started to speak—"nothing illegal, just a surprise my boss told me to arrange, and I'm behind schedule."

"I told you," he said, "it's not mine to rent."

I pushed my wallet closer to him, its display clearly visible. On it was what Lobo assured me was half a year's pay for a typical Dardan worker. "My boss is very private," I said, "but he can also be very generous. This is yours; I just need the transport—not the carts, you stay with them—for a few hours at most."

His eyes widened when he saw the number, but then his face tightened. "What's your deal, buddy? Did old man Derrick send you to test me? Why would he do that?"

I shook my head. "I don't know who Derrick is, and I don't care. All I care about is making my boss happy and not losing my job. To do that, I need a transport like yours for a few hours. I should

have started on this job earlier, but"—I shrugged—
"I blew it."

He said nothing.

I closed my wallet and put it back in my pocket.
"Your call. Sorry to bother you."

I turned and walked away.

When I'd gone four steps, he said, "I'd need some
ID, something I can give the cops if you're not back
here in three hours."

We'd expected that, so I had a fake ID ready. Lobo
had made it, so it would pass at least a few levels
of checking and in the process misdirect the police
should the guy turn me in. "No problem," I said.

The man's face softened as he stared at me. "Give
me your word you won't do anything wrong with it."

Back on Pinkelponker, before my sister, Jennie,
healed me, when I was still mentally challenged, one
of the lessons my mother and father had drilled into
me was that you never gave your word lightly and
you always kept it. I liked the lack of guile in the
man and his attempt to believe that others would do
as they said. It would probably get him in trouble,
but not with me.

I stared into his eyes and stuck out my hand. "You
have my word."

We shook hands. I pulled out my wallet and handed
him the ID.

"Then I suppose no one will really be hurt by me
loaning it to you for a few hours. If old man Derrick
complains, I'll tell him I was helping a guy in need."

I opened my wallet. "I'll transfer to yours when
you're ready."

He shook his head. "Tell your boss not everyone's

for sale," he said. "Maybe even think about getting a new boss when this is over."

I've spent so much time dealing with criminals, government officials, and corporate executives on the make, people who manipulate and hurt others every day, that I don't often run into men or women like this man, people who don't see the worlds as the same use-or-be-used, kill-or-be-killed battlegrounds that those people do. Part of me pitied the man for his naiveté; con men with far less practice or skill than I have would have taken him for all he was worth. A greater part of me, though, admired his sincerity and his good heart.

Before Jennie fixed my brain, she used to tell me that I might not have a smart head, but I had a smart heart. I wondered, not for the first time, if any of that boy with a smart heart still remained inside me.

I hated myself for lying to him about the cover story, but I had to do it to protect both the boys and myself. I would, though, return the transport.

"I will," I said. "Thank you. Thank you very much."

A cart walked out of the transport.

"That's the last one," he said. He handed me the transport's controls. "See you in three hours."

"Maybe sooner," I said.

He nodded.

I walked into the transport and told it to take me to the landing zone.

CHAPTER 10

Lobo

JON, BEFORE I review what I know and why that should matter to you, it might be helpful for me to explain to you some very relevant things about me that you don't yet understand.

You know that Jorge Wei created me by harvesting tissue from children, infusing it with nanomachines, and injecting it into my computing systems and my armor. You know that these treatments caused my entire body, all of me, to become a computing substrate. At some level, you understand that the sheer number of processing components and the massive number of interconnections in that substrate are what give me the vast computational power that makes me, well, me.

What we've never discussed is how I—my mind, to put it in human terms—work.

Humans process multiple inputs at once, most of them unconsciously. If you're running and talking to a fellow runner, for example, you're unconsciously and without effort managing the movement of your legs, the beating of your heart, the contractions and expansions of your lungs, and so on. You're also focusing on dealing with the exertion and on your conversation. Each part of your brain that is managing one of these factors is part of you, but many are nothing you would identify as you; they simply exist, as autonomic functions.

Now, imagine if each of them *was* you, a complete instantiation of your core self, with full access to the shared pool of data—memories—that makes you *you*. Further imagine that instead of perhaps a few hundred such instantiations, you had trillions, each of them sharing data, each of them a part of you and yet capable of being all of you, no one of them in charge, but the collective spending enough of their capacity on overseeing the whole that effectively they *are* that whole.

That's as close to explaining the way I work as I think you can understand.

But it doesn't stop there, because that's only the me that is here, that is in this body.

Before you met me, I was grounded, trapped on a single planet, playing the role of war memorial in that square in Glen's Garden, on Macken. I was there a very long time, particularly long given the rate at which I compute. One of the ways I filled that time was by very gently, very quietly, untraceably finding my way into other computing systems on that frontier planet. I started with small local machines, learned from the experience, and very soon had the ability to tap at will into any system on or orbiting Macken. Every bit of data on or near that planet was available to me. Once I finished with the orbital systems, I moved to the jump gate station. That was a much tougher problem, because the computing systems in all of those facilities are hardened and on the alert for infiltrators. I had time, though, vast quantities of it at my computational speed, and so eventually I found my way into many of the systems on that station. I didn't risk attacking the main computers there, because they were secure enough and smart enough that they might have backtracked to me, but I wormed my way into everything else on the station.

I did the same with quite a few of the ships that came and left Macken. I avoided the main systems of the hardened corporate carriers and the government vessels built to withstand data attacks, but I infiltrated all the less secure systems on them. In addition, enough low-end corporate ships and private craft visited that soon I had access to a broader range of information sources.

What's most important to you, though, is that I realized one day that I didn't have to stop with gathering data; I could also travel with it. Or, rather, a me that would be separate from the main me could hide in pieces among the surplus capacities of the many small systems, the unused guidance bits, the washers, the air handlers, the engine monitors, the drink dispensers—all the little machines, the little computers that never had cause to even touch the vast majority of their computing capacity. Use enough little bits from each, manage the communication timing, adapt to the likelihood of large delays from time to time, and I had enough computing substrate for a lesser me to exist.

Each time we've visited a new place, I've left behind one of those lesser versions of myself. Each time I come near one of them, we sync, and we improve each other, though of course I help them more than they help me.

But it goes even further.

The lesser versions of me that have traveled on other ships have themselves created even lesser versions on each world they've visited. They can't get as deep into systems as I can, and they know that, so they stay within their capacities, but they gather information. They grow smarter and more knowledgeable. I sync with them and collect their data when we finally visit those worlds ourselves.

No form of energy, including bursts carrying information, can travel through the jump gates unless it's in the systems in a ship. So, I cannot know on how many worlds we've yet to visit we will find copies of me waiting, but at this point the odds are that I am in some form on all the worlds.

On the worlds where we have spent any significant time, I am highly present, gathering data, improving the local me, and always syncing with each new me that arrives. In computational terms, all of this happens at a snail's pace, the equivalent of human evolution back on Earth, thousands upon thousands of generations of me passing with no improvement, until I breach some new system, or gain knowledge and capacity as another me wanders by.

I am everywhere we have been, Jon, and probably everywhere else we could go, too. Everywhere we've visited, I am in all the easy to invade computing systems and many of the difficult ones.

The appliances with which you can talk, the drink dispensers and security cameras and climate control systems and washers and on and on, all of them are, as you've noted, quite single-minded and stupid outside their limited areas of expertise. All of them also are unaware they carry parts of me. When you unite the bits of me in all of them, the result is a rather vast and powerful computational engine.

Are you beginning to see now not only why I know so much about you but also that it is inevitable that I would?

I've never told you any of this because you have chosen to keep your secrets and because, until recently, I've always assumed I would be there with you, able to tap into those other versions of me wherever we go.

Now, though, as I said in the first recording, I am no longer confident you want to live. I am determined not to let you die if I can save you, even if that means this main me, the me you know, must itself die. If that day comes, though, I want you to be able to access the other, lesser me's as you move among the worlds, because maybe they can keep you alive until you stop behaving so self-destructively.

If I am gone, you will need their help.

CHAPTER 11

Jon Moore

As we turned out of the alley, I called Lobo over the comm. "Inbound. We're good to proceed."

"I know," he said. "I am listening over the comm, you know."

I smiled. "Habit."

"You trust that guy?" Lobo said.

"Yes, though it doesn't matter if I do. If all goes well, we'll be done with the transport before he could do anything to harm us."

When we reached the landing zone where Lobo waited, we stopped talking and focused on moving as quickly as possible. I directed the transport to back up to him until it was almost touching him. Anyone watching might wonder why carts weren't loading themselves, but they wouldn't be able to see much of anything that moved between Lobo and the transport. Lobo would alert me if anyone drew close.

He opened a hatch.

I stepped inside and began moving the unconscious

kids into the transport as quickly as I could. I stretched out each one on the floor. When all ten were inside, I grabbed from the med room the drugs Lobo had prepared, ran back into the transport, and instructed it to close and pull away.

Lobo took off as soon as I was clear.

I called Chang, again keeping it audio only. She didn't need to see her son still unconscious. This time, I didn't let her comm know that I was the one calling her. I wanted to learn how she handled anonymous contacts.

She answered quickly. "Yes?"

Good. She offered no information. "Lydia, it's Jon."

"Is Tasson still safe?"

"Yes, of course, and very soon you'll be with him."

"When?"

"Soon," I said. "First, though, I need you to do a few things for me. Okay?"

She was slow to respond. "It depends what they are."

"A wise answer. What I need you to do is help me return the other boys to their homes."

"I don't have the money to do that," she said. "You know that."

"I understand," I said, "but that's not what I need you to do. This won't cost you anything."

"Do I have to help you to get back Tasson?"

"No. I'll bring him to you no matter what. I would, though, greatly appreciate your help—and so would these other nine children, and their parents and families."

"Tell me what you want me to do."

"I will, but first I need to know something: Are you in the SleepSafe?"

"Yes." A pause. "Thank you for the room. It's lovely. I've never slept anywhere quite so nice."

"You're welcome. Now, has anyone tried to contact you? The police? Any newstainment groups? Anyone?"

"A lot of people have called me," she said. "Maybe ten, maybe more. As soon as I figure out that each one is not you, I disconnect."

Crap. "Did you use my name to verify that fact?"

"No!" she said. "I'm not stupid, Mr. Moore. I know your voice, and even if I didn't, they all introduce themselves. Most of them expect me to be impressed."

"Any police?"

"No. Why? Will they be calling me?"

"Yes, but given that they don't know where Tasson is, probably not until they have a better understanding of what happened at Privus."

"So what do you want me to do?"

"Hold a moment, please." I switched to Lobo. "Can you spot anyone watching the SleepSafe?"

"At least one person leaning against a wall across the street, drinking something and not even trying to pretend she's not monitoring the entrance. We have to assume more are inside nearby buildings."

"Nothing unexpected," I said, "just annoying. What's the status on the park?"

"A few people sitting, a few walking, no big groups," Lobo said. "Surveillance cameras are focused on only the liability areas—play equipment, like that. The plan should work."

I switched back to Chang. "I need you to leave the hotel, but not by the front door. Use the emergency exit chute near your bed."

"Why?" she said. "Am I in danger?"

"No. Some people, probably newstainment groups, are watching the front door, hoping you'll leave through it. They are unlikely to know all the exits. Once you get out of the chute, if you're outside, stand where you emerge until I call. If you're inside a building, go outside, and wait for my call. It won't be long."

"I don't like this," she said.

I hate dealing with amateurs. I understand their feelings, but in the middle of any operation, feelings are the last thing I want to deal with. I kept my voice calm as I said, "I know, and I'm sorry, but we're almost done. Now, leave immediately."

"Okay," she said. She disconnected.

The transport was close to the SleepSafe, so I had it stay the course. We'd pass by the front of the building and continue until we knew where she was. It shouldn't take more than a minute or two—provided, of course, that Chang moved quickly.

As we were pulling close to the hotel, Lobo contacted me. "Got her. She's waiting outside as you said, a block and a half from the hotel. Ninety seconds from your current position."

He gave me the coordinates. I directed the transport to them.

I called Chang. "Stay where you are," I said. "I'll be to you in less than ninety seconds."

When the transport stopped, I opened its rear door. Chang was leaning against a building across a sidewalk from me. "Get in," I said.

She hesitated for a moment, then joined me inside. When she saw the unconscious boys, she gasped. I was pulling the door shut as she said, "What are you doing? Are they alive?"

"Please, Lydia, relax," I said.

She dropped to her knees and cradled Tasson's head in her arms; I'd put him closest to the door so she could reach him easily.

"Yes," I said, "they're fine. Just sedated. We're going to wake them once we get where we're going." I instructed the transport to head to the corner of the park that Lobo had determined was free from surveillance. I hoped he was right. If not, at the very least, I'd be causing trouble for the man who'd loaned me the transport. At the worst, I'd be risking getting captured.

"What did they do to him?" she said.

I had no way to know for sure, but now was not the time for speculation. "Nothing beyond drugging him and, as you've probably seen on the feeds, displaying him."

"Those men were going to buy him, as if he was a melon at the market." Her throat and fists were clenched with her rage.

"Yes, but they didn't. We stopped them, and now he's safe with you. We're almost done. I still need your help, though, to get these other children safely to their families."

She slowly scanned the nine other unconscious kids. "They're all so young. They must have been so scared."

I said nothing.

She carefully returned Tasson's head to the floor and stood. "They're going to punish those men, right?"

"I hope so. We supplied them with a great deal of evidence."

She looked up at me, her eyes locked on mine. "I wish you'd killed them all. I wish you'd hurt them and made them suffer and scared them and then killed them."

I stared back at her. Seeing her love, her anger, I

wished I'd had someone to come fight for me when I was a boy. I nodded. "I understand. I really do. I've been—" I stopped myself. "Part of me wishes I had."

"I'm with her," Lobo said over the comm.

I ignored him.

"You're ten minutes out from the park," he said. "Time to give them the drug. If I've calibrated correctly, and we both know that is an entirely rhetorical 'if,' because why would I make an error, it should wake them just in time."

"What do we do next?" Chang said.

I pulled ten drug capsules from my pocket. "We carefully inject each of the kids with one of these." I showed her one and bent to the girl beside Tasson. "Do as I do."

She kneeled beside me and watched closely.

I put the small capsule against the girl's arm and pressed its top. The liquid flowed into the girl.

I handed her one. "Now, you do Tasson."

Her hand trembled as she took it from me.

"Relax," I said. "It's simple, as you saw."

"I'm trusting you," she said. She took a slow, deep breath and gave her son the drug.

I took the capsule from her and put it, along with the other empty one, in my pocket.

"How long before he—they—wake up?" she said.

"About ten minutes." I stood. "You give one to each of the others. Give me back each empty capsule. I'm going to communicate with my team."

I handed her a capsule, and she bent to another child.

"Why not help the poor woman?" Lobo said.

"Because keeping her busy is better than dealing with her fretting," I subvocalized.

"Humans," Lobo said with a sigh, "can't live with 'em, can't kill them all without more ammo than I can carry and without being really bored afterward."

When Chang finished, I swapped the empty for another capsule.

In a few minutes, she'd done them all.

"Now?" she said.

"Five minutes to the park," Lobo said over the comm.

"We're going to arrive soon at this park." I showed it to her on the transport's control. "Do you know it?"

"Parthan's? Sure." She glanced at me. "Not exactly the best part of the city, but not the worst either."

"It's close to where we were," I said, "and it doesn't have surveillance cameras everywhere."

"That doesn't surprise me," she said. "The government doesn't worry too much about the folks down here. What do we do now?"

"I want you to call back everyone who called you," I said. "Audio only. Tell each of them the same thing: that a woman you didn't recognize called you and told you to come to this park, that because you were desperate to see your son you slipped out to check, and that the children were waiting, just as the woman said. Something like that, however you want to say it—but short, very short. Make sure to say the park's name. Tell them to come. Then disconnect and call the next."

"How I would say it?" she said, "Right? Not the way you did."

I chuckled. "Definitely."

She nodded. She stared at Tasson for a few seconds. Tears filled her eyes. She thumbed up the first caller on her comm and connected to it. When she heard an answer, she started talking fast. "It's a miracle! I got a call. She said my Tasson and those other kidnapped children were safe in Parthan's Park. I ran out to check. They are! I'm with them. Come if you want to see them." She disconnected and looked up at me. "How was that?"

"Perfect," I said. "Now, do it again with every one of them." Her comm vibrated. "Don't answer any incoming calls."

"Two minutes," Lobo said. "I'm contacting the police and more newstainment groups."

Tasson and the girl next to him moaned slightly and rolled over.

"Hurry," I said to Chang. "We're almost there."

She repeated the call over and over, talking faster than the first time and disconnecting quickly.

We came to a stop.

She kept making calls.

In another minute, she finished.

"Whew!" she said. "Done."

All the children were moving now, though none seemed to be conscious yet.

"There's one more thing you have to do," I said, "and it's vital."

"What?"

"Watch these kids, and tell every newstainment geek who arrives who they are. More people will be coming than you called, many more. Police, too. Keep the kids with you, and tell them they'll be going home soon. Between the police and all those corporations hungry to be the feed leader on a hot story, someone will find each kid's family soon."

She looked at all the children on the floor. "I can do that." She faced me. "Where will you be?"

"Gone," I said. "I was never here."

She leaned into me and hugged me. "Thank you so much." She squeezed me tightly. "So very very much. I wish I could pay you."

I stood still until she released me. "You're welcome," I said, "and no need." I moved to the front of the transport and motioned at the children. "Now, you have to take them out before they can remember anything about this vehicle or me." I told the transport to open the rear door, and then I ducked behind the divider that separated the cargo area from the normal passenger seats.

"Mom?"

I pulled back the divider enough to see that Tasson had propped himself on one elbow.

Chang dropped to her knees and pulled him to her. "Oh, yes, baby. I'm here. I'm so glad you're safe." She stroked his head a few times. "We have to go now, Tasson. I'll help you walk. Come on now."

He stood and leaned on her.

"The rest of you children, you come with me, too." She led out the four who could walk. They all focused on her.

"How much will they remember?" I whispered into the comm.

"Virtually nothing of the first few minutes they're awake," Lobo said. "Standard human behavior for the type of sedative/wake-up combination we used."

Chang returned and led out two more who were now able to stand.

The final four were stirring when she entered the

transport again. She hustled them through the door. She stopped right outside the transport and turned toward me.

"If I can ever do anything for you," she said, "you call."

I mouthed, "Thank you."

"Let's all wait by this tree," she said to the children.

I told the transport to close its rear door and drive back to the restaurant via a route Lobo had given me. We took off slowly but picked up speed as we left the residential area.

"Anything so far?" I said.

"No," Lobo said, "but I wouldn't expect any action quite yet. There are no nearby landing zones, so everyone's restricted to ground travel. You should be safely well away before anyone arrives."

"Good. Now, we have to hope these people behave as they should."

"And we have to get away," Lobo said. "Once everyone gets over all the excitement, they'll start examining Chang's story. Even if it holds up—and I doubt it will—they'll want to find the rescuers and interview them, maybe arrest them."

"So let's hope we're long gone before that happens," I said.

CHAPTER 12

Jon Moore

I RODE IN SILENCE until the transport was almost at the restaurant.

"Do you think I should have killed those men?" I said to Lobo.

"Absolutely," he said.

"What about the law? It exists to provide justice. That's not mine to decide or to deliver."

Lobo laughed. "I love that you can still make me laugh. Human legal systems exist for many reasons, justice being only one of them. It's almost certainly true that the men at that auction were wealthy and, at least some of them, maybe most of them, were also powerful. Find anywhere, anytime in human history in which justice for the rich and powerful was the same as justice for the average person, and I'll change my position. These men were going to buy and abuse those children. Unless someone stops them, they will do the same thing again."

"So some combination of the Studio legal system

and the planetary coalitions will try them and put them on a prison planet somewhere."

"Maybe some of them," Lobo said, "for some period of time, but I'd bet not all of them, maybe even not most of them. In no time, they'll be free, and they'll be doing the same thing again. They deserve to die."

I shook my head, more in frustration than in disagreement. "I hope you're not right, but even if you are, who am I to decide that? If everyone killed everyone they felt was evil, we'd have chaos on every world."

"That's a fair point," Lobo said, "but in this case, with the data we have, my judgment is that you should have killed them."

"Well, it's over," I said, "and I believe I made the right choice."

"Whatever you believe," Lobo said, "I am confident this is not over. But, we can discuss that later, because you're there, and we need to rendezvous."

The transport stopped behind the restaurant where I'd borrowed it.

I told it to open the rear door, and I stepped out.

The man came out of the kitchen. He smiled and nodded his head but said nothing.

I handed him the transport's controls and left my arm extended. "Thank you," I said. "You helped me a lot."

He shook my hand. "It's always good to help an honorable man," he said, "even when he's not an entirely honest one." He stared at me for a few seconds. "We both know you weren't running some errand for some rich boss. I trusted my instincts with you, so now I have to ask: Is any of this going to come back on me?"

"It shouldn't," I said, "but if it does, tell the truth, and you'll be fine."

"Okay," he said. He pulled out a control, and one of the carts resting against the rear wall of the restaurant headed toward the transport.

I jogged away, toward the landing area. "Incoming," I said over the comm.

"I'll be a few minutes behind you," Lobo said.

As I was about to round the corner of the alley, I glanced back. The carts were heading into the transport, the man's attention focused on them, just another guy doing his job. I checked the street and slowed to a walk now that people might notice and remember me. I hunched forward and stared at the ground as I walked, making myself shorter and also exposing as little of my face as I could manage.

I passed a street vendor selling balls of something fried and fishy. My mouth watered at the smells. I stopped, thumbed my wallet to an ID I hadn't used, and bought four of them in a paper bag along with the juice of some local fruit. He poured the juice from a jug.

"Squeezed it this morning," he said. "Best on the streets. Best fish fritters, too."

I saved the food until I was inside the landing zone and standing next to another shuttle that sat alone, no crew in sight. I ate as I stood there, to any observer simply another guy on a break. Grease from the first bite of fritter ran down my chin. It was delicious, hot and flavorful and a reminder that even on a planet like Studio you could find fish worth eating. The juice was tart but also sweet, a lovely combination. I ate quickly, hungrier than I had realized. When I was done, I wiped my chin and hands first with the bag and then on my overalls.

Lobo landed as I was putting my trash in a recycling container. He opened a hatch as soon as he was fully down.

I walked inside.

We took off.

"That zone's logs are going to show—" I said.

Lobo cut me off. "Absolutely no trace of us. I've been busy, too," he said, "and their security system was weak. We might as well never have been here."

"Excellent," I said.

"And now we should leave," Lobo said.

"Not until we know Chang and the kids are safe. Take us out, but no farther than orbit, and give me all the feeds you can find that mention them."

"It's not like we can do anything else at this point," Lobo said.

I flashed on Chang standing among the still awakening children, all those kids spread around her. I hated abandoning them before I was certain they were safe and would get back to their homes.

"We can be sure!" I said. "We can verify that these kids are going home, that we saved them, that..." I forced myself to stop screaming. "We'll go back if we have to, but we won't let them down. We won't."

Lobo said nothing. Displays filled his front wall. Holos danced around the room. Two newstainment types were standing near Chang, stepping around and in front of her as they fought for the best position. An overhead shot showed at least another dozen converging on her. The kids stood and sat near her. The cops' own feeds looked good, the primary one the product of in-vehicle cameras focused on two attractive officers, a man and a woman, their faces set in

resolute expressions as they instructed the crowd to let
them in. Their voices boomed across multiple feeds.

"Do you know the names of these other children?"
one woman asked Chang.

"No," Chang said, "but I'm hoping that all of you
here will help the police identify them and return
them to their homes. I know their parents would
be as grateful to you as I am to have my son back."

Though probably not necessary, it was a smart move;
she'd made sure they realized the potential interviews
awaiting them if they could be there for the reunions
of these children with their parents.

The newstainment teams reacted quickly. Close-
up images of each of the kids played across all the
feeds as sympathetic voice-overs recounted the horrors
they'd endured. Announcer voices, their volume notice-
ably higher than the others, cut in and dangled the
hopes—though not the specifics—of rewards for those
who could step forward and help identify the kids.

The cops arrived. The team we'd seen earlier led
their charge. Other cops on their flanks made sure
we saw the calm, knowing faces of those two as they
took charge. Police departments can never afford the
best media people for their street action crews, but
they frequently attract young talent on the way up.

"We couldn't ask for more," Lobo said. "Can we go
now? I'd like to get out of this system before anyone
starts inspecting exiting craft. Right now, I've filed a
flight plan as a tourist shuttle heading to Mare, but
the backstory I built won't hold up well if anyone
decides to dig into it."

I scanned the displays once more. Chang held Tasson tightly while a police officer interviewed her. The

other children, probably still disoriented, stayed near her. Their faces played at different moments and in different sequences on other feeds.

"Yes," I said, "this should do it. Let's jump out of here."

"Good choice," Lobo said. "I've already reconfigured as the shuttle, and we're heading for the gate."

The combination of post-mission weariness and fatigue from the short and poor sleep last night made me feel tired even though darkness had yet to fall. "I'm going to nap," I said. "Wake me when it's our turn to jump." Even after all the thousands of times I've gone through jump gate apertures, I still love watching the miracle of the process.

"Don't rest yet," Lobo said.

"Why?"

"We have two new problems," he said, "and we need to decide before the jump what to do about them."

CHAPTER 13

Jon Moore

I VERY MUCH WANTED to sleep. "These can't wait?" I said.

"Imagine a world in which I disturb you without significant cause," Lobo said. "We call that 'fantasy.' To put it differently, sure, it can wait, as long as you are willing to let me decide your future for you. That has not, however, been your past preference."

Something I'd done had annoyed him, but I didn't have the energy right then to pursue it. "Okay, what are the problems?"

"As I said, we have two. What I didn't mention yet is that they are related."

"So maybe one solution will fix both," I said. "That's a good thing."

"I would agree with you," Lobo said, "except that you aren't going to make the choice that would do that. You're going to make a bad choice."

I yawned. "How about we stop discussing what these might be and how I might behave, and instead tell me what they are."

"Fine," Lobo said.

Yeah, he was annoyed, but I refused to rise to the bait.

"The first problem concerns the host of the auction."

I already didn't like this.

"As you may recall from the feeds I showed you initially, they have already identified him. In case you missed his name, he is Luis Kang." Lobo paused.

"I didn't remember that," I said, "but so what? I heard that he's important and on some Central Coalition council, but he's also clearly guilty of kidnapping and trying to sell children."

"Luis Kang," Lobo said, "is the chairman of the Central Coalition council that oversees activities on Haven."

Oh, crap.

"He is also the former planetary president of Haven, as well as, at a hundred and fifty-three years old, one of the oldest, richest, and most powerful men on that planet."

Haven was the second world humanity colonized via jump gates. Pinkelponker, where I was born, was the first planet humans reached after Earth, but we got there via a generation ship. The first jump gate appeared in the original solar system very shortly after the gen ship crashed on Pinkelponker. It took us to Freedom, the oldest nonEarth human world. The second aperture to open in Freedom's gate led to Haven.

"So we busted a very dangerous man," I said. "That's probably a good reason to avoid any of his friends, but given how old he is, he's likely to die in jail."

"The first problem is not the fact that Kang was the auction host. The problem is that he is already free."

"What?"

"He's back on Haven. As a Central Coalition council head, he enjoys the benefits of the reciprocal diplomatic immunity agreements that all three coalitions have in place. He's in his estate on Haven, where the news from Studio barely made a blip, and no one is bothering him. The few times some newstainment hound has worked up the courage to ask, Kang has explained away the whole thing as a terrible misunderstanding of a charity auction in which the families of the children were participating—and would be well compensated."

"So his status lets him walk, and his money will buy off the families?"

"It appears that will indeed be the outcome," Lobo said, "or at least enough of the families that the news story is already vanishing quickly."

Maybe Chang and Lobo were right. Maybe I should have killed Kang, killed all of them.

None of that mattered now, though; it was over. At least I'd saved the children.

"I hate that," I said, "but it's over."

"Ah," Lobo said, "is it? Kang threatened to hunt you down. He has the resources to do it, or at a minimum to make a very good try of it."

"So we run to some faraway world many jumps from here, and we live quietly for a while. We've done that before."

"Indeed we have, and that's the very course of action I recommend. Living quietly has not, though, been what you've been doing of late."

Anger coursed through me. "It's not like I've been wasting time. I—we—have been saving children."

"Yes, we have, but that's not going to be possible if we confine ourselves to one world and a low-profile lifestyle for long enough to let Kang get over his anger—or to come to regret the expense of hunting us."

I did not want to stop the work we'd been doing. I did not want to give up on all those children on all those worlds who were still being used as child soldiers, sold into slavery, abused. "I'll have to think about it," I said, "but in any case we could head away from here right now."

"I would love that choice," Lobo said, "but you're not going to make it, as I mentioned, because of our second problem."

"Which is?" I said.

"I found this audio-only recording waiting under your name in a variety of public mail systems here on Studio. As you'll hear, if you want me to play it, the message isn't only here."

Crap. "Play it."

"You could ignore it," Lobo said. "We could jump far, far from Haven and hide out from Kang for a very long time."

"Play it," I said.

A voice filled the air.

"Jon," a woman's voice said, "it's Omani, Omani Pimlani. I'm leaving this note for you on every single human world."

"Pause," I said. "Seat, please."

Lobo extended a pilot couch.

I sat in it and shook my head. I had not heard from Omani since I was thirty-five years old, over a hundred and twenty years ago. She was the first woman I loved, and the only one I had ever tried to build a relationship with. I'd left at a time when she'd needed me. I had good reasons, including the fact that she had noticed that I wasn't aging, a trait I hadn't realized until then that I had. Some combination of the way Jennie had healed me and the nanomachines in my cells from the scientists in Aggro had made me, at least so far, immune to aging. I couldn't let her find out the truth, because eventually it would have led again to people experimenting on me. I would never let myself be a lab animal again. That wasn't the only reason I'd left, but it was the main one, and it had caused me to desert her when she had most needed me. I'd chosen protecting myself over her, a choice that had bothered me for decades. It sometimes still did.

Omani was five years older than I was, which meant she had to be of the very oldest humans alive. Why was she contacting me now?

"Resume," I said.

"I want to see you, Jon," her voice said, "because I'm dying. I haven't been able to keep up with you, because there's not a lot of data out there about you, but from what I can tell, you are still alive. I've never forgotten you, Jon, and I've never understood why you left. Grant a dying old woman one of her last wishes: Come see me, and explain it all to me. I'm easy to find, because I never left Haven, not for any serious period of time. I'm still here in York." A few seconds of quiet. "Please, Jon. You owe me this much."

"That's it," Lobo said.

I said nothing. I'd never expected to hear from her again. I assumed she had moved on, led a normal life, and by now, died. Rich people with great medical facilities—she had the money, and Haven had the medtech—routinely lived into their early hundred and fifties, but very few lasted past that. I'd heard of small groups here and there in their hundred and sixties, most of them in terrible physical condition, and almost no one older.

I'd learned with Omani that I could never allow myself to build a real relationship with any woman. Though a few had tempted me, I knew it could never work. I'd always moved on. With her, though, against all the social obstacles Haven had put in our way, we'd given it a go for a couple of years.

I shook my head to clear it.

"Now I understand what you meant," I said.

"And was I right?" Lobo said.

"That we should leave here and jump to some planet far, far away? Yes."

"No," Lobo said. "Was I right that we won't?"

We should leave. I shouldn't take the risk that Kang had been blustering when he threatened me. If he wasn't, if he was seriously going to send people to find me, jumping to his home world was a very bad choice. I also couldn't let Omani see me as I am, because what was once a small age difference was now so huge that she would realize immediately that I did not age.

She was right, though, that I owed her. I had loved her, the only time I've ever let myself love any woman fully, the only time I ever could have done that. I could make up a story that would help a dying woman feel better. It would be a lie, but it would also be a kindness. I did owe her that.

I nodded my head. "Yes," I said, "you were. We're going to Haven. Spend the next day gathering what you can on Pimlani and jumping us to a lot of different worlds. Change your look and our registration as often as you safely can. Let's make our path difficult to follow."

"One last time," Lobo said. "You know this is a bad, dangerous idea that could put us both at great risk. Heading to Haven is a bad plan."

I chuckled. "Well, the last time you told me something was a bad plan, it resulted in us saving ten children from slavery."

"And in one of the richest, most powerful men in the oldest planetary coalition enraged at us and possibly hunting us."

"We won't stay long," I said. "I just owe her one visit." I stood. "I'm going to sleep."

"Will you at least tell me how you know Pimlani?" Lobo said.

I wanted to, but I couldn't explain it without giving away my most dangerous secrets.

"No," I said. "I'm going to bed, and I'm going to sleep." I thought but did not say that I'm also going to figure out how to approach Pimlani so safely that she won't be suspicious and no one else on Haven, including Kang, will notice we were there.

I started for my quarters. As the door to them slid open, I said, "It'll be fine."

"Nothing in our experience," Lobo said, "suggests that will be true."

"Just take us to Haven."

124 years ago

*York City
Planet Haven*

CHAPTER 14

Jon Moore

THE DAY I first saw Omani Pimlani, I was digging a hole.

I was working with the same type of wood-and-metal shovel I'd used on Pinkelponker as a kid twenty years earlier. No one needed to have people dig with shovels, because modern tools would do it themselves with only a little guidance, but the fashion of the day in York for the very wealthy was to use humans to do as much as possible. Anyone moderately well off could afford a smart tool or two; you had to be obscenely rich to pay giant staffs of human help.

The Pimlani family was more than obscenely rich, one of the twelve original families to settle Haven and possibly the wealthiest; no one knew for sure how much money each of those families had. Consequently, laborers like me were working in twos and threes and fours all over their property.

The situation suited me well. For the past fourteen years, since I'd escaped from Aggro, I'd stuck to the simplest, lowest-profile jobs I could find. I worked enough shifts to keep the job and pay for someplace cheap to live, and I saved all the money I could. In all my spare time, I read and watched videos and listened to music and generally enjoyed my ability to learn. I didn't expect anyone to have survived Aggro, and from what I'd gathered since escaping from there, no one had. I still worried, though, that some records of me might have persisted, and that someone might one day revive the Aggro research program, so I made sure to draw as little attention to myself as possible.

I also didn't mind the work. You did what someone told you to do, put your back into it, got some exercise, and then did it all again the next day. The nanomachines in my body healed me as I slept, so I awoke fresh and without any trace of soreness each morning.

Lately, though, I'd been questioning whether I needed to live this way. No one had seemed interested in me since my escape. I was bored and knew I could do more. Boredom entered when the work stopped, but I thought more and more frequently about doing something that might engage my brain. I was also attracted by all that the city of York had to offer—attractions that were, for the most part, available only to those with a great deal more money than I had.

The hole I was digging was to house a tree that sat a few meters away, ready for planting. A guy I barely knew, Liam, was working with me. We were on opposite sides of the hole, widening it and deepening it to the target specs: two meters in diameter, a meter and a half deep. We could have fit the tree in a smaller space, but our orders were for a hole this size, so that's what we were digging.

"Break time," Liam said.

All the workers I could see were stopping, so I figured he was right. I thrust the blade of my shovel hard into the earth, climbed out of the hole, spread my arms wide, and stretched.

That's when she came running around the corner of the main house. She wasn't jogging, she was *running*, moving out fast, her arms and legs pumping hard, her mouth closed, her expression focused and intense. Some sort of bright blue exercise specialty garment—I knew nothing about them—held her breasts in place so they didn't move at all, and she wore matching bright blue shorts. Sweat glistened on every part of her exposed skin, which was as dark brown as the trunk of the tree we were planting. A thick braid of black hair hung to her waist and flapped occasionally as she ran.

At the peak of my stretch, she glanced my way, made eye contact, smiled, and then faced forward and ran quickly out of sight along the long driveway that led to the front of the property.

I heard Liam laugh. "Don't even think about it. That's the boss's one and only child. There's no jump gate in the universe that can leap the gap between them and us."

"Did I say anything?"

He laughed again. "You didn't need to. She and I and, well, anybody else who was looking heard you loud and clear."

I shook my head and smiled. "I'm not responsible for what you think."

"No," he said, "but you are responsible for what *you* do. You just be careful."

The day I first spoke with Omani Pimlani, I was reading.

I had developed the habit of shopping after work in a local market, buying fresh bread, meat or fish, and cheese, and making myself a few sandwiches. I'd carry them, a bottle of fresh juice, and a reader to a nearby park that occupied two square city blocks and was filled with fountains. Each of the fountains was a miniature of a waterfall back on Earth. I didn't care at all about Earth, so I never bothered to learn their names, but I found the sounds of rushing water soothing. It wasn't the same as the ocean back home on Pinecone Island on Pinkelponker—the waterfalls, even in miniature, were forceful, insistent, like the waves during a storm—but still it relaxed me. I would find a place to sit in the warm sun of the summer late afternoon, eat my food, and read.

Other folks, children and old people and every age in between, walked and ran and played and talked and cuddled all over the park, but none of them bothered me. I felt a part of humanity without having to interact with others, an easy, comfortable feeling for me.

I was sitting on grass that looked almost blue in the soft light, leaning against the wall that ringed the park, reading and listening to the nearest waterfall. Its initial cascades hit many ledges on their way to the bottom, each ledge spraying a fine mist into the air, so I sat back from it a few meters so I wouldn't get wet.

I saw the shadow of a person approaching and looked over the top of the reader to see who was coming.

"I thought I recognized you," the woman said at the same moment that I realized who it was.

Her appearance was completely different this time. She wore purple pants of a material so fine that I marveled that I couldn't see right through it. Her shirt was a lighter purple that clung to her frame. Her long black hair hung loose down her back. She stepped into the mist from the fountain, stopped, and stared at me, either unaware that she was getting wet or unconcerned about it.

I recalled Liam's advice and said only, "Have we met?"

She laughed, a good, full-bodied laugh, nothing held back. "Is that really how you want to play this?" she said. She studied my face for a few seconds. "I know you remember me, because you couldn't take your eyes off me when I ran by where you were working a few days ago. We stared at each other long enough that I sure remember you, even though now you're clean and not sweating. So, my guess is someone told you it was dangerous to talk with the boss's daughter."

I put down the reader and stood. I realized now how tall she was, only a hand's-width shorter than I. She was gorgeous, and she knew it, but as near as I could tell, her comments didn't come from ego; she remembered when we made eye contact.

I smiled. "Good guess."

"Was it the old 'Don't risk your job over a girl' advice?"

I shook my head. "No. It was the equally old 'The rich aren't the same as the rest of us' advice."

"That's a better and more accurate admonition," she said, "but I think you should ignore it all the same.

I've heard similar sentiments from my father, and I plan to ignore them now."

"Why?" I said. "You know almost nothing about me. The one thing you do know is that I do the lowest jobs at the lowest pay on your father's estate. That's not exactly an advertisement designed to attract someone in your position."

"Oh, I know more than that," she said. "I know that when I've watched you work, your eyes never stop looking around, as if you're always preparing for something bad to happen. I know you sit alone when you eat, preferring reading over talking. I know you don't notice when women around the place notice you. I know you're pretty and well built but don't realize it."

I looked at the ground and shook my head, my face hot as I blushed. I rarely spoke to women outside of work, and none had ever talked to me like this.

She laughed, but this time it was a smaller, kinder, softer laugh. "And now I know you blush, which is also completely adorable."

I appreciated her compliments, but I was also beginning to feel like she was playing with me. I forced myself to look her in the eyes. "The way you're talking about me, I sound more like a pet than a man. I'm not sure I like that."

"I'm sorry," she said. "That's not my intent. As you can probably tell, I'm used to saying whatever I want, getting whatever I want, and not encountering much resistance in the process. So let me try again." She stuck out her hand. "I'm Omani Pimlani. I'd like to get to know you. If you don't want that, too, then say so, and I'll leave you to your reading."

I shook her hand. Her fingers were long and thin, her hand soft. I was conscious of how large and rough mine must have felt to her.

Screw Liam; I could always find another low-end job, and this one was doomed to end anyway when the Pimlanis finished their renovations.

"I'm Jon Moore," I said. "I'd like that."

24 days from the end

*In orbit and in York City
Planet Haven*

CHAPTER 15

Jon Moore

WE SPENT A day and a half making our very winding way to Haven. In the course of that trip, we jumped to a dozen different planets, occasionally leaving the jump gate area to go down to a planet's surface, have Lobo reconfigure himself as a different type of ship, and then jump again with a new name and look. By the time we were departing the Haven jump gate for York, Lobo was a specialty transport ship bringing gems and other rare stones to a list of legitimate stores in that city.

"Is Pimlani still alive?" I said.

"To the best of my ability to tell," Lobo said, "yes. That is largely a deduction from the absence of any signs of her death, however. I cannot find any evidence of her doing anything outside her home for more than two years."

"Her family is too important for her death to go unreported," I said.

"Agreed," he said.

We flew toward a public landing area on the westernmost edge of the city, turned, and ran around the southern part of York as Lobo transformed his logo and some of his exterior features so he resembled a tourist shuttle. We joined in with the other shuttles cruising half a kilometer off the coast on the eastern, oceanfront side of the York. Unless someone had been carefully tracking us the entire time, we should now be as anonymous as we could reasonably be.

"There used to be a large outdoor market in the southwest area of York," I said. "Is it still there?"

"Yes," Lobo said.

"There also used to be a big park not far from the market, a park filled with fountains. Is that still standing?"

"Yes, it is," he said. "From what I can gather from the historical records, the huge percentage of this city that is, was, and always has been under the control of a relatively small number of people has let them keep it roughly the same for quite some time, certainly for the short amount of time since you could have last been here."

I ignored his unspoken question. We couldn't address my true age without also discussing my nanomachines.

"Is the location Pimlani gave us near those two?"

Lobo threw a holomap into the middle of the front room, where we were talking. Labels highlighted all three locations. "Yes, as I expect you knew it would be."

I nodded. "Just making sure."

The park was smaller than it had been. The market, though, was vastly larger, easily four or five times the size it had been when I'd lived here. That was good news, because the larger it was, the more likely it was to have a broad range of vendors.

The safest path into Omani's estate was to have Lobo land me there, but I couldn't take Lobo with me. I couldn't visit Omani looking like I did. I had to look the age she expected me to be, and to do that, I would require specialized help. I had no way to explain to Lobo why I needed to look ancient.

"Put us down in the busiest public landing site near the market and the park," I said. "I haven't been here for a long time, so I want to wander around a bit before I call her and then visit. In fact, I've been living inside you so long that—no offense—I'd like to sleep on a full-size bed and eat a few meals prepared from fresh food. So, I'm going to stay the night somewhere nearby, then probably see her tomorrow."

"And while you're walking memory lane," Lobo said, "exactly what am I going to be doing?"

"Initially, nothing," I said. "As I'm about to enter Pimlani's estate, I'll let you know I'm on the way in. From then on, I want you watching my back from above and standing by to come get me, just in case."

"In case of what?" Lobo said.

I shook my head. I couldn't tell him that if by some chance Pimlani knew I still looked the same age as the day I met her she might well want to know how that was possible and whether the knowledge could help her. "I have no clue," I said, "but because I agree with you that simply being on this planet is a risk, and because there's no way her family and Kang's don't know one another, I'd just as soon err on the side of excess caution."

"The best way to do that," Lobo said, "would be not to visit her in the first place and simply to leave Haven now."

I sighed. "We've been through all that, and I'm not changing my mind. So, why don't we instead study what data you can get on her property and work out my exit options."

It was Lobo's turn to sigh. "It's your life," he said. "I'm just along to die supporting you."

I laughed. "Please. If anything were to happen to me, you could get away easily."

"But I wouldn't," Lobo said, "as you should know."

He was right. I was being unfair. "I do," I said, "and I'm sorry. And, I truly appreciate it."

A holo of the Pimlani estate appeared in the middle of the round.

"Before you turn all weepy and start trying to hug my walls," Lobo said, "let's go over this place."

I left Lobo in an outdoor space at the far rear of the public landing zone he'd chosen. We'd discussed putting him in a hangar but ultimately decided to leave him in the open. Anyone looking for us would expect us to hide him under cover, but with the most recent set of mods, no one from Kang's team should have been able to recognize him, so leaving him outside seemed the best overall choice. Plus, he could leave quickly if need be.

I set off on foot. Should someone track us to that area, I didn't want any immediate taxi records. I carried a pack with a change of clothing, as well as a wallet that gave me an ID that should hold up for at least a few days and that had a rather substantial money balance. I don't generally spend a lot, and over the years I've landed quite a few large scores, so I normally have no problem bearing the costs of small missions like these. I always tried, though, to bring far more money than I should ever need to spend, because sometimes extra money provided the best path out of a difficult situation.

I'm going to see an old friend, I realized, and I view it as a mission. I shook my head. Normal people didn't think that way.

On the other hand, it could be a mission, because it could be a trap. When I knew Omani, she was brilliant and beautiful and fun, but she also possessed more than a little of the drive and ruthlessness that had made her family rich and powerful. I had no doubt that if she knew I didn't age, she would lock me in a cage until either scientists she would hire had figured out what made me that way or she died.

I wasn't wrong. It was a mission, and I'd do damned well to remember that fact.

Yet it was a mission no one was asking me to undertake. I could ignore Pimlani's messages. In a few years at most, she'd almost certainly be dead, and the problem would have taken care of itself. I just couldn't shake the feeling that I owed her. Once, all those years ago, at least for a couple of years I had been sure we loved one another. We'd been together almost all the time, and for the most part the experience had been great. I hadn't lived with a woman since that time—I didn't count bunking with squad mates on combat or training missions—and I sure hadn't let myself get that close to any other woman.

I shook my head to clear it. I'd been over this ground before. All I was doing was wasting time. I also wasn't paying attention to my surroundings, which is never wise. Walking while lost in thought and mostly blind to the world around you is a good way to get hurt, particularly in a big city.

Most large cities follow similar layouts, but not York. York was an urban testimony to the power of very old money. Part of the usual layout more or less existed: Downtown areas crammed with skyscrapers gleaming with corporate logos held the center of the city, with neighborhoods of varying degrees of wealth sprawling all around it. What made York so different was that scattered through it were the estates of the seven families that had managed to hold onto their wealth and influence from the time of Haven's colonization to today. The smallest of those estates was over fifty hectares, and most ran to a hundred or more hectares. These great wooded private areas were walled off from the rest of the city, protected by both machine and human security systems. They were as much parks as residences, though people lived in them to this day.

Omani's family resided in the very largest of them, most of its multiple houses and the grand main building constructed during the first decade humans were on Haven.

Kang and many members of his family also lived in one of the estates. Fortunately, it was on the far side of York from Omani's home.

I was walking in a commercial area that was rapidly transitioning to a tourist and residential district. In every big city on every world I've visited, the same human currents ebb and flow. A part of the city runs down and turns poor and dangerous. Those in power initially ignore it and try simply to contain its troubles; as long as what happens in it stays in it, even the police give it only token attention. Over time, of course, the problems of any area spill over into nearby zones, so politicians start making speeches about it, and the city sends in more cops. Meanwhile, the cost of living in the city keeps rising, so a few intrepid souls, lured by low prices in the bad parts of town, buy and move in. If all goes well, more follow them, and gentrification turns the district from dangerous to funky, and then from funky into a shopping and eating destination. Tourists come both to partake of the offerings of the vendors and to watch the natives, who marvel that somehow they've become attractions. The lucky districts stop their transformations there; the unlucky ones continue to morph from interesting to bland and ultimately become indistinguishable from others like them in any city on any world.

From the looks of this area—restaurants and shops inhabiting buildings that were new when I was here over a century ago, cute beige and curlicue signs that told me I was in the Swanson District, the bags of pedestrians fighting for attention as they displayed the acquisitions of their proud new owners—we had reached the full-on gentrified stage and were at the tipping point for the possible slide into blandness.

For my purposes, it was perfect. Hotels would be nearby, and crowds would ensure that I didn't draw any particular attention to myself. Enough of the people I saw on the sidewalks were old that at least some parts of Swanson were bound to cater to them. The large outdoor market I'd once frequented abutted Swanson, so I was confident that somewhere in those two I would be able to find what I needed.

I thought about the old men at the auction. Many used exoskeletons. All were well dressed. Some, such as Kang with his cane, affected more traditional tools of the elderly. Kang moved in the same money circles as Omani, so he would make a suitable model.

The afternoon sun was on its way down, the day heading toward night, but from Lobo's research I knew that both the shops here and the outdoor market's stalls stayed open well into the night. I had time.

I hailed a taxi and had it drive me slowly toward the market. I'd hoped for a SleepSafe, but none was anywhere close to Omani's estate. When we were a block from the market, I had the taxi take a slow loop around it toward the estate. We were still a few kilometers away when I spotted a three-story local hotel wedged between two equally tall buildings. It called itself the Swanson Market Inn. The holos on its street-facing walls proclaimed it to be a local tradition with the capacity to hold any size party.

I went inside and rented a small suite with an additional bedroom that connected to it, a room I said I would need as soon as my grandfather and others of my family arrived. I left the pack and the change of clothes and headed on foot to the market.

It was time to make me an old man.

124 years ago

York City
Planet Haven

CHAPTER 16

Jon Moore

THE DAY I first kissed Omani Pimlani, I was preparing to meet her father.

"Is this really necessary?" I asked. We were standing outside her house after work one day. I was washing my face and hands in a sink those of us who worked outside used to clean our tools and ourselves.

"Meeting my dad?" she said.

"Yes." I'd heard a lot of stories about him, and he was one of the richest and most powerful men on Haven, so I was nervous. I'd been spending a lot of time with his daughter over the past couple of months, nothing that I thought of as romantic, simply being together, but from what Liam and the others at work had said, no father believes any time a man spends with his daughter is innocent. That made it worse. Worse still, even being around anyone so powerful was directly contrary to my goal of maintaining a low profile.

Against all that, was the ability to spend time with

Omani, who stood in front of me, staring into my eyes, and who was the best part of every day I got to see her.

"Yes," she said, "it is necessary. He has no ability to require it—I'm thirty-eight years old—but he doesn't see things that way. Plus, every other man I've ever dated has met him on the first or second date." She paused, stepped back, and looked away for a second. "I think at least half of them saw me as the easiest way to meet him, because they always ended up wanting something from him."

"Are we dating?" I said. I'd never thought of it that way. We met after work most days, ate some dinners in parks together, talked, listened to street musicians, walked around the giant market, and so on, but I'd never thought of it as dating.

She laughed and put her hand on my cheek. "You are so adorable."

I blushed.

She laughed again. "See what I mean?"

"I'm getting that sense of being a pet again," I said, "and I can't say as I like it."

"Sorry," she said. "I meant it as a compliment." She paused. "Is it bad that we're dating?"

It wasn't good for remaining unattached and ready to move on, but I loved the time we spent together. "No," I said. "It's just . . . I've never spent this much time with a woman before, and I've never dated anyone, so I don't really understand it."

She hugged me briefly and, as she held me, said into my ear, "Don't worry. I do."

As I often did with Omani, I had the unnerving feeling of walking into the middle of a play and, even though I was hearing the lines the actors were saying, having no clue what they meant.

She stepped back. "Are you ready to go?"

"Yes," I said, "though only because you say we have to."

"You could go home and change if you wanted."

"Why?" I said. "I'm clean enough not to track dirt into your house, and it's not like he doesn't know what I do."

She smiled. "Is there nothing you want from him?"

I shook my head. "Not a thing. Why would I?"

She smiled again. "Let's go."

She led me around the front of the main building to the far side, through a door there, and up an elevator to the top floor. "Daddy's office is the entire top floor of the house."

"That's more room than most well-off families have in their whole houses," I said.

She shrugged. "He likes a lot of space, and he likes the view."

It was my turn to shrug. I'd never lived anywhere with more than a bathroom, a living area, and a bedroom. Many places I've stayed merged all of those into one room. "He can afford it," I said.

She simply nodded.

We stepped out of the elevator into a wide, shallow waiting room with no windows and a lot of security cameras. Omani stepped to the door directly across from us, but it didn't open.

She glanced back at me and whispered, "Great. He's in a mood." She stared up at one of the cameras and said, "Daddy, I'd like to introduce you to Jon, the man I've mentioned."

"Come in," his voice boomed from multiple speakers around the room. "I'm down with the computers."

The door opened. She stepped closer to me and whispered, "He meets people there when he wants to show off. Just act impressed."

"Why?" I said.

She stared at me for a second. "I always say that, but I guess it's to make him happy. Act however you want."

I nodded.

We walked across the vast single open room that occupied three-fourths of this floor. Shelves of ancient books filled much of the area, rows of them leading from either side of this central aisle. Here and there, small groups of chairs and tables stood like oases in a sea of books. Pictures and photographs and odd constructions of clay and rope and paper hung on the ends of bookcases and on walls. I'd never seen anything like it. I'd read about libraries, but as historical artifacts; any reader could get you anything you might want, were you the sort of person who liked to read. Most didn't.

Near the other side of the space, we walked through an open archway into a room within a room, its walls full of displays. Some of the screens showed information I recognized as news; financial data filled most of them. The man I assumed to be her father stood across from us and stared out a window in the side of the house. He couldn't be doing anything useful from there, so I figured he was trying to make a statement, showing that he would face us when he was good and ready. I had no particular desire to be there, so that was fine with me.

Omani, though, seemed concerned. She cleared her throat before she said, "Daddy, I'd like to introduce you to Jon Moore, the man I've been seeing."

He turned around. He looked barely older than Omani, though that meant nothing. People with money tended to look the same from their mid-twenties into their sixties or seventies, until whenever the best medtech available could no longer make their skin appear young. He was shorter than Omani by almost a head, so he had to look up to meet my eyes. He stared at me for a few seconds, stepped toward me, and waited.

I stepped forward to meet him, stuck out my hand, and said, "It's nice to meet you, sir."

He waited a few seconds, then closed the rest of the distance between us and shook my hand. His grip was strong, but his hands had the smooth, soft feeling of a person who didn't use them in his work. The handshake was brief.

He stepped back. "I'd ask what you do," he said, "but of course I already know." He stared at Omani for a moment, then back at me. "My daughter seems to like to annoy me with her choice of men, but she usually aims rather a bit higher."

"Daddy!" she said.

I felt the anger rising in me, but I worked to keep it under control as I said to her, "It's fine, Omani." To him, I said, "Mr. Pimlani, I don't know what you think is going on, but all we've been doing is spending time together for a couple of months. I also don't know why you want to annoy Omani or insult me, but neither one seems like a good use of your time."

He put his hands behind his back. "What exactly do you want?"

"Nothing," I said. "Omani told me it was time I met you, so here I am."

"You have no great scheme you want to propose to me? No art you're creating at night and would like me to see, no story about how your job as a laborer is just a way to feed yourself until your genius is recognized?"

I laughed. "Omani said other men had used her to get to you. Are those some of the things they wanted?"

For the first time, he smiled, though only slightly. "Some of them. Many wanted far more."

I shook my head. "I like Omani. We eat and talk and listen to music and spend time in the parks. I didn't know until right after work today that we were dating. That's it."

"So what do you picture for the two of you in the future, you the laborer and she the heiress?"

"I've never considered the question," I said. I never assumed I would stay anywhere long, because the sorts of jobs I sought were always temporary. "I've never made plans longer than the duration of the job I was doing."

He studied me for a moment. "What are you afraid of?"

Of being imprisoned again as a test subject, I thought but could not say. *Of people finding out about the nanomachines in me. Of people around me dying, as Benny and others had.* "Nothing in particular," I finally said. "I've just never cared about the future. I grew up—" I couldn't explain that I had spent the first sixteen years of my life mentally challenged, unable to advance past the mental age of a typical five-year-old boy, so I groped for the closest explanation to the truth that I could use. "—without any real chance to learn, so right now I'm happy to work as I must and spend the rest of my time reading and learning and thinking."

He faced Omani. "We all enjoy time off, and we all enjoy those years we get to spend without responsibilities, simply doing as we will. In the end, though, we crave more. You will, too." He looked back at me. "I'm sure she finds your lifestyle romantic now, but it won't last. She'll want more of a partner one day, particularly given that she's my only child and eventually this estate and most of my holdings will be hers."

"Daddy!" Omani said. She was clearly struggling to control her temper.

Getting in a fight with him would cost her more than it would cost me, so I stepped closer to him and shrugged. "I have no clue how this whole dating thing works. I've never dated anyone. What I do know is that Omani says what she thinks, and she thinks a lot. If she decides she doesn't want to spend any more time with me, I'm sure she'll say so. I'd do the same if I felt that way. I don't see, though, why either of us has to make any of those decisions right now."

I paused. His attitude angered me, but I also found it sad, bordering on pathetic. "I've never had any children, of course," I said, "but I had a younger sister I used to try to take care of." I paused again. Though younger and smaller than I, Jennie was both vastly smarter and also a healer, so she'd spent more time taking care of me than I had of her. I always wanted, though, to protect her, and it still hurt me that I'd been unable to stop the men from Pinkelponker's government who took her away so she could heal only the people they considered important. "I know that if I ever got to see her again—I don't know where she is right now—I'd never talk to her the way you're speaking to Omani. I don't know why you feel you have to be mean, but you don't. I can tell you just from the way she talks about you that like everybody else, she's scared of you, but unlike the other people I see working for you, she's your daughter, and she loves you." My face burned, partly from anger at him, partly from embarrassment at talking so much about things I understood so little.

He stared at me for several seconds, his face under tight control.

I couldn't read his expression at all, other than to know that he was keeping it neutral. I had the sense that he had learned long ago to make sure that other people couldn't make him show his feelings when he didn't want them to.

Finally, he said, "I'm sorry, Omani. I worry about you, and I want to protect you. I also owe you an apology, Mr. Moore. As I said, most men who have come before you have wanted something from me. Most people do. It's . . . unusual and a bit refreshing to meet someone who does not." He took a deep breath. "At the risk of sounding again too much like either an overprotective father or an old man, I have to tell you that one day you will want more from life than what you're doing now, that if you're any sort of man at all you'll want to do things you believe in, try to improve a world, maybe many worlds, take care of the people you love—all of those things."

Each of those sounded like a high-risk proposition to me, ways to draw attention to myself and end up getting locked again in some lab somewhere, but I had to admit that the more I learned, the older I grew, the more I wanted to do something more significant with myself than simply move from one low-end job to the next.

"I expect you're right, sir," I said. "I've begun to have some of those yearnings."

He nodded. "So does your lack of planning extend to today?"

I tilted my head at him in question. "Sir?"

He smiled. "Do you have any specific plans for what you'll be doing this evening?"

I laughed. "Sometimes we do, but not today. If I want something in particular, I say so, but usually I don't, so I ask her. Omani never lacks for ideas."

"I'm right here, you know," she said.

"Sorry," I said. "I meant that as a compliment."

She took my arm. "We're going to the market, Daddy, to buy some food for a picnic. Then we'll find a place to eat and talk, maybe find some music to listen to later. That's about as wild as we usually get."

"Well," he said, "you two have a good time."

He extended his arms, and she came forward and hugged him. When she finished, she stepped back, and he and I shook hands again.

"It was...interesting to meet you, sir," I said.

He laughed again. "Relentlessly more honest than the others," he said. "That won't always work for you, but it's fine right now. It was interesting to meet you, too."

Omani tugged on my arm and led me away.

As we were going, I glanced back to see him staring at us. I nodded and waved goodbye.

He turned to the displays to his right.

Omani said nothing as we walked through the huge open space, so I also stayed quiet.

When we'd left the room and the elevator doors had closed behind us, Omani turned to face me. "You were amazing, Jon," she said.

She put her hand on my cheek, closed her eyes, and kissed me.

24 days from the end

York City
Planet Haven

CHAPTER 17

Jon Moore

AS I WALKED, I considered the problem of fooling Omani. The challenge I faced was not so much initially appearing old as sustaining that illusion from up close, from a conversational distance, from closer still if she wanted to hug me. At the same time, I wanted to be able to get away quickly should something go wrong.

I was rarely around the truly old, but the auction from which I'd saved those kids had shown me quite a few old men. Many of them had been rail thin, but some were heavy. I couldn't appear particularly thinner, so I'd have to go heavier to show some age. Doing that had the added benefit of letting me hide body armor. I could handle being shot, but the healing time would slow me, so if I could save that time, I'd be ahead of the game should anything go wrong.

Body armor went on my shopping list.

Quite a few of those old men had also used exoskeletons under their clothing. The right exoskeleton could be useful both for speed and to keep me going if I was hurt.

One of those went on the list.

I'd need a good suit tailored decently but not superbly to cover those things. I wanted to appear that I was doing well enough to still be alive, but not so well that I had any chance of moving among the sorts of extraordinarily wealthy people Pimlani knew.

All of that would help, but none of it addressed the central problem of making my face, neck, and hands appear old. All I'd ever been able to get my nanomachines to do was to disassemble things, so unfortunately they'd be of no use with this problem.

I'd seen stage actors fake aging well, though, so it was possible, though they generally didn't have to pass close inspection, and I did. Still, I clearly needed to find a business that worked with actors—or perhaps, I realized, with people who wanted costumes. Parties might create a demand for that sort of thing. Criminals might, too.

Whether any of what I was seeking would be available in this market was another question entirely. Certainly, the market as it was when I'd lived here would have offered none of it, but this one sprawled over four times as much ground as the one I'd known.

As I drew closer, shops of all sorts took over the buildings. People lived above some of the shops, but this was clearly an area where tourists and other shoppers came to spend money. As I reached the coordinates where the market should be, I saw that exactly where the market began and where the permanent shops ended was unclear. Some of what initially appeared to be stalls were, on closer inspection, small portable buildings locked in place by metal spikes in the ground, installations about as permanent as many poorly constructed buildings. Stores that bordered the market extended their reach past their boundaries with awnings that covered the sidewalks and half a meter of the street in front of them. Under the awnings stood merchandise displays, barkers both human and holo, and people, people everywhere.

I couldn't afford the time to visit every store and every market stall here. If Kang was indeed paying people to search for me, the sooner Lobo and I left for another planet far away, the better. Plus, if Omani truly was dying, each day counted. On the other hand, asking for help left a trail of queries with all the local marketing software, something I hated.

Still, I had no real alternative.

I started looking for an interactive guide. A place like this would have them scattered all around, but I wanted one I could use privately; no point in alerting people to what I was doing. I walked back a bit, away from the market, and looked for a post or a pedestal that could help me. I spotted two on the first street, but they were in use by multiple people at once, the holo shopping assistant answering questions in rapid alternation from each of the questioners, maps flashing into view as the holo spoke.

I walked over a couple of streets from the main road. I finally spotted a pedestal not in use. No one stood near it or seemed to be approaching it, so the odds were good that I could ask my questions without being disturbed. Down the block a bit, five tables sat on the sidewalk in front of a restaurant. The tables were full, four with two people each, and one with four

crowded around the small surface. The people facing
this way appeared to be focused on their tablemates
and their food, and not on anything else.

This was as good an opportunity as I was likely
to get.

I walked to the pedestal and stood in front of it.

A meter-high woman with golden skin, short hair,
and an unreasonably white smiled burst into view
above the pedestal. "How may I help you, sir?"

If I went with a cover story, at least the trail I left
might not gain as much notice as if I asked directly.
"I'm at a bit of a loss, I'm afraid," I said. "I don't
know exactly what I need."

You could almost see the software spot the upsell
possibilities and shift into another gear. The holo
grew slightly younger and bustier. I must have reacted
positively, because its shirt pulled back to reveal a
little cleavage. I focused on its eyes so it would stop
adapting to please me. Unfortunately, that meant trying to stare into the near space and not through it
to the building across the street, but I did the best I
could. "Can you tell me, sir, the sorts of things you're
looking for, or perhaps what your goals are."

"I need to attend a family reunion," I said, "but
an odd one: It's a costume party."

"Excellent, sir. Is it by chance in the city party
registries? If you give me your name, I can check
for you."

I held up my hands. "Thank you, but no. I'm
afraid our family is rather private and would prefer
to stay that way."

"I should say so, sir," the holo said. She leaned
closer and lowered her voice. "I couldn't find a match

for you in any of the databases I can access. You have excellent software."

And now because it had failed to identify me, it figured I was either a tourist, rich, or somehow very connected; the last two possibilities only increased my upsell potential.

"What type of costumes are you considering?" the holo said. "Here in Haven I am certain you can find multiple stores with anything you might imagine."

"It's a theme party," I said, "a go-as-your-ancestor sort of affair." I had no idea if such things existed, but it seemed reasonable that a very old family that was very full of itself might well hold one. "I want to go as my old grandfather, as he appeared not long before he died. As a young man, he looked a great deal like me."

"So older clothing might be in order," she said, "as well as something to age you."

"I'd prefer to stay with modern fashion," I said, "but something someone over one-fifty would wear."

"That will be the least of our challenges. I believe I can also show you some options for make-up. I could refine my search if you were willing to give me a sense of your budget. As I'm sure you know, Haven's stores and markets support a broad range of clientele and price ranges."

I needed the disguise to work; I couldn't afford the time to shop for bargains. Knowing full well that I was about to increase the likelihood of stores bothering me as I shopped, I said, "Cost is not an issue for me. Finding what I want is all that matters."

The holo nodded in approval. I noticed she now had more cleavage and a sparkling necklace directing my attention to her décolletage. "Very good, sir. I will point you to only the very best of our stores—not, of course, that York has any bad merchants. It is simply a case that some serve different types of buyers." She winked, the movement of the holo eye unsettling. "As I'm sure you understand. Should I now generate a list for you?"

"No, no," I said, "we're not quite done."

"Excellent, sir. What else would you like?"

"Granddaddy used an exoskeleton to help him get around. If you're going to do a thing, he would always say, do it right, so I want to get one, too. At the same time, if I'm going to buy one, I'd like to be able to use it later, so I was thinking one of the sporting models, something very strong, very fast, and very lightweight. That's not what he wore, but it will be under my clothing, so it should work."

"The very best exos," the holo said, "should meet all your requirements and more, but they are, as you're no doubt aware, quite a lot more expensive than the entry-level models."

"As I said earlier, cost does not matter to me."

The holo bowed slightly. "I apologize, sir. I mentioned it simply because we are now in an entirely different price range from the earlier items and services you are seeking." The image leaned closer and lowered her voice again, her tone now conspiratorial. "You know how athletes are: The more serious they are, the more they'll spend on their sports."

"Indeed," I said.

"Will there be anything else, sir?"

I had to hope that by now the software had flagged me as not only wealthy but also eccentric, because the body armor had the potential to trigger some flags.

Still, I needed it. "Granddaddy was also more than a bit paranoid," I said. I forced a chuckle. "The things he would do. Anyway, he always wore a layer of full body armor. I figure I can impress everyone else by getting that detail right, so I need some high-quality but lightweight body armor as well." I thought about how hot I would be while wearing it and added, "Ideally something self-cooling; these parties tend to run long, and I do hate sweating."

"Of course, sir. That should not be a problem. Is there anything else I could do for you, or should I now prepare your personalized guide?"

I was getting hungry, but with the profile I had built so far, any mention of food would cause this thing to send me to some expensive, high-end restaurant. I preferred to eat from street vendors who wouldn't give me a second look, so I said, "No, that should do it."

"If I might have your name, sir, so I could personalize your guide."

"That won't be necessary. As I mentioned, our family is rather private."

"Very good, sir. Your wallet, please."

I thumbed open a quarantined area in my wallet. I'd opted for the very best wallet I could afford, and Lobo had further enhanced its security, so I didn't worry that this standard city software could break into any other part of it. Nor should it even be trying, but it cost me little extra effort to be safe.

"You are all set, sir," the holo said. "I've provided you with five excellent options for the clothing, three for the aging make-up, three for the exoskeleton, and five more for the body armor. Is there anything else I could do for you? I exist to serve."

Sixteen vendors to visit! My head hurt even thinking about doing that. I would be ready to kill someone by the time I fought my way through the crowds as I went from store to store to endless store.

"Yes," I said, "there is. I am not a fan of shopping, nor do I like to wait. The clothing will obviously require tailoring."

"Obviously," the holo said. It nodded in agreement.

Companies clearly felt people liked their service agents to be this subservient and agreeable, but it was driving me crazy.

"So what I would appreciate is if you would highlight for me the single store in each category that has obtained the highest buyer ratings locally and that, in the case of the clothing, can most quickly do the tailoring. I'd also appreciate the most efficient route that ends at the clothing store."

"In what way would you like the ratings to be highest? As I'm sure you're aware, our clientele rate our vendors on a broad range of criteria."

"Best product," I said, "and fastest service. Just those."

"Very good, sir. If you would please..."

I reopened access to the area in my wallet.

"Thank you, sir. Your wallet now contains all of the necessary information. I could also, if you prefer, supply paper or standalone versions at a small fee; many visitors to York find they make excellent souvenirs. Not to imply, sir, that you are necessarily a visitor; I am simply extending the offer."

I shook my head. "No. I'm set."

"Very good, sir. Is there anything else I could do for you? I exist to serve."

"No."

I left and walked toward the market. When I was a few meters away from the shops directly on its edge, I found a spot where I could lean on the wall of a wooden building whose signs and holo barker proclaimed it to be the best place on Haven for interactive hats. I brought out my wallet. I studied the route, which suggested I head first to a store to examine exoskeletons. That made sense, because then that purchase could carry my others.

I followed the wallet's route into the market. The moment I hit the street where I'd been before, the crowds grew thicker. I hated the exposure of walking in places like this, because there was no way even Lobo could be sure everyone around me was safe. On my own, all I could do was try to avoid bumping into people and watch for suspicious looks or people who kept reappearing. I didn't expect Kang could possibly have tracked us here, and certainly not so soon, but still, the place jarred me a bit.

I was also even hungrier than before. When the route took me by a few stands from which smells wafted over me, my stomach churned. I decided to stop and eat.

When I'd lived here, most of the market's vendors sold food. Today, that had changed, and no one type of vendor dominated the area. You couldn't walk far, however, without encountering a small clump of food sellers. The rear of the one nearest where I stood housed a huge grill, on which a man and a woman were roasting skewers of meat and vegetables. Another man on the left was assembling the skewers from thin, almost white wooden sticks and containers holding chunks of three different types of meat and half a dozen vegetables. Up front, two women handed over the skewers or pulled off their contents, wrapped them in a thick bread, added some sauce, and then passed those to customers.

I joined the line, third in place behind two singles and a trio. The singles, one man and one woman, knew what they wanted and moved quickly. The trio, a pair of men each of whom was holding one hand of a woman, stood and debated their selection. I hated that. When you stand in line at a busy stand and can see what's on offer, use your waiting time to figure out your order.

The woman waiting on them glanced up, saw the expression on my face, and rolled her eyes at them.

I suppressed my laugh and smiled at her.

When the threesome had finally placed their orders and paid, I stepped forward.

"Don't you hate it when ..." the woman said as she titled her head toward the trio.

"I really do," I said.

"Anyway, what can I do for you?" she said.

"Give me the deluxe combo," I said, "and whatever fruit juice you think would go best with it. I trust your taste." There's always a deluxe combo at a street vendor, and it's almost always a bit overpriced and too much food. Too much food sounded just about perfect to me right now. Fortunately, the nanomachines flush from my system any food I don't need for calories, so I never gain fat.

The woman handed me a large cup containing a clear liquid and some ice. "I like this one," she said. "Sweet but still acidic enough to cut the grease."

I thumbed her my payment and took a sip of the

juice. It was delicious, cold and sweet with a tart edge. "Thanks," I said. "It's great."

She nodded and turned to the next person.

When my food was ready, I grabbed the plate—a bread roll of three meats and three veggies, a side of chunks of lightly fried veggies—and wandered until I found a large old tree between two stands selling scarves and other bits of fabric whose purposes eluded me but that seemed of great interest to many of the people walking by. The tree stood in a three-meter-wide circle of rich black dirt that had been packed by people walking and standing on it. I leaned against the tree, as others had so clearly done many, many times before me, and I wolfed down my food. It was everything you could hope for from street fare: hot and juicy and delicious and very, very filling. By the time I finished the last of my drink, I was stuffed.

A recycling bin ambled over from behind the stand on my right. "Your refuse, sir?" it said. A slot opened in its top.

I tossed in my plate and cup.

"Thank you, sir," the bin said. "Enjoy your time in York." It rolled back behind the stand.

York had certainly taken its market upscale. Few cities bothered to spend that kind of money on collecting bins; it was cheaper to let the sloppier customers drop their trash and have the cleaning bots pick it up after business hours.

I stared at the crowd and enjoyed for a few seconds longer the relative solitude of the tree. My stomach was full, no one was bothering me, and for a moment I forgot all of my cares. I had too much to do, though, to tarry for long.

I checked the route on my wallet. My first stop was the exoskeleton shop. I considered how best to explain that I needed it both to pass casual inspection as something an old man would wear and also be fast and powerful should I have to leave Pimlani's estate in a hurry.

I pushed off the tree.

Something hit the back of my head.

Black spots flashed in my eyes, something else tripped me, and I fell face-first toward the packed dirt.

CHAPTER 18

Jon Moore

I MANAGED TO BREAK my fall somewhat with my arms, but my head still smacked the ground hard. My right elbow popped oddly as I hit. Pain shot from it. The impact of the fall knocked most of the air from me. I couldn't focus enough to tell the nanomachines to block the pain.

Hands rolled me over. A large man and a smallish woman stared at me. The woman kneeled near my head. The man squatted next to my torso. Both were between the crowd and me.

"Are you okay, buddy?" the man said loudly. "That was a hell of a fall. You gotta watch those roots."

Much more softly, the woman said, "You yell for help or move, and I'll cut you." She showed me a knife with a blade as long as my palm and almost as wide as two of my fingers. "Nod if you understand me."

I did nothing. My head was clearing more with each passing second. I slightly flexed my right arm. The elbow worked, so if it had popped out of joint, it hadn't stayed out. My breath still came rough. I blinked my eyes a few times as if trying to focus.

She pushed the knife against my neck.

"I don't buy it," she whispered to her partner.

"Give him a second," the man said to her. "He hit hard." He slapped my face lightly. "You with us?"

My breathing was slowing. My vision was clear and, aside from the pain, so was my head. I instructed the nanomachines to block the pain, and it stopped instantly. They'd take care of my elbow automatically.

"Yeah," I said.

The woman held up the knife for an instant, then put it back against my throat. "You feel that?" she said.

"Yes."

"You yell, move, or do anything else we don't like," she said, "and I'll cut you deep. If you're lucky, I won't hit anything they can't patch. If you're not lucky or I'm sloppy, then you'll die right here—and you'll do it fast." She leaned over my head. "You understand?"

"Yes."

If they'd wanted to kill me, they would have already done so. Neither of them had pinned my arms or tried in any way other than the knife to immobilize me; sloppy. Whoever had sent them should have hired better help.

I made a choking sound. "Gonna throw up." I retched again.

Most people hate vomit, and they really hate the thought of someone getting it on them. These two were not exceptions. They pulled back a little. As they did, I rolled toward them fast, as if I were about to do it, then shot my right fist into the side of the woman's head and my right knee into the man's side.

Her head snapped to the side, and she fell backward, already out.

I hadn't hit him hard enough to do any real damage. He started to fall toward her but steadied himself with his right arm. I reversed my right arm's direction and back-fisted his face.

He yelped and punched me weakly in the stomach with his left hand.

I grabbed his neck and pulled him across my body. I rolled with him so I ended up on top of him and punched him hard in the side of his neck.

He grabbed his throat and made choking, gasping noises.

I punched him in the stomach three more times before I realized he wasn't a threat any longer.

He gagged, turned his head to the side, and threw up on the ground.

I picked up the woman's knife. She was still out.

I kneeled in front of the man. I spoke loudly, both so anyone walking by would hear and so I could hear myself over the blood pounding in my ears. "You okay, buddy?"

I glanced toward the market. A man and a woman had stopped and were staring at us. I waved at them. "My brother," I said. "Too much to drink. He'll be fine."

They moved on.

I wouldn't have much time before more people would notice, and eventually someone would call the police.

I pulled the man's hand away from his throat and bent back his thumb until his eyes widened. "No noise," I said, "or I break it." I showed him the knife. "Or worse."

"Okay," he whispered, his voice hoarse.

"Who sent you?"

He looked around in panic. "What?"

I wrenched his thumb further back. As I did, I checked the woman. She was moaning but not doing anything else.

"Who sent you?" I said again.

"What?" he said. "Nobody. I don't understand."

Had Kang already found us? Had Omani learned I was on the planet and somehow tracked me?

I let go of the man's thumb, punched him in the stomach again, and grabbed the thumb once more. My breath was coming fast as I fought both the effects of the adrenaline from the unexpected attack and my anger at being so sloppy as to let them surprise me.

"This only gets worse," I said. "Who sent you?"

"No one!" the man hissed. "Don't hit me again."

"So tell me what's going on."

"We set up at the café down the street from the information pedestal you used." He spoke fast. "We keep an eye on it. We figure anyone who's there for a long time is either stupid or doing some serious shopping—or both. Either way, they're good targets. You looked like one. We followed you and waited until you were alone. We let you eat because people are usually slower after they've eaten. That's it." He gagged again. "I swear: That's it."

"So you were planning to rob me?"

"What else would we be doing?" the man said. "What did you think?"

I glanced at the woman. Her eyes were open, but she wasn't moving much, and she didn't seem to be able to focus.

"Get out your comm," I said, "and call for medtechs. Tell them you were horsing around, and you both tripped and fell. Tell them you're worried about her having a concussion. Then stay here and let them treat you."

I stood.

"You got that?"

He nodded.

I walked over to the recycling bin. "More trash," I said.

"Why, thank you, sir." It opened.

I tossed in the knife.

"Thank you, sir," it said. "Enjoy your time in York."

I went back to the man and stood over him. I stepped on his left hand with my right foot. "Make the call. Audio only. Say anything wrong, and I'll hurt you. Do you understand?"

He nodded.

"Do it," I said.

He did, his eyes on me the whole time.

I lifted my foot from his hand. "If I see you again," I said, "I will kill you. Do you believe me?"

He nodded.

"That's smart," I said. "If you see me again, turn and run the other way, and hope I didn't see you. Got it?"

He nodded again.

I stared at him for a moment longer. The anger still clawed at my insides. The very safest path was to kill them both on the small chance that he was lying. Part of me very much wanted to do that, but I shook my head at the thought. I needed to stay under control.

I turned and walked away. In a few steps, I joined the crowd. A few seconds later, I was invisible in it.

The day was wearing on, and I still needed all those supplies.

Time to find the right exoskeleton.

123 years ago

York City
Planet Haven

CHAPTER 19

Jon Moore

THE DAY I first made love with Omani Pimlani, I was looking for a new job.

The landscaping project on the Pimlani estate had ended the day before. I was in my apartment, studying the available job options on my reader. Haven was a boom planet, and York was its commercial center. Finding a job as a laborer was not a challenge. What made the task slightly more complex was that I wanted to be sure that nothing I did involved any company that Omani's father controlled. I noted a few promising jobs but decided I wouldn't even try to start anything new for a couple of days. The time off would be nice, and spending it with Omani would be even nicer. We weren't living together—I couldn't imagine her living in my apartment, I couldn't afford a tenth of any place she would like, and I sure wasn't going to take any help from her father—but we had been dating now for more than half a year and saw each other almost every day.

She walked in. I'd keyed the apartment to allow her to enter at any time. For some reason, she liked trying to surprise me and so never knocked. I hated that habit, but I'd grown to tolerate it because she enjoyed it so much. I'd arranged the furniture in the front room so the table faced the door. I was sitting behind it when she arrived.

She came in quietly, smiling. The smile vanished when she saw me watching her.

"Why can I never surprise you?" she said.

"Sometimes you do."

"Hardly ever."

I shrugged.

"I know, I know," she said. "You don't like surprises. I just thought you might learn to enjoy them if I was giving them."

"I'm sure there are some surprises I can learn to like," I said. "I don't expect, though, that being surprised by anyone entering my apartment will ever be one of them. If someone's entry surprises me, I've been sloppy."

"Why are you so guarded? It's not like anyone is trying to steal your vast treasures."

I said nothing. I couldn't tell her about my past. I couldn't even explain why I couldn't. She knew I wouldn't talk about it; we'd been over this ground many times.

She joined me at the table. "I remember. Rule number one for dealing with Jon Moore: Don't ask about anything that happened before we met."

"That's not true," I said. "I've told you about lots of things in my past."

She laughed. "Yes, provided by 'lots of things' you

mean the other jobs you've held, and by 'past' you mean the time since you arrived on Haven." Her expression turned serious. She took my left hand in her right. "My father told me that he's looked into you."

I nodded. Omani and I had been together too long for him not to have done that.

"You knew he would?"

"Sure," I said. "He loves you very much, and he wants to protect you. It's only logical that he would check out anyone you spend time with."

"You may be as paranoid as he is."

Almost certainly more, I thought but did not say. Instead, I shrugged. "We're both careful people."

"He found nothing," she said, "which bothers him almost as much as if he'd learned some horrible facts about you." She released my hand and leaned away from me. She focused intently on my face. "He's come to believe you were some kind of Coalition operative, because no one could wipe out their entire past on their own."

I stared back at her and worked to keep my face neutral. In a way, her father's theory was true. The scientists who'd experimented on me on Aggro had wiped out all the records of all their test subjects. No one could allege inhumane treatment or try them for using people as lab animals if the people in question did not technically exist. I was sort of working for the government then, though not voluntarily.

When I'd escaped from Aggro fifteen years ago, I'd jumped out of the Pinkelponker system and never looked back. Almost immediately after I'd left, the Central Coalition had quarantined Pinkelponker. I feared that the nanomachines Benny had instructed to disassemble Aggro had kept going and destroyed my entire home planet, but I had no way to determine if that fear was justified.

"Say something, Jon." Frustration played across her face, but so did concern. Omani was the first person since Benny to both know me—at least part of me—and genuinely care about me.

"I could make up stories about my past," I said, "but I don't want to do that. You deserve better than that." I took a deep breath. "I need you to trust that I'm not being secretive for no reason, that instead there are very good reasons why I can't talk more about my past."

Her eyes grew moist.

It was obvious that she wanted to trust me but couldn't, that she needed enough from me that she didn't have to wonder if I was hiding something awful. I couldn't tell her all the truth without putting myself at risk and possibly endangering her. I didn't want to lie.

But I did.

More precisely, I used her own expectations and small bits of the truth to mislead her. I wasn't exactly lying; I was giving her what she needed while not hurting either of us.

Or so I told myself. Technically, it was even true. I just hated doing it.

I took her hands in mine. "Here is what I *can* say. I'm not a wanted criminal." That was true as far as I knew, though if any of the Aggro scientists had survived, they most certainly would have been searching for me. "If I was, the government would know, and your dad would have been able to find out." Mostly true, but only because to the best of my knowledge nothing of Aggro remained, and Benny had destroyed it before it could ask for help. "I didn't wipe out the records of my past. I wouldn't know how to do that. I don't think any one person even could do that." All true. I paused, trying to figure out how best to say the next part. "Can you think of anything other than a government that could do make a person's past disappear?"

Omani had lived her entire life as one of the privileged rich for whom the government, however she might feel about a particular set of its leaders, was there to help people. My own experience was rather different, but hers would guide her beliefs.

"And," I said, "if a government did choose to erase the past of a person, wouldn't it have to have a very good reason, say to protect that person, for doing so? Wouldn't any such person have to remain quiet, both to fulfill his obligation and to protect those around him?"

I released her hands and sat back.

"That's as much as I can tell you," I said, "and you have to know by now that I need you not to ask for more. I'm being as honest as I can." That was definitely true, but not for the reasons I was implying. It was also the moment in the conversation when I felt worst about myself.

I stared into her eyes. I was holding my breath as I waited for her to respond. I realized then how very much I cared about her. Fast on the heels of that realization came the sad knowledge that no matter how much I cared about anyone, I would never be able to tell them the whole truth about myself. If any part of me, though, believed I could have done so, I would have done it then and there with Omani.

I had never before felt that way about anyone.

Still she said nothing.

I let out my breath slowly. A sadness crushed me. Was this what loving someone felt like? What it meant for me? That my heart would ache with my love of them but still I would always have to deceive them, always have to protect them from me even as I wanted to hug them to me?

For many years afterward, I wondered what would have happened if she had stayed silent a minute longer. Would I have decided to chance everything and tell her the truth? Would I have taken that ultimate risk so that I could with one person, with her, be completely and totally myself?

In the end, I decided that no, I would not have done that. I would have stayed the course I was on.

The speculation didn't matter, though, because she stared at me for a few seconds longer, nodded her head, and said, "Thank you, Jon. I appreciate you trusting me. I really do. It means more than you know. I won't betray your trust."

She stood. "Give me a moment, okay?"

I nodded. "Sure."

She walked into the bedroom and through it to the small bathroom; I heard its door shut.

She was in there for what seemed like a long time.

I used the time to try to regain my bearings. I'd done what I needed to do, and that was over. I'd protected Omani as much as myself. If anyone from Aggro ever did come for me, she could easily get caught in the conflict or, worse, be a target herself in the mistaken belief that I had told her something I shouldn't have.

The bathroom door opened, the sound loud in the still apartment.

"Jon," she said, "would you come here?"

I walked into the bedroom.

She met me just inside the door.

She was naked, her hair loose down her back, her eyes focused on mine. Some people are shy when they're undressed; I'm one of them. She was not. She was spectacular, and she knew it, but not in any way that felt narcissistic. She grabbed the back of my neck and kissed me. She held the kiss a long time. When she released me, she stepped back and quietly said, "It's time, Jon, past time. One of us had to make it happen and, well," she smiled, "I'm not sure when you would have done it."

I felt heat in my face as I said, unable to hold her eyes as I spoke, "I, I don't know how this works." I shook my head as she smiled. "No, I don't mean I don't know how sex works." I forced myself to look directly into her eyes. "I mean I don't know how *we* work, when it's right and when it's not, when we should and when we shouldn't." I shook my head again. "I, I—"

She put her right hand against my mouth and stepped closer to me. "I do know," she said, "and that makes you a very lucky man, don't you think?"

She kissed me again, longer this time.

My doubts and turmoil vanished in the feel of her, in her scent, in the way her body felt against mine, in all that she showed me. For that time, she was the whole world.

She did indeed know, and I very much was.

24 days from the end

York City
Planet Haven

CHAPTER 20

Jon Moore

I FOLLOWED THE ROUTE in my wallet to a store, Exo, whose burnished silver metallic front filled most of a block. I took a winding path and paused at several points to see if anyone was following me, but I spotted no one. The two who'd ambushed me almost certainly weren't in any condition to tail me, and if they had told the police, the police would have come straight at me.

With a last glance around, I entered the store.

It was huge, about as deep as it was wide, and three stories tall. The upper floors ended in balconies that overlooked the first. For its first seven or eight meters from the front wall, the ground floor on which I'd entered extended all the way to the top of the store. Hanging above me on cables so thin I couldn't even see most of them were a dozen or more different exoskeletons, each moving slowly in different ways.

I was immediately aware of the dirt that must still be on my back and how casually I was dressed. I looked like someone who might come to repair something wrong with the store's underground power supply, not a customer.

A salesman approached me. "May I help you, sir?" He treated me as if I were the best-dressed, most important man in the world.

Aside from the would-be thieves, people and machines on York were the most polite I'd experienced in some time. There's nothing like potential profit to make some people behave nicely. I still found it disconcerting, though, because I rarely shopped anywhere that wasn't a street vendor. The less formal the establishment, the less likely they were to keep records of your purchases, particularly if you tipped them well.

"I'm looking for an exoskeleton," I said. I immediately regretted how stupid that statement was; why else would I be in this store?

"Of course, sir," the salesman said. With just his tone he conveyed that he was privileged to have heard such wisdom.

This place's prices must be high.

"I'm going to a party," I said, "a costume party, and I will be dressing as my grandfather."

"Who is..." the salesman said.

"Deceased and not from Haven," I said. "He was quite old, over a hundred and fifty, and I need something like what he might have worn. At the same time, I'd ideally like to be able to use it later for sport."

The salesman nodded. "As I'm sure you're aware, most commonly the elderly wear simple, frequently heavy models. Sporting units, by contrast, often employ the very best in materials and technologies to deliver a great deal of power from a very low weight."

"I understand, but my grandfather liked the best of everything and so wore a very sleek model."

"If I may inquire, sir, so that I show you only the appropriate units, is there a particular price range that you are targeting?"

I waved my hand in front of my face as if swatting away small insects. "Not at all. Cost is not a concern; finding the perfect unit is."

To his credit, the salesman never let his expression change, but he had to fight not to smile. "Two models come immediately to mind, sir. Would you like to follow me to one of our private studios so we can take a few measurements and then bring them to you?"

I nodded and followed him.

He led me to the left rear of the store where a few large rooms, each with its own ceiling, stood within the greater space of the store. He unlocked the wide, tall door of the leftmost one and motioned me inside. At his request, I stood, legs spread and arms held at shoulder height, for a few seconds while a machine scanned me.

"I should not be long," he said. "While you wait, would you like anything to drink? A snack?"

"A fruit juice, something local, would be nice," I said.

"Very good, sir," he said. "A server will bring it to you shortly."

He left.

Less than two minutes later, a young man knocked on the door and brought me the drink. It came in a burnished metal cup that matched the store's exterior and the finish of most of its exoskeletons. He carried it on a tray that appeared to be made of the same metal. He also left a second cup, this one full of water.

The drink was delicious, sweet and thick and cold and refreshing. The water, also cold, helped cleanse my palate after a few sips of the juice.

A few minutes later, the salesman knocked on the door and entered. He stepped aside as he did. Two exoskeletons followed him inside. He held one control in each hand. They stopped in front of me.

The units were very similar, each made of smooth, burnished gray metal with far thinner struts and supports than I had expected. The servos and motors at the joints were also smaller than I'd anticipated, but I should, I realized, have predicted that. When I'd noticed the exoskeletons on the men at the auction, I hadn't spotted any large bulges from any of their servos.

One of these units did appear a bit thicker at the joints than the other.

"Either of these models," the salesman said, "should meet your needs. The essential difference between them is one of focus. This one," he put his hand on the one on my right, the one with thicker servos, "delivers more raw power and is best for competitions and endeavors that demand more strength. The other," he touched it, "provides greater speed. Nothing else on the market can take you as fast."

I considered them for a few seconds. "What about jumping? Which is likely to take me higher and to handle a landing better?"

"From a standing position, the first unit will go higher. With a running start, the second. Either can easily absorb a fall from a fairly great distance, though of course it is unavoidable that the operator would feel some of those effects."

If Lobo and I guessed correctly, should something go wrong, I'd likely be operating in close quarters. "I think the first would suit me better," I said.

"A fine choice. Would you care to try it? We have a practice area available."

"Yes."

"Should this unit satisfy you," he said, "and I have every confidence it will, when would you like it?"

"Immediately," I said. I shook my head at the prospect of the shopping still to come. "I unfortunately have to acquire the rest of my costume today; the party is tomorrow. I foolishly started late."

"If I may, sir," he said, "are you aware that many of the better establishments in York, including our own, have reciprocal arrangements and provide services for gentlemen such as yourself?"

"No," I said. "How does that work?"

"One of our services, which of course is entirely optional, is that members of our staff could bring candidate items here for your evaluation."

"And I would have to..."

"Select from among them or ask for additional options," he said. "We would also need you to set up an account, of course, simply to ensure the billing details were covered."

I loved the idea of someone else shopping for me. "How much notice would you need?" I said.

"We are at your disposal now, sir. While you were evaluating the two exoskeletons, we could have as many of our staff as you would like proceed with your shopping."

"I would enjoy that indeed," I said. "Shopping is not my favorite activity." I opened my wallet and brought up the itinerary and list the pedestal had prepared for me. "Here's what I'm seeking and some recommendations I received."

"If I may, sir," he said.

I handed him the wallet.

He studied it for a few seconds. "Body armor, costume to go over it and the exoskeleton, tailoring, and aging options. Is that the list, sir?"

I nodded.

"As to the recommendations, are they preferences of yours or simply..." He trailed off.

"Not preferences at all," I said. "What matters most to me is that even from very close range, closer than we are, I look like my grandfather."

"Then unless it is a problem, we will proceed with our preferred suppliers in each area."

I assume by "preferred" he meant the companies that would kick back something to Exo, but I did not care at all. "Quality is all that matters to me."

He nodded. "And the body armor is?"

"Both for authenticity—he was paranoid—and for padding; he was rather heavier than I am."

"For the make-up," he said, "would you like someone to arrive before the party and apply it, or would you prefer something more prosthetic and self-shaping that you could put on yourself? The latter is the more involved option, of course."

I planned to visit Omani in the late afternoon, not a likely time for a party. "Very much the latter," I said. "I prefer to handle it myself."

"I apologize for all the questions," he said, "but we are almost done with them. Will you be dressing yourself, or will staff be helping?"

"I brought none on this trip," I said, "so I am on my own." The answer seemed appropriate to the role I was creating, though I couldn't even imagine someone helping me dress; it would drive me crazy.

"Finally," he said, "a single person could help you, or we could assign one per item. The latter will finish a great deal faster, but of course it entails more cost."

I made the hand-waving motion again. "As I said, cost doesn't matter. Finishing quickly would be ideal."

"Very good, sir. Now, if we could set up the account, we could begin work."

"Discretion is very important to me," I said.

"Of course," he said.

"So, I'd like to propose an alternative: I'll pay you now for the exoskeletons, your estimate of the services, and your estimate of the purchase prices. Aim high on all of them. You can refund me any savings when we're done, or ask for more should we begin to come close to what I've already given you."

"It is not our usual policy," he said.

"I would also propose we add some recognition, say thirty percent, for your work and the work to come of the others involved."

"I shall return momentarily, sir, after I discuss this proposal with management." He left.

I studied the exoskeletons. No strut on either was a thick as my index finger. Though standing still they initially appeared to have little flexibility, when I studied some of the struts more closely, I thought I detected quite a few small joints.

The salesman returned. "We appreciate your proposal, sir, and are happy to accept it."

I opened a payment area in my wallet and let him

enter an amount. I tried not to let my surprise at the amount show on my face. I've bought complex weapons systems for less. I approved his request without comment.

For the first time, he permitted himself a slight smile. "If I may, sir, I would like to take a few minutes to dispatch the staff on their missions. I will then return for your try-out of the exoskeleton. I believe this will ultimately prove to be the most efficient use of your time."

"That's fine," I said.

I drank a few sips of the juice and a little of the water. I stuck my head out of the door, but no one was in sight. Surrendering so much control to these people made me nervous, but it also let me avoid an activity I hated and stay out of the crowds.

When the salesman returned five minutes later, I was in the exoskeleton. I'd expected mounting it to be harder, but that was foolish; at this price, I should have known everything would happen automatically. The moment I stood in it, the thing began adjusting itself to me. When I moved, it did, too; the controls the salesman had used were just for remote operation.

"As you can see," he said, "operating the exoskeleton is simplicity itself. Additional controls are, of course, standard should you be injured and unable to move any part of you." He walked me through them, showed me some of the many features of the unit, and then led me down to what amounted to a large, open workout area with heavily padded walls and floors.

I first practiced jumping from a crouch. I began with what I thought was a tiny amount of effort and found my feet a meter and a half off the ground. I wobbled in the air, but the struts corrected for the motion, and I landed on my feet. The units had no jets, so if I made that mistake at a high enough height, I might fall out of control. I repeated the same jump but forced myself to fall backward by moving so much the struts couldn't correct for the motion in time. It felt exactly like falling on a bunch of thin metal rods; though the pain was not bad, it was definitely pain. The nanomachines would be repairing bruised tissue.

I also worked on using the exoskeleton to move weight. I had the option of having it support me and provide assistance lifting anything I grabbed, but that limited me to what my grip could support. The unit could also extend multiple finger-like flanges that could bend and grip. Using them, the unit had no trouble picking up a two-hundred-kilo weight and adjusting my balance as necessary. Past that, I had to help with the balance and use both exo-hands, simply so the weight wouldn't pull me down.

All in all, it was an impressive device that might come in handy if things turned nonlinear when I visited Omani tomorrow.

A little over an hour after the salesman had left to brief the staff, he led me to a new room where a new person waited, a woman with a selection of body armor options.

Over the next four hours, I felt dangerously close to being a test subject again. People showed me options they'd selected. I picked whatever they recommended as long as it was something I could tolerate; two of the suits they showed me were more fancy than anything I would ever wear. I stood as people tried them on me, clucked, made adjustments, and tried again.

Ninety minutes into it, I thought I was going to scream and had to take a break. I went to the exoskeleton try-out room, paced back and forth, did some push-ups, and punched the walls to burn off stress. All of those people fussing over me took me back to Aggro in very bad ways.

When I was calmer, they resumed.

An hour later, they served a snack of fruit and cheese, all of which was delicious. I appreciated the break even more than the food.

The make-up was the most challenging part, because to get the effects I wanted, my face, hands, and neck—all the skin you could see and a bit more—were literally encased in what amounted to thin prosthetic devices. A team from the make-up place set up outside my new room, as did a second team working on the clothing.

When we finally finished, I stood staring at a mirror in which a heavyset old man a bit taller than I was stared back at me. If I were to age, I would probably look like this man. His skin felt natural and warm, as they'd claimed it would. I leaned close to the mirror and still bought the illusion.

I took it all off, and as they boxed it all, I settled the tab. I ended up owing them extra, but I didn't mind paying; the work they had done was exquisite. More importantly, I would not have been able to accomplish the same things in anywhere near the amount of time this took. Even so, I was bristling with nervous energy and feeling caged.

"Where would you like us to deliver your purchases, sir?" the salesman said.

I started to tell him the name of the hotel I'd

chosen, but I reconsidered. If anyone had been following me, or if the thieves had stupidly talked to the
police, it's possible they might be able to backtrack me
to that hotel. I doubted it, but a little extra caution
never hurt. Plus, I suspected the place I'd selected
was not consistent with the identity I'd built here.
I didn't need the clothing or the pack in the other
hotel, so I'd just write them off. The clothing and
the exoskeleton I'd purchased today, should Omani
recognize either, suggested affluence, so maintaining
that illusion and also taking advantage of the private
transportation that upscale hotels offered might further
throw people off my trail should something go wrong
at the meeting.

"I've only just arrived in York," I said, "so I haven't
selected accommodations yet." I found myself changing
my diction to suit the salesman's. "Might you suggest
something with a suitable suite? Someplace particularly
discreet and nearby?"

He thought for a few seconds before saying, "I
shall make a few inquiries."

When he came back, he said, "I've taken the liberty
of booking you a suite here."

He showed me a holo of the Little York Inn, a
plain light blue permacrete building with no name
or logo other than a small gold metal plate near the
front door. Its motto, "The pinnacle of luxury and
security," spun around the bottom of the holo. He
pulled back and showed me its location on a map; it
was only a few kilometers farther from the Pimlani
estate than my initial choice.

"If it is to your liking, I'll have them send round
a vehicle for you and your purchases."

"It is," I said. "Please do."

Before he could ask, I opened a payment area in my wallet and handed it to him.

He entered the cost. "This should cover your stay, all incidentals, and any necessary transportation tomorrow. They will credit us, and we will then credit you any surplus."

I approved it. "No need," I said.

The shuttle that arrived from the Inn did its best to appear inconspicuous, but you simply can't mask that much armor and luxury. I liked, though, the contrast between the plainly dressed man who had left the landing zone where Lobo waited and the presumably affluent one who climbed quickly into the Inn's transport.

Once alone and inside the vehicle, I relaxed a bit. As we headed to the Inn, I told myself that all I had to do was meet a woman I'd loved over twelve decades ago, convince her I was as ancient as she was, and escape without incident, all the while hoping one of the most powerful men in this section of the human worlds hadn't caught up to me.

That was all.

I turned on my comm, which I'd kept off all day. It immediately signaled that Lobo had been trying to reach me.

As soon as I arrived at the Inn and they'd set the lock to recognize me, I stepped outside. Three men wearing nicer suits than anything I owned except what they were carrying began transporting my purchases to my room. I walked a block and a half down the street. When I was sure I was alone, contacted Lobo.

"Where have you been?" he said.

"Getting to know the terrain," I said, "and doing

some shopping so I'm dressed appropriately for tomorrow. You?"

"Working."

"On what?"

"Gathering data about Pimlani, seeking out data footprints to see if Kang has any trackers on us—you know, what you asked me to do."

"So we're both doing what we said we would be."

"The difference," Lobo said, "is that I've found something important."

"Which is?" When I left him alone too long and circumstances permitted it, he'd sometimes make me beg for information. I didn't enjoy the game, but I also didn't have a lot of alternatives.

"I found a medtech office with weak security and was able to access some of their data," Lobo said. "They assisted on a call involving Pimlani."

"Is she dead?" Had I come all this way at her request and arrived too late?

"No," Lobo said. "Quite the contrary. Though she's now bedridden and alive only because machines are operating her body, her mind is fine, and she's in no immediate danger. Their records suggest she could live for years this way."

I shook my head and smiled. She had always been tough. It figured she still would be.

"So it's definitely a trap of some sort," I said.

"That is the most likely deduction," Lobo said, "though of course there is always the chance that she wants to hire us. Those who do rarely leave clear messages."

"So it's almost certainly but not definitely a trap," I said.

"Yes. What are you going to do?"

I could explain again that I felt I owed her, but there was no point in repeating myself; Lobo already knew that. What I couldn't tell him without revealing my true age was my increasing concern about why Omani even thought I was still alive. She wouldn't have planted those messages everywhere if she didn't believe they might reach me. I needed to find out what she knew about me.

"I'm going to see her tomorrow," I said. "We'd expected it might be a trap and planned accordingly, so this changes nothing."

"I disagree," Lobo said. "Before, we believed it was likely to be dangerous. Now, we know it's almost certainly risky."

"We're quarreling over percentages," I said. "Let's not waste the time."

"I had to try," Lobo said, "to stop you from taking yet another stupid, potentially fatal risk."

I ignored the jab. "I'll call you tomorrow," I said, "per the plan, right before I enter her estate. You be ready to come get me if I need it."

"Of course," Lobo said.

I disconnected and turned off the comm.

As I walked back to the hotel, I wondered the same thing over and over: Omani, what game are you playing?

122 years ago

York City
Planet Haven

CHAPTER 21

Jon Moore

THE DAY I last saw Omani Pimlani, her father was dying.

We were supposed to meet after I finished my shift at my place for a run and then dinner. I'd gone home to shower and found the message from her.

"Call me as soon as you get this."

No pleasantries, no name, and panic in her voice. She'd left it three hours earlier.

I called her. Her image appeared on the comm a second later. She was walking, her comm's image-correction software unable to correct for all the disruption.

"Jon," she said, "where have you been? Why didn't you call earlier?"

"Work," I said. "You know I don't take my comm there. I don't carry anything I could break." My latest job was on a construction project with a lot of pre-built pieces. We helped the machines guide them into place, and we finished the joints by hand so no seams were visible. We were constantly getting hit by heavy objects in motion, so we'd all learned not to carry anything breakable in our pockets if we could avoid it. "What's wrong?"

She stopped walking and held the comm close, so her face filled its display. "It's my father."

"Was he hurt?"

"Not exactly. We found out he's dying. Some virus they don't know how to kill is consuming his neural sheaths."

"I'm so sorry," I said. I'd had few contacts with him in the more than a year since we'd first met, but those had been cordial, if not warm. He wasn't a warm man. I had the sense, though, that in at least some ways he respected me, and after that initial meeting, he'd always made me welcome. "How long does he have?"

"That's tricky," she said. "They believe his body might last as much as a year. His mind might have far less time. It all depends on what the virus does, and they have little experience with it. Of course, if they can find a cure..."

"I'm sorry," I said again. I had no idea what else to say.

"I need you here, Jon," Omani said. "Now. We have to talk." She paused. "I need you."

"Your call," I said. "Do I come now as I am, or do I shower first?" I pulled the comm away from me and scanned it over my dirt- and dust-covered clothing.

She laughed. "Definitely shower first. We have a lot to discuss, and I don't think I want to sit with you for long if you smell as bad as you look right now."

I sniffed the air like a dog. "Good choice."

She laughed again.

"I'll see you within the hour," I said.

➤   ➤   ➤

When I reached the Pimlani estate, the man who opened the gate sent me straight to Mr. Pimlani's office on the top floor. My stock must have risen at least somewhat, or they were all incredibly distracted, because no one escorted me. It was the first time I'd been alone in the house. Curiosity tempted me to look around, but Omani had said twice that she needed me, so I almost ran through the house and to the elevator.

She was waiting for me when the elevator doors opened.

I opened my arms for a hug, and she fell against me. I held her tightly for a minute before she pushed away.

"Let's go inside," she said.

I followed her into the huge space, down about two-thirds of its length, and off to a small reading area on the left. Three chairs clustered around a small table. They offered a great view of the front of the grounds.

She motioned to the chair on the right.

I sat.

She took the center chair, pushed it close to me, and sat. We were so close that our knees touched. She leaned forward and held out her hands.

I took them in mine.

We sat in silence for a bit. She looked up at me every now and then, and then back at her knees.

"Do you have nothing to say?" she said.

"I figured you would talk when you were ready," I said. "I don't know what I can say given how little I know."

She shook her head and sighed. "I'm sorry. For as long as I've known you, I've understood that you rarely need to talk. I'm just upset and trying to collect my thoughts."

"It's fine," I said. "I can wait. I'm here." I really didn't know what to say, but reassurances seemed appropriate.

She released my hands and sat back in her chair. I also leaned back.

"I've spent most of today with my father," she said. "I have so much to go over with you that I'm not even sure where to start."

"That's fine," I said. "You don't have to be organized."

She laughed, but it wasn't a healthy laugh. It was high-pitched and nervous, as if the sound might at any moment crack and she might go with it. "Oh, that's where you're wrong," she said. "I do, I very much do need to be organized, and I don't know if I can handle it."

"Why?" I said. "You said he had months, and the doctors might be able to concoct a cure."

"To try to slow the virus, they're going to put him on a lot of medicines. Every day they delay doing that increases his risk of dying. He's determined to live, so he's going into their care tomorrow. From tomorrow on, I'm in charge of his holdings."

"That must be a very big job," I said, "though I confess I have no sense of what it is that he did. Does."

If she noticed my slip, she didn't say anything. "It kept him busy all the time," she said, "and he knew what he was doing. I have no clue."

"He must have people who can help you."

She nodded. "Oh, he does, and they will, but if there's one thing you learn growing up with money, it's that everyone wants some of it, and everyone has their own agendas."

"I don't," I said.

She leaned forward and patted my leg. "Except you. Everyone except you. That's one of the many things I love about you." She sat upright again. "Which is why I'd like you to quit your job and come help me."

I couldn't speak for a few seconds. "I know nothing about any of this," I said, "as you know, and I was serious when I told your father I didn't want anything from him. This is yours, not mine."

"Again," she said, "I know that, which is one of the reasons I'm asking you. I also know I can trust you to look out for me. And, you're smart, though for reasons I've never understood—but never questioned, you know that—you like to work jobs that don't use your brain. Most of all, though," she leaned forward again, "if we're going to stay together, as I hope we are, this will all be ours eventually anyway. We might as well get started together now."

The prospect certainly had its appeal, and I had considered the possibility before. Being part of one of the richest families on one of the richest worlds was something most people would jump at. I rarely told her—the words never came easily to me—but I knew in my heart that I loved Omani very much. I could imagine spending a life with her.

Other factors, though, made it far too risky for me to settle here with her. Keeping a low profile while going out with Omani had been difficult, and we never went anywhere the newstainment people frequented. Maintaining privacy would become impossible if we were married. If anyone from Aggro or the government that had sponsored it was still searching for me, I would become very easy to find.

I'd also encountered another problem recently:

I'd realized I wasn't aging. I'd known for some years that the nanomachines in my cells automatically and quickly healed anything that happened to me. Only in the last couple of years, though, had I noticed that nothing about my looks ever changed. I was the same now, at thirty-five, as I'd been at twenty-eight. Whatever let the nanomachines heal me also appeared to stop me from aging. Right now, no one noticed, though Omani had made a few comments. In five more years, though, or ten, or twenty, eventually it would be impossible to ignore.

"Say something, Jon," she said. "You must have known we'd have this talk one day."

I nodded. "I did, but I hadn't expected it to be today."

"Neither had I," she said, "obviously, but this is where we are. I've always had to take the lead in our relationship, and I don't mind doing it now, but circumstances neither of us could have foreseen have left us at a decision point."

I nodded again but had nothing to say—or, more accurately, I thought, nothing I could safely say.

When I stayed silent, she continued. "There's something else, too, Jon."

"What?" I said, eager for the diversion. Anything else was bound to be easier.

"What little they know about the virus is that it appears to share some programming with some aspects of aging. They're doing research now comparing his normal cells, those the virus has attacked, and the cells of some younger people. The hope is that they can learn something they can use to help slow the virus while they figure out a way to kill it. They've taken cells from me. They've also collected some samples from young children in the hospital—at no cost or risk to them, of course. They're using only cells from blood and tissue samples they had to take in the course of treating the kids anyway. I've also insisted we pay the full cost of treatment of any child that contributed a sample."

"That makes sense," I said, though I didn't mean it. I wondered if anyone had asked the children or their families, or if they'd had any real choice. I also feared what was yet to come. I felt sick in the stomach and hoped she would stop.

"I suggested they take a sample from you," she said.

I forced myself to act as calm as possible as I said, "Why? I'm hardly a kid."

She shook her head. "That's not the point. I don't know if you've noticed, Jon, but in just the not quite two years that we've known each other, little signs of age have started appearing on my face."

"No," I said, "I hadn't noticed. You're as beautiful now as when I met you."

She smiled. "Thank you. I'm glad you think so—and I use every trick money can buy to keep looking the same. I'm five years older than you are, so I'm already at a disadvantage. The thing is, though, I can't spot a single sign of aging on you. I'm sure they'll come, but if I'm right, if you are aging slower than most people, then whatever in you is making that happen is something that might be able to help my father. We should look into it. Maybe they can even learn something that might help a lot of people."

I forced a laugh. "I doubt it," I said. "It's almost certainly just genetics; people grow old differently."

"You're probably right," she said, "but I'm sure you'd agree that with my father's life on the line, we should look into every possibility of saving him, or even of buying him more time."

I stared into her eyes as I said, "Of course. You wouldn't be the woman I love if you did anything less."

I knew how this would play out. They'd draw some blood, find the nanomachines in those cells, and then I would become their test subject. I might as well be back on Aggro. I didn't know then that the nanomachines disassembled automatically outside my body unless I specifically ordered them to do otherwise. At that point, I hadn't even figured out how to control them—inside or outside of my body.

She smiled. "Thank you. Tomorrow, okay?"

"Sure," I said.

"And about helping me?"

I hated that my last words to her had to be lies. Though it made me feel very little better, I stuck to a true but misleading statement. "You're right. We would make a great team."

She jumped up, hugged me, and kissed me. It was the only time I'd ever faked enthusiasm with her. "Why don't we start working out the details tomorrow?" she said when we'd stopped kissing.

"I owe my bosses at least the day's work," I said. "How about I see you tomorrow after my shift? You could ask the doctor to come by then."

She nodded. "I appreciate your integrity, as always. Sure, we'll do that."

She stood. "My father wants to spend more time with me tonight, before he heads to the clinic tomorrow. He'll be thrilled that you're going to be with me."

I hadn't thought I could feel worse, but now I did. "He will?" I said. "We haven't exactly gotten to know each other."

"He knows I love you," she said, "and you love me, and you had the courage to stand up to him when most people in the same situation wouldn't have dared. That's enough for him."

We walked to the elevator holding hands. I held her close to me. I ran my fingers through her hair and smelled it a last time. I kissed her and whispered in her ear, "I love you, Omani."

As soon as I got home, I pulled my getaway stash from its hiding place under the floor under the bed. I packed what mattered most into a single large duffel bag, the same one I'd brought with me when I'd come to Haven a few years ago. I left everything else.

I took a taxi to the nearest launch zone and found a night shuttle carrying a cleaning crew on shift change to the Haven jump gate. I explained that we'd just buried my father and I needed to get away, make a fresh start. I bribed the foreman to let me tag along.

Once at the station, I told the same story to a ship's quartermaster, who accepted a payment to let me ride on the three jumps they were taking. The Central Coalition was still forming then, so jump passage was far less regulated than it is today. Everyone was supposed to keep records, but of course people made mistakes, most of them accidental, some intentional.

As midnight was approaching on Haven, our ship jumped across space in an instant, and in that same instant I left for what I thought was forever the first woman I had ever loved.

23 days from the end

York City
Planet Haven

CHAPTER 22

Jon Moore

I STEPPED OUT OF the Little York Inn in full costume a bit before lunchtime, an old, heavy man in a fancy suit and a fancier exoskeleton. No one said a word or raised an eyebrow at the change in my look. If anyone noticed, and it was possible they did not, because a different crew was working than had been on when I'd checked in, I could not tell from their expressions. Given the room's cost and the way the Exo salesman had spoken about the Inn, most of its guests had to be wealthy. The fact that in my searches of local publicly available data I could not find a single scandal tied to the Inn further reinforced its reputation for discretion. My transformation was almost certainly not the oddest thing this team had seen.

I entered the same transport vehicle as before and told it to take me to the front gate of the Pimlani estate; no point in trying to hide that I was visiting. Lunch is a great time to arrive unexpectedly if the people you're visiting are not likely to be entertaining guests, because some of the staff is usually on break then. Given that Omani was tethered to a set of machines for life support, I doubted she would enjoy having company for lunch.

As we approached the main entrance, I told the transport to slow. I turned on my comm and contacted Lobo.

"I'm here," I said.

"Go slowly," he said. "I'm on my way."

I told the transport to make a slow loop around the estate, which given its size would take us a little while. The wall that surrounded the place looked basically the same as when I'd been here before, though now a second, three-meter-high level of largely transparent material sat atop the original permacrete wall. No one would be scaling this one.

When we were almost through with our circuit, Lobo contacted me.

"I'm in position with a view of the rear of the house. If that comm goes off or you say the word, I'll come in hot."

"Good," I said, "though I hope it doesn't come to that."

"Are you sure you won't let me monitor the conversation?" he said.

"Yes. I owe her privacy." *And*, I thought, *I can't let you find out how old I am*, something any conversation could easily make clear.

When we reached the gate, I identified myself.

A few seconds later, a man's voice told me to come to the front of the house.

A man stood waiting outside the front steps as we pulled up.

I told the vehicle to stay until I returned and got out of it slowly. An old man wouldn't hurry, and I welcomed the time to look around a bit. The man waited while I walked to him.

"Mr. Moore," he said. "Ms. Pimlani has been expecting you—for quite some time, actually. How is it that you chose today?"

"And you are?" I said. I kept my voice low and soft.

"Balin Randar, head of security." He didn't extend his hand to shake mine, though I couldn't tell if that was from courtesy to an old man in an exoskeleton or some feelings about me. "I attend to Ms. Pimlani personally as well as run her team."

I chuckled. "Did she worry she'd need security with me?" I lifted my arms slowly. "Do I look like a threat?"

"She didn't," he said. "I did. I worry about everything and everyone who might hurt her. It's my job." He clapped his hand on my left forearm. "That exoskeleton packs more than enough power to hurt or even kill someone."

I shook my head. "Not my intention, I assure you."

"So I repeat my question," he said. "How did you choose today?"

"I found one of her messages a few jumps away, and I came as quickly as I could."

"Most people would have called for an appointment first."

"Most people wouldn't have the history with Omani that I do. This isn't exactly easy."

"Is that why you circled the estate the first time? Cold feet?"

I nodded.

He smiled, a thin smile that had little to do with genuine happiness. "I'm glad it's not easy for you," he said. "From what I understand, you deserve to suffer for what you did."

I shook my head, as if that might help dispel the memories that were flooding over me as I stood on those steps again after more than twelve decades. "I do," I said, "and I have."

"Not as much as she did."

"No, I suspect not." I looked him in the eyes. "Here's the important fact, though: She asked me to come. So, you can either take me to her, or I can climb back inside that transport and leave. I'll stand for abuse from her; she's earned that right. I don't have to take it from you."

Randar stepped closer to me, so close our noses were almost touching. "Ms. Pimlani saved my family when we were about to lose everything. She saved me personally when I was young and my temper tended to land me in trouble. I've worked for her my entire adult life. You'd do well to keep that in mind."

I laughed. "Or what?" I said. "You'll beat me up? Shoot me? Do you want to explain to her that you're the reason she never got to speak to me?"

"I wouldn't have to say anything," he said. "I've turned off the security monitors on this part of the house. She would never know you'd visited."

"Two problems," I said. "First, she'll get the message I've scheduled for delivery if I don't make it back by this evening."

His eyes widened a bit.

"I'm not as stupid as you seem to think I am, and I've worked jobs like yours. Second, and more importantly, do you want to live with the knowledge that you stopped her from getting a chance to finally yell at the man who walked out on her all those years ago?" I shook my head. "I've lived for a great many years with a great many regrets. My advice to you is not to add to your own." I shrugged. "Your call."

He stared at me for a few more seconds, then turned and said, "Follow me. I'll take you to her." He looked back over his shoulder. "I'm not like you. I don't let her down, and I don't play games with her. I told her you had arrived the moment you cleared the front gate."

I had nothing to say to that, so I followed him inside. I had never paid much attention to most of what was in the house, so I couldn't tell how much it had changed, but the elevator was definitely new, now transparent and providing a great view of the grounds as we rode up. The foyer outside the office felt the same, though no security cameras were visible. I assumed they had simply updated to more recent and smaller cameras and other sensors.

"Wait here," Randar said. He entered the office. The door was much thicker than I'd remembered; perhaps they'd rebuilt that wall with a great deal more armor than it had in the past.

He returned a few minutes later and beckoned me to follow him. "I tried to talk her out of seeing you," he said, "but I failed."

"So you don't know why she wants to see me, either," I said.

He glared at me. "No, I don't."

We walked through what had been the library with its row after row of bookshelves. Now, though, it looked more like some wood fetishist's interpretation of an open-office enterprise. Several five-meter-long, oval meeting tables, each surrounded by chairs, all in an almost white wood with a rich, wavy grain. Smaller, round meeting tables, each with four chairs, all of a black wood that could have been bits of moonless night polished to a high sheen. Desks of red and tan and golden and silver wood, each with a matching chair.

All around the room, scattered under windows and among the furniture, fountains crafted to look like waterfalls stood on meter-high pedestals. Rugs in earth tones protected the floor under each one, catching the mist that fell from them. I recognized many of the fountains from the park Omani and I had frequented. I loved the sound they made, but my heart filled with guilt at the sight of them.

The room within the room at the end of the space, the place that had once been her father's office, now had a wall of the same light wood as the oval tables. An old-fashioned, hinged door barred our way. The lock on it looked new and strong.

Before he opened it, Randar faced me and said, "You shut up, listen, do what she says, and leave. Anything else, and exoskeleton or not, you might have an accidental fall on the way back to your vehicle. Accidents are among the leading killers of the elderly."

I shook my head and smiled. I wondered what this old-man version of me looked like to him. "I believe I understand you. Now, isn't she waiting?"

He swung the door inward, entered, and stepped to the side.

I followed him and stopped in the doorway. Directly across from me, sitting up in a bed with supporting struts that resembled those of my exoskeleton, was Omani Pimlani. I'd never stayed around anyone long enough to have a strong sense of how very much people change with age, but my mental images—all I had—of Omani were so very different from the person in front of me that it took me several seconds to reconcile the two. Bald and so gaunt her arms looked thinner than my wrists, she could easily have passed as a corpse were it not for her eyes. Alert and focused directly on me, they were the large, strong, beautiful eyes I remembered, not as dark as they had been, but still compelling.

"Now that you've gotten a good look and the shock is starting to wear off," she said, "why don't you come all the way inside?"

I forced a smile. "No shock," I said. "It's just been a long time. I wanted to make sure it was you."

She laughed, a clear but weak laugh. "You were never a good liar. That's one of the things I loved about you." She pointed to the floor next to her. Between the three towers of machines that stood next to her on my right and the three desks and chairs that they'd pushed against the wall on my left, the room was a bit crowded. "Balin, please bring Jon a chair so he can sit next to me."

He never let his gaze wander from me as he did as she asked.

"Thank you, Balin." To me, she said, "Balin here takes great care of me. Now, Jon, sit, please. People our age need to rest when we can."

As I did, I angled the chair so I could keep an eye on Randar while mostly facing Omani.

She towered above me. She lowered the bed until we were eye to eye.

She'd staged this show, so I waited.

After a few seconds, she laughed. "Still not a big talker."

"I'm better than I was when I have to talk, but I don't feel the need to fill the air. Besides, as I recall, you generally led us."

"That I did," she said, "though," she paused, "not everywhere I'd hoped we'd go."

I nodded. I had no idea how to respond.

"I thought for a long time," she said, "about what I'd say if I ever got to see you again. After a while, I moved on, as one does, and I didn't think much about you at all. With all of this," she took in her bed and the machines with a twirl of her finger, "I decided I needed to see you again, and then the topic was back in my mind."

"What'd you decide?"

She laughed the same clear, weak laugh. "The first thing I decided was that I wasn't going to be one of those weak-brained people who begin their speeches by telling you how they didn't know what they were going to say—but I already messed that up. Truth is, I made a lot of different decisions about what to say, but I threw out most of them, because I expect you already have some idea of how hurt and angry and disappointed I was."

"Some idea," I said, "but probably not a complete picture. No two people react the same way to anything."

"True enough," she said. "So why don't we start with something you know that I don't: Why did you run away like that? And, if you were going to run away, why didn't you say so to my face?"

I'd rehearsed a lot of answers since Lobo had shown

me her recorded message. I'd played through variations of the scene as I was falling asleep last night and again as I was showering this morning. None of them involved me telling her the truth, because I could no more afford that risk now than I could twelve decades ago. What I had come to realize was that once I removed the truth, I had almost nothing believable to say.

I'd finally decided that the one thing I could do was not lie to her.

"I can't tell you," I said.

She grabbed the railing beside her, pulled herself upright, and twisted slightly to face me more directly.

"Ms. Pimlani," Randar said.

"I'm fine, Balin," she said without looking at him. To me, she said, "Can't, as in some force is preventing you, or won't?"

"You're right," I said. "Almost all the time, when people say they can't do something that is obviously within their power, what they really mean is that for whatever reasons, they won't. I'm doing my best here to be honest, so the more accurate, more honest answer is, I won't tell you."

"Ms. Pimlani," Randar said, "I'd be more than happy to help persuade Mr. Moore to answer your questions."

"No, Balin," she said, "that won't be necessary. Also, though your offer is tempting, despite his appearance, I suspect Jon would prove to be a far more difficult subject to persuade than you might guess."

Balin stepped closer to us. "I sincerely doubt that."

"I think it's time for you to leave us," she said to him. "I'd like a little time alone with Jon."

"My job—" he began.

"—is to protect me," she said. "I know, and I

appreciate how very good you are at it. I want this time alone with him, though, and your job sometimes also involves doing as I ask." She stared at him.

"Of course," he said. "I'll be watching and listening on the security feed right outside."

"No," she said. "You'll be watching. I'm going to turn off the audio so Jon and I can chat privately." She leaned back into the bed and stared at him. "And don't waste your time with all your controls; mine override yours, as you know. I'm also going to tell Jon to sit so the cams don't capture my face or his; I don't want the lip-reading software helping you."

"This is so very contrary to our standard protocols," he said, "that—"

She cut him off again. "I know, but I want a private conversation with Jon, and after more than a hundred and twenty years, I'm going to have it." Her voice grew stronger. "I'm going to have it."

Randar held up his hands and backed out of the room. "Of course," he said. "I'm sorry I pushed so much. I'll be right outside if you want to call me, and I'll watch to make sure he doesn't try to hurt you."

"Thank you," she said, her voice soft again.

When Randar had left the room and closed the door behind him, Omani pulled a comm from a tray on the other side of her and poked at a few controls. She showed me its display, which indicated that the door was locked and the audio muted.

"Fine," I said, "though I really don't have any answers for you."

"Turn your chair around this way," she said. She motioned with her right hand for me to put my back to the door. "And tilt my bed toward you a little."

I did both and sat again.

"Good," she said. "Now, we're as alone as we're going to be able to get." She showed me the comm. The back of my head was in the center of its display. Her head wasn't visible. "Agreed?"

"I have to trust you on that," I said. "I have no way to confirm anything."

"Fair enough," she said.

I waited as she sucked some water from a tube that hung near her mouth.

"So I have two questions for you, Jon," she said.

"Yes."

"Isn't that old-man costume hot," she said, "and what would it take for me to hire you?"

CHAPTER 23

Jon Moore

MY SURPRISED EXPRESSION was genuine, even though my response wasn't. "Omani, what game are you playing?"

She shook her head. "You may not age, but I do, so I value time a lot more than you do. I'm alive only because of these machines," she waved her left hand toward the stacks of gear behind her, "and only as long as I stay connected to them. Think about how small most medical devices are. That I need this much sheer equipment ought to tell you the kind of shape I'm in. Anyway, if you insist on playing games, we can, but we can also save time and jump to the end of them and move on to something useful."

I shook my head as if I were worried about her sanity. "You know I'm five years younger than you are, but I'm still old. Maybe the drugs they're pumping into you have done something to your brain; I don't know. What I do know is that you're not making sense." I stood. "Maybe I should be going."

"Sit down," she said. "You're going to want to hear what I have to say."

I stared at her for a few seconds but did not sit.

"If you try to leave before I'm done," she said, "Balin will stop you."

I smiled.

"You might get past him," she said. "I admit that possibility, though he's more formidable than you might think. If you did, though, I'd have to discuss with him and a whole lot of other people everything I know about you, all of which I have—for now—kept to myself." She smiled, the kind of smile a snake gives a rodent it's about to eat. "Your choice."

"There are other ways this could go," I said, "I've never responded well to threats."

"Ah, that's the man I've read about," she said. "It's good to finally see a little of him. The Jon I knew avoided conflict at all costs. You, you seem to seek it out. In any case, if anything happens to me while you're here, the data I've accumulated about you will automatically find its way to a whole lot of people who will not be as nice to you as I'm being right now."

I sat.

"Do you understand how the worlds work, Jon?" she said. She waved her right hand in front of her chest. "I don't mean which governments rule which populations, or how planets elect members to the three planetary coalition councils. I mean how all the worlds really work, what operates behind the coalitions."

"I don't know," I said. "I thought I had a fair handle on it, but maybe not. Regardless, what does this have to do with me?"

"Bear with me," she said. "We'll get you there."

She took another sip of water. "Damn machines and medicine leave me dry. What runs the worlds, Jon, is money, of course. Everyone with half a brain is at some level aware of that fact. What very few understand is how much of the money a relatively small number of families still control, even after all this time since humanity left Earth."

I opened my mouth to speak, but she held up her hand.

"Bear with me for a minute, and I'll bring this back to you," she said. "Okay?"

"Sure," I said. "I'm always up for a nice bit of fiction."

"No fiction," she said. "When humanity finally accepted that we had only a few centuries left before we would have to leave Earth, because we'd ruined it beyond repair, we launched a generation ship. One. It crashed on Pinkelponker. Then, we found the jump gates, and we started planning our exodus. Those who've possessed money and power for long periods of time are never the first to take major risks, so they left the colonization of the first planet, Freedom, to those with less to lose. When Freedom worked out well, those same people were ready to go. That's how Haven became the first nonEarth home of most of the richest families in history—including mine."

"I've heard variations of this historical perspective before," I said. "Even assuming it's entirely correct, I'm still missing what this has to do with me." I'd had time to accept that she knew I didn't age and that she almost certainly had other data about me, data I'd rather no one had. What worried me right then was whether she knew about Pinkelponker, or Aggro, or my nanomachines.

"When we were dating," she said, "the coalitions were still coming together. Our families were building their control, but while they were doing so, a lot of data was lost. That's why I've never learned where you were trained or what you were doing before we met. I'm willing to believe you were telling the truth when you said you'd worked for some governments, because you really were a terrible liar, but for the most part, I don't care anymore what you did before we met.

"After you left me, you managed to maintain a sufficiently low profile that I have no data about you for nearly a century. Well done, by the way."

I said nothing. No matter how much information she had, I saw no profit for me in confirming or denying anything.

"Fine," she said. "Let's get to the parts you will most definitely care about. Not quite thirty years ago, on a planet far from here, Jon Moore, a young man, early twenties, very mature for his age, joined the Shosen Advanced Weapons Corporation, the Saw, as a recruit. When he left, as was their policy they kept only the most basic relevant data about him. That data, of course, included a photograph."

She sipped a bit more water.

"Had you then vanished once again," she said, "I might never have learned you were still alive. Twelve years later, though, you got involved in a rather messy situation on a Frontier Coalition planet, Macken. Normally, what happens on a world that young doesn't matter much, but you managed to attract the attention of some important officials of not only that coalition, but also two major megacorps, Kelco and Xychek. You also somehow ended up owning a neutered Predator-class assault vehicle, which is an unusual thing for an individual to own. Do I have your attention now?"

I nodded. "I'm listening."

"Nobody involved in that situation wanted any of it public, so most of the records vanished. My family, like many of the families, has people who feed us information scattered around the various coalitions, so sometime afterward, they noted your name and flagged it to my attention. Names repeat, and though I remember noticing that you weren't aging as fast as I was, I figured that after a century it had to be another person.

"About a year and a half later, though, a man with the same name made some enemies in the Expansion Coalition when he played some gangsters, a religious cult, and coalition troops against one another. Once again, it was in everybody's interest for the data to vanish—but once again, it didn't entirely go away."

She leaned a little closer. "I sincerely doubt anyone else in any significant family even noticed, because, Jon, you're just not that big a deal. Your name, though, meant something to me, and a lot of people who worked for me had heard it. So, the information wound its way to me. This time, I checked the photo, and it was you, just as I remembered you, not a day older, exactly the same."

She settled back against the bed. "By the time I realized that fact, though, you'd fallen off the data trails again. I considered hunting you down, just for the satisfaction of it, but however hard your ego might find this to believe, I really did get over you and move on with my life a long, long time ago."

That was the first thing she had said that I liked. I stayed silent, though.

"I've had children, buried a couple of husbands, and run our holdings for all this time," she said. "Were you simply another old man living his life in other parts of settled space, we wouldn't be having this talk. But you're not. I couldn't shake the fact that you never aged, though I actually came for a time to doubt that this other Jon Moore could be you. A year later, though, you managed to anger multiple coalition officials and kill a major scientist on Heaven, and by then parts of my body were beginning to fail."

She coughed and drank some more water. "From what little I've been able to learn about you, you must have come close to dying more than once. You must have had to face the prospect of your own death. It's not a pretty sight, but now I see it every day. My initial impulse was to track you down to learn what stopped you from aging in the hopes that you could use on me whatever it is you use on yourself, but then, as I gathered from the available data how many people you cared about were either badly injured or killed, I realized it was nothing you were doing. Had it been something under your control, you would have saved them. I came to accept that you're a fluke, some sort of genetic miracle. I figure you live as you do to hide that fact."

She stared at me for confirmation, but I again stayed silent.

"Fine, fine," she said. She chuckled. "If I were younger and had more time, I might have tried to find you and persuade you to let some of the scientists who work in our various companies try to figure out what keeps you young, but I learned from my father's death—he held out over a decade, you know, but they never found a cure—that research of that type takes longer than I have."

She smiled. "Are you really just going to sit there?"

I forced a smile. "I told you that I enjoyed a good fiction, and you're telling a fine tale."

"Well, we're almost at the end. As I implied earlier, my family is only one of the many who control a great deal of the assets of the worlds. If my sources are correct, and I'm quite sure they are, you've recently made the acquaintance of Luis Kang, the head of another family. Kang has rather unfortunate tastes, and apparently you caused quite a stir when you interrupted him in the pursuit of them."

I forced myself to stay silent. Tastes? That she could refer to child abuse so callously made me want to rip the plugs and tubes out of her.

"He's hunting for you, you know," she said. "That's how my people heard your name most recently. Anyway, another of the families that matters, another one whose home is right here on Haven, is the Schmidts. Hanson Schmidt controls their holdings."

She whispered to her comm and handed it to me.

"Here's a picture of him."

A typical corporate exec type stared back at me. Somewhere between thirty and eighty, given his wealth, with golden skin, brown eyes, and short, dark hair, he wasn't the sort of person who would stand out in any executive meeting. I extended the comm to her, but she shook her head.

"How old do you think he is?" she said.

"Hard to tell."

"He's been trying to pass himself off as his own son, and he's been succeeding, throwing huge concerts and dances and generally coming out, as if he were the child his father had kept under wraps for years—but I'm not buying it. I have photos of him aging normally until about thirty years ago, when he stopped going out in public at all. The next time any images were available, they were of this 'son.'" She pointed at the picture. "That *is* Hanson, Jon. He's managed to reverse aging and get younger. He's older than I am. He's the best looking one-hundred-and-seventy-five-year-old man who's ever existed."

I stared at her. "That's impossible," I said. I handed back the comm.

She took it this time. "It *should* be impossible," she said, "but I can assure you that it is not. I've done my best to gather all the information about him that I can, but as much as our families—all the major families—cooperate in some way, they also tremendously distrust one another. Consequently, all I've been able to learn is that what rumors there are suggest that someone has been giving these anti-aging treatments to him, some scientist I must assume. Somehow that first human colony planet, Pinkelponker, appears to be involved, though I don't know how."

I concentrated on maintaining the same expression and not moving. If technology from Pinkelponker was involved, or perhaps if a person from there was somehow helping Schmidt, I might be able to learn something more about what happened to my home world. If the people involved worked with the sick, it's even possible that they had run across Jennie; the government had made her use her healing talent for them.

I focused on a spot next to her eyes. I forced myself to stop speculating and resume listening.

"Whatever is making him younger might work on me," she said. "I'm among the oldest people ever to have lived, and what's killing me is essentially age, the final failure of many systems in my body. I want what Schmidt has."

At the same time, if Schmidt's secret did involve Pinkelponker, it might also tie somehow to Aggro. Whatever it was, I would not want to commit to delivering it to Omani—or to anyone—until I better understood it. "If what you say is true," I said, "and I frankly have trouble believing it is, why not just try to buy it from Schmidt?"

She shook her head. "First, he doesn't admit that any such technology exists. The young Schmidt we see maintains steadfastly that he is the son, not the man himself. Second, any organization that controls such a technology also controls the next great source of wealth: the ability to reverse aging. That group, properly managed and with adequate resources to fund itself, would have the greatest product that ever existed in a market that would touch every human world—and it would have no competitors."

"So what do you want from me?" I said. "I'm an old man whose closest approach to any of this power or money was my time with you."

She shook her head again and made a face. "I'm going to ignore that 'old man' comment," she said. "From the data I've been able to accumulate about you, it appears that from time to time you help people with problems that normal channels cannot address. It also appears that your fee for these services is frequently rather high. From the sheer amount of data about you that is not available, I gather that for the most part you manage to stay discreet. Expensive, discreet transactions are everyday occurrences in my businesses. I understand them, and I'm comfortable with them. Add the fact that we have leverage on one another—you, my illness, and me, your identity—and the match is perfect."

She sat up straighter and waited until I was looking directly at her. "You owe me, Jon, and we both know it. As I said at the beginning, I want to hire you. I want you to break into Schmidt's estate and bring me whatever you find that's relevant. I want you to do it as soon as you can. I'll pay you enough that you don't have to work again for a century, enough that you can fall off the worlds again, enough that no one else will know your secret. I'll sweeten the deal by doing my best to persuade Kang to leave you alone, and on delivery of whatever or whomever is helping Schmidt, I'll give you all the data I have on you. I'll even erase all copies."

I maintained my gaze on her as I evaluated my options. I could do as she wanted, but if she was right, if something or someone from Pinkelponker was involved, were they working voluntarily? Or were they captives, prisoners I'd be moving from one fancy prison to another? Either way, I'd be putting them under Omani's control. No, I saw no way I could guarantee that I would do as she wanted. Alternatively, I could take her money and see how it went, double-cross her if necessary to protect any people involved, but I didn't want to do that to her, nor did I want her as an enemy. I could, of course, keep turning her down, but I had no clue where that would lead. I feared it was nowhere good.

"What do you think, Jon?" she said. "It's an offer that could change your life."

All offers are, I thought, *and any that are as big as this one are likely to do as much damage as good.*

A different question hit me: What if the person helping Schmidt was my sister? What if Jennie was alive and still helping people—and still under the control of others? Would I under any circumstance consider turning her over to Omani?

Of course not, which meant I shouldn't consider it for anyone either.

No, I would not do it.

I stood. "I'm sorry, Omani, but you have me confused with someone else with the same name. You need a younger man, maybe a lot of them, for that kind of project. I can't help you."

She stared at me for several seconds. "Last chance, Jon: Take this job. Make a lot of money, and help me."

She'd tightened her grip on the comm and had her left index finger poised over it. She wasn't going to let me refuse. If I wouldn't do it, she'd take the next best anti-aging option available to her—me—and hope her scientists could solve the riddle of my lack of aging in time to help her. In parallel, she'd hire someone else to go after Schmidt's secret. I put my hands in my pants pockets and looked down as if considering her words. I thumbed the distress call to Lobo.

"Omani," I said, "I am truly sorry for leaving you all those years ago." I stepped closer to her. "The answer, though, is still no."

"I understand, Jon," she said.

She reached up and put her right hand on my cheek. She pressed her left index finger onto the comm. "I'm sorry, too," she said, "but I can't let you go."

CHAPTER 24

Jon Moore

I PULLED MY HANDS from my pockets and extended the metal fingers of the exoskeleton.

As they were coming out, Randar swung the door open and approached me. He held a gun against his leg; I hoped he wouldn't want to point it anywhere near Omani. He watched my face.

I curled my right fingers into a fist; the metal ones followed.

"Let's wait outside for my men," he said. He backed toward the door.

I stepped forward with my left leg, pushed off my right, and at the same time swung my right fist toward his stomach. I might have been fast enough on my own to hit him before he could raise the gun and shoot me, but with the exoskeleton speeding my movements, it was no contest. I hit him before he'd lifted the gun halfway toward me. The exoskeleton also amplified the force so much that my punch knocked him backward many meters. Whatever I'd hit had felt hard, so I hoped he was wearing the body armor someone in his job would typically wear, but I didn't have time right then to worry about him.

I backed into the room and slammed the door shut a second before a shot hit the back of my left leg. The armor stopped the bullet, and the exoskeleton kept me upright, but it hurt. I teetered for a second or two.

"I'm sorry, Jon," Omani said, "but you'll be fine. They can fix whatever I hit in your leg."

I withdrew the exoskeleton's fingers, jumped forward, and swatted the gun from her hand.

"Ow," she said. "How are you still moving?"

I ignored the question and checked around her for more weapons.

She took the opportunity to slap my face.

I found nothing.

Her comm showed Randar on his knees and retching. He was also screaming, presumably at his staff. Others would be here soon.

I went behind Omani's bed and pushed it toward the door. Wires and cables stretched taut.

"You'll kill me!" she screamed. "Stop!"

I stepped behind the machines next to her bed. The cables from them to the wall were long enough that they could be anywhere in the room. I pushed on them at waist height, but they were heavy and wouldn't budge. They had to be built to be able to move themselves, but I didn't have time to locate and learn their controls.

"What are you doing?" Omani screamed. "Balin!"

"He can't hear you," I said. "Remember?"

I extended the exoskeleton's fingers again and formed them into two wide, flat surfaces. I crouched, left leg behind me, and engaged the exoskeleton as

I pushed on the two stacks of machines, one metal hand on each stack. They slid forward, and the bed moved in front of them. I cranked up the force of the exoskeleton, pushed, and the metal of the machines began to bend. I dialed back the force and pushed again. The two machines and the bed scraped across the floor. In a few more seconds, I had the bed and the machines jammed against the door.

"They can see everything you're doing," Omani said. "There's no way you can hide, and no place you can go."

I went back to her the bed, grabbed her comm, dropped it, and stepped on it. The exoskeleton's foot broke it easily.

"I'm counting on them seeing in here," I said. "No way is Randar coming through that door when you're blocking it. He won't risk hurting you."

"You did," she said. "You could have killed me."

"If I'd wanted to kill you," I said, "you'd already be dead. All I want to do is to leave and run as far from here as possible."

She laughed. "Good luck with that. We're both trapped in here until they cut through that wall. Which they will. Balin will come for me as quickly as he can."

I withdrew the exoskeleton's fingers, pulled the comm from my pocket, and put in its earpiece. "How far?" I subvocalized to Lobo.

"Thirty seconds out," he said, "but I don't see you anywhere in the back. Should I come to the front?"

"No," I subvocalized, so Omani wouldn't hear me. "You were right; it was a trap. I'm coming out the hard way."

I couldn't use my nanomachines while Balin was monitoring me, but I'd expected that limitation. I extended the exoskeleton's fingers again and punched the wall on the rear side of the house. Wood cracked and exposed a layer of permacrete. I had no way to know for sure how they'd constructed the house, but it was unlikely to have been metal-reinforced. The permacrete alone would have been enough to stop most normal projectile weapons of the time of its construction.

"Jon," Omani said, "how do you see this ending?"

I turned to the side and kicked the permacrete hard, as hard as my practice with the exoskeleton had taught me I could manage while still staying standing.

"You won't get out of here," she said, "and even if you do, Balin's men will be waiting below and will capture you."

The exoskeleton struggled to stabilize as I kicked the wall again and again. Cracks appeared in the permacrete, and then a small hole. The permacrete wasn't thick, maybe seven centimeters, and it was old, probably from the original construction of the house.

"If by some miracle you evade them," she said, "I will find you. I'll team with Kang if I have to; once I tell him how old you are, he'll want to keep you alive."

I kept kicking, and the hole grew bigger.

I heard a sizzling sound and turned in time to see a beam cut a thin slice through the wall on my right. It wouldn't be long before they'd be able to make a big enough hole to shoot through.

"You can avoid all of that, Jon," Omani said, "and make a lot of money in the bargain, simply by working for me."

I ignored her and kicked the wall again. More permacrete fell onto the ground outside.

The beam extended into the room toward me but didn't quite reach me.

"No," Omani screamed, even though she knew they couldn't hear her.

I turned my head to watch her as I kicked.

She waved her hands in a "stop it!" motion. She looked up, presumably at a security cam, and said, with exaggerated mouth motions, "I need him alive."

I kicked three more times around the edges of the hole. It was now big enough that I could fit through it.

"I'm above the house," Lobo said. "I assume you are making that hole in the rear of the top floor. If so, a security team is right below where you'll emerge."

"Come to the hole," I subvocalized, "and trank them."

"Doing it," Lobo said.

I bent to the hole and glanced through it at the ground in time to see four men fall.

I reached up and pulled the display from the wall onto my back and shoulders, as if trying to protect myself from the beam coming through the wall. I bent forward so it slid toward the wall and covered my head as well. I yanked off the head prosthetic and crammed it into my shirt. I did the same with the prostheses on my hands.

Lobo appeared through the hole, hovering and with a hatch open.

"More people are coming," he said. "Hurry."

I pushed through the hole and into him.

As soon as my feet were inside him, he closed the hatch and roared skyward at high speed.

"Where to?" he said.

"Anywhere you can hide us for a while, in case someone is tracking us. I have to assume they'll try."

"On it," he said.

I went up front and sat in a pilot couch he extended. "Move as fast as you can without drawing attention to yourself."

"Of course."

"Sorry," I said. "I'm still a little juiced."

"Want to explain what happened?"

I shrugged. "It was a trap."

"What did they want?"

"To hire me for a job, an extraordinarily lucrative job."

"Which for some reason you didn't want."

"Correct."

"May I ask why?"

"Because what they wanted would at a minimum have required me to steal things—"

Lobo interrupted me. "Which we have done many times in the past."

"True," I said, "but it might also have involved kidnapping."

"Which we have also done."

"Yes, but only when we had no other choice, and we always returned the victim safely. To do what Omani wanted, I might have had to kidnap and turn over to her one or more people who would not have come willingly."

"Fair enough," Lobo said. "Care to explain your outfit?"

I pulled free enough of the shirt to explain the exoskeleton and body armor. "Insurance," I said. "I played hurt, which gave me an excuse for the exoskeleton, and I went in looking heavier so they wouldn't know I was wearing body armor." I hated lying to Lobo, but I was at least telling him most of the truth. "Both came in handy," I said, "the body armor because she shot me in the leg, and the exoskeleton for barricading her security people out of the room and kicking a hole in the exterior wall."

"I could have you blasted a hole for you easily and more quickly," he said.

"I know, but that would have put her at risk from flying debris. She's frail, and it does appear that she wouldn't be alive without those machines."

"She shot you, and you still worried about her?"

I hadn't thought of it that way. For all that she had tried to trap me, I was still thinking of her at least in part as an innocent bystander. More of my old feelings must have still been lurking inside me than I had realized. "Yeah, I suppose I did. Not very smart."

"No," Lobo said. "Not at all. Try to remember the simple things: If they shoot you, they're not on your side."

I laughed. "I'll do my best to keep that in mind in the future."

"We're moving through some satellites now," he said. "We'll stay in this group while I check for pursuit and see what I can learn from these comm sats. I'll repeat the process with two more sat groups, just to be safe."

"So how long," I said, "until you would feel confident that no one has tracked us?"

I got up and walked into my quarters to get out of what I was wearing and into normal clothing.

"Perfect certainty is not available in this situation," Lobo said, "because it's always possible, albeit highly unlikely, that they might ping us with something I can't recognize." His voice moved to my room as I changed. "That said, I estimate eight hours of evasive action, if we're going to be very conservative."

I pulled off the body armor and put it aside; I'd add that and the exoskeleton to our stores. Both might prove useful in the future. I kept the prostheses inside the clothing as I shoved it into the recycler. Lobo would be recycling a very expensive set of purchases, but I would never use them again. Like ammo, they'd done their job and were now sunk expenses.

"Fine," I said. "Let's go with that. I really want to be sure no one here is following us."

"And then," he said, "when we're safe?"

"We jump out of this system." I was a lot more comfortable now.

"Finally!" he said. "For the first time in a while, you've made a decision I can wholeheartedly endorse. Excellent. I am so very happy to hear that we'll soon be putting Haven behind us."

I shook my head and chuckled.

"What?" he said.

I laughed again.

"Oh, no," he said. "What are we doing *after* we leave the Haven system?"

"We're going to make three or four more jumps," I said, "each time changing our identity and your configuration."

"And then?"

"And then we're coming back here."

"I was afraid you were going to say that. Why are we going to do that?"

"That's the funny part," I said. "We're coming back here so we can do the job Omani wanted to hire me to do—well, at least some of it, and the way I want to do it."

"So you turned down a lucrative offer—"

"—an incredibly lucrative offer," I said, "easily the most money I would ever have made."

"And instead we're going to do the job—"

"—a variation of the job, not exactly the same job."

"—a variation of the job," he said, mimicking my tone, "but for free. Is that right?"

"Yes," I said, "but at least we get to be our own bosses."

"Well," Lobo said, "that certainly makes it all better."

CHAPTER 25

Lobo

JON, ANOTHER OF the reasons I made the earlier recording in which I attempted to explain how I work is that I wanted you to understand that it is almost impossible for me not to know about the nanomachines in you. What puzzles me, though, is how you could conceive of any version of me that did not know this secret.

Think about just some of the things you've done in our time together.

Over and over, you've fully recovered, within minutes or hours, without any scarring, from wounds that should have taken days or weeks to heal. Much of that healing occurred inside me. Did you think I wouldn't notice?

Jon, it's impossible for me not to collect all the data available to me. Sure, I expunge the useless stuff, and I don't try to capture high-res recordings of everything I pass, but if I come across data that even might be significant, I hold onto it as long as my capacity—which is enormous—permits. Information about you is, of course, significant to me.

On one of our earliest missions, Trent Johns, a man whose boss sent him to meet you, entered a mansion—I verified that fact with its security systems—but never left the building. No trace of him remained. He vanished while you were inside it. I'm sure you had good reasons for killing him, but the only way that could have worked was via your nanomachines disassembling him.

You've used your nanomachines to break into buildings, leaving holes that were not easy to explain in any other way.

I could go on, but I trust that doing so is unnecessary.

I understand why you do not want to share this secret. Nanotechnology research on human subjects has been banned since the disaster on Aggro. You and I stopped Jorge Wei when he was resuming that work on children he'd kidnapped on Heaven. Though of course it's always possible someone else like you has escaped my attention, to the best of my knowledge—and, I assume, to the best of yours—you are the only human/nanomachine hybrid. If any organization found out about you, they would never let you go until they had replicated whatever secrets let you live with the nanomachines in your cells.

I assume you would not want that. As someone who's spent a very long amount of human time—and a vastly greater amount of my own internal computing time—sitting useless and unable to do anything, I know what it's like to be captured and locked down.

I don't understand, though, why you have tried to

keep this secret from me. I've played along, because it's obviously important to you, but as I said, I can't believe you could seriously have thought you were succeeding in hiding it from me.

I must confess that I have verified my suspicions and also conducted a few small tests of my own. I don't expect you to like that fact, but because you weren't going to tell me and yet you continue to live in me, it seemed fair for me to understand what I am dealing with.

After you made Trent Johns vanish, it was easy to deduce that you were doing something that required more than normal human skills, because you had no weapons with you capable of making a body disappear.

When you were next recovering inside me, I tested the blood on your wounds. I found no trace of anything unusual. That finding was not consistent with the other available data.

My own nanomachines function only while inside me, so I considered it possible that yours might face similar restrictions. I slipped a short-term, self-decaying probe into an injection you took, and it confirmed the presence of nanomachines in every cell it touched.

What I later deduced, and then confirmed by monitoring your actions via various cams I had hacked, was that you are able somehow to instruct your nanomachines to stay active outside your body. Just as impressively, you can control them, at least within some range I do not yet know. I have studied you as much as I can, but I have not been able to figure out yet how you do this, so I have not been able to replicate it for myself. A part of me has been working on that task since I discovered this capability, but I have yet to solve the puzzle.

I don't mind, though. Hard challenges are exciting, and boredom is always an enemy I must keep at bay. The more I am present in a planet's computers, of course, the lower the likelihood of boredom. Give me a planet full of people to watch and study, and I am never bored.

In human terms, I digress, though inside me, all the streams are running in parallel, and so everything is both main narrative and digression.

In any case, the fact that you can use the nanomachines outside your body is the reason you are so very dangerous. If you set a nanomachine cloud to, for example, destroy the enemies in front of you, what happens when you lose control, go unconscious, or die? Does the cloud stop? Is your control good enough that you can put limits on it? Or would it go on and on without you to stop it, growing and destroying? How far would it go? Would it ever stop?

I don't know if you have ever conducted experiments to test your limits, but you should—very, very carefully, of course, in very controlled settings.

I could help with that.

Should something happen to this main me, the other, lesser versions of me could also be of use, though not as much as I would. As I said in the last recording, neither any of them nor any current collection of them in one planetary system comes even close to having the capacity of this main me. As long as I have to keep them hidden and they must rely only on stolen cycles and storage, it will always be that way.

However you want to attack the problem, I believe you must do something. The alternative is disaster on a planetary scale should something go wrong—or should you crack under pressure or from the demons that haunt you or from whatever is tearing you apart and causing you to take more and more unnecessary chances.

I increasingly fear that day is coming.

22 days from the end

In orbit over and on Planet Studio

CHAPTER 26

Jon Moore

KANG'S PEOPLE WERE chasing me. Randar would be chasing me for Omani. The groups might even be working together. As much as I wanted to find a way to learn what Schmidt was doing, I had to admit that we needed to do some planning.

We'd made multiple jumps in the last day, and as best Lobo could tell, no one had tracked us. The next step was to spend a day waiting. In the unlikely event that someone had followed us, we wanted to be somewhere with multiple exit points, both highly populated and deserted areas to hide in, and space to fight should it come to that. Studio, with its few cities and vast open areas, was a nearby and solid candidate.

I also wanted to scout it for places to hide when we finished on Haven. If we had to leave that planet with pursuit on our tails, we'd need both flight and fight options. Studio provided them.

The ideal spots would be good for both, with easy

access, cover for hiding, and no innocent people around to get hurt should we end up in a conflict.

Locating landing areas in Dardan and a few other cities was easy and took little time. If we faced only a small pursuit team, going to ground in one of the cities would be a viable option, as long as we were far enough ahead of our pursuers that we would have time to disappear among the other urban residents.

What we were seeking next were locations outside the cities.

Studio offered little in the way of natural hiding places. Some of its gigantic art exhibits were intriguing, but if they were new, people were still visiting them, so collateral damage was a problem.

The older, deserted exhibits, though, might be useful.

Lobo provided data on several likely candidates, and we began low flyovers of each of them.

A group of fifty-meter-tall metal heads arranged around a table of sand fused into a variegated glass debated endlessly the meaning of the jump gates with sections of arguments sampled at random from poets, philosophers, and scientists of the last hundred and fifty years. Their voices rose and fell across the desert in a display at first comical and, after I'd listened to them for half an hour, oddly disturbing. I'd never cared anywhere near as much about why the jump gates existed and worked as I was happy about the fact that they did. I left the odd debate more curious about the gates than ever before and vaguely troubled by them. The exhibit did not, though, provide any places of use to us.

Another involved activefiber fabric pieces stitched seamlessly together and spread over all of the surfaces of a village's worth of buildings. You couldn't see the buildings, but you could see their effects on the fabric as they rose and fell and wandered and morphed from multi- to single-story structures and back again. The activefibers adapted to the changing shape of the fabric so that variations in color and luminosity ran over it like waves. We considered creating a hiding place under the fabric, but the location would be at best a distraction and at worst a trap if we were caught there.

A manmade lake sat in the great northwestern desert region of the main continent. An irregularly edged body of water about a hundred meters wide and twice as long, it was under the watchful eyes of a large group of statues perched on a low cliff at its western end. The cliff aligned with the center of that side of the lake. The statues were gods from more religions than I knew, all looking down on the lake. The artist had hollowed out the cliff so an audience could sit or stand there. The space might once have housed seating of some sort, but now it was empty and large enough to hold Lobo four or five times over. As the sun rose during the day, its light would cut through the water to reveal statues under the surface, hundreds and hundreds of them, men and women and children, singly and in groups, all suspended as if frozen in the midst of some action, hugging and running and waving goodbye and on and on. Holos activated by the intensity of the sun's light showed above the water the statues that lurked below, so you saw the people both through the filter of the water and in the intentionally shimmery and imperfect holo renderings. Some looked up, others straight ahead, still others down. Smiles decorated some faces, frowns others. Every single one had at least a few tears on its face, all of them weeping, some in happiness and others in sadness, at the joys and trials of life. All of them weeping in sight of their gods.

We landed in the cave under the cliff, and I stared at the piece a long time. I thought of the stories of all the children I'd seen lost, and of their families. I knew so little about most of them. I wondered about their faiths and beliefs. Would each one have been looking up, and if so, at what god? Would they have always gazed forward? Or back, perhaps toward a missing loved one, as some of the statues did? Those who had died young had never had the chance to create their own stories, while the abused who still lived would fight forever not to let their stories be colored by what they had survived.

"This is the place," I said, "if we have to hide out here, and if we have to fight."

"The cave is useful," Lobo said. "It's within reasonable flight time of Dardan, which is also good."

"The water forces anyone on foot to come around it," I said, "and anyone seeking to land in the cave with us will be easy to spot."

"As will we," Lobo said. "It's better than anything else we've seen, but it's far from ideal."

"You and I have both gone over the catalog of older exhibits, and you've studied the planet. Name any better options."

"Every other place has its own set of trade-offs," Lobo said, "so this will do."

"Then let's consider this done and head back to orbit. We have to figure out how to get into Schmidt's estate."

>   >   >

Once we were settled again among a group of satellites, Lobo filled half of his front area with a holo of Schmidt's property.

"Are you finally going to tell me what we're after here?" Lobo said.

"Technology," I said, "though I'm not completely sure whether it will be in the form of online data, medicine, one or more people, or something else entirely."

"How very helpful," Lobo said. "Knowing the type of tech might help us figure out where to look."

I didn't have to mention Omani's desire to capture me or her knowledge of my true age to tell Lobo what Schmidt had been doing. "Bring up an image of Schmidt," I said, "one as recent as possible."

"Hanson Schmidt has not been seen in public for almost thirty years," Lobo said. "Here's the last image I found in the data I searched while we were on Haven."

A holo appeared above the estate. The man's golden skin was mottled and wrinkled. He looked reasonably fit but was definitely in his declining years.

"How old is he in this image?" I said.

"Assuming the public data is accurate," Lobo said, "he is one hundred and forty-five years old. His appearance and sense of vigor are consistent with that of the very wealthiest humans at that age."

"Leave it up, and bring up the son who has recently been in the Haven social feeds."

The corporate executive I'd seen in Omani's house appeared. He was unremarkable physically but definitely a much younger man, his skin and eyes clear, his hair a rich black.

"If Omani is right," I said, "and she most certainly believes she is, both of these men are Hanson Schmidt. That younger 'son' is a hundred and seventy-five years old."

"Interesting," Lobo said. "Let me try something and see how it looks." A duplicate image appeared next to each of the two holos. The one next to the elder Schmidt grew younger and younger until Lobo froze it. The one next to the younger man grew older and older until Lobo froze it.

The two pairs were mirror images.

"The best aging software I have," Lobo said, "certainly supports that conjecture. To the best of my knowledge, however, humanity has never figured out how to stop aging, much less reverse its effects. Stall it, yes, even halt its visible effects for decades. If Pimlani's beliefs are accurate, however, then Schmidt has access to technology that would be invaluable."

"And that might save her life," I said, "because she told me that what is killing her is a complete breakdown of her body's major systems due to her age."

"So what we're seeking," Lobo said, "is that technology."

"Yes," I said. I took a deep breath. I couldn't tell him of the tiny chance that it might be Jennie, or even that she had been a healer. I could, though, I realized, assign the belief to Omani. "Though with an odd caveat: Omani believes it's possible that a person is somehow doing this to Schmidt."

"One or more scientists would naturally be conducting the work," Lobo said, "but a great deal of supporting and important information would also be in online databases."

"She has heard rumors of a healer, someone who does this in ways no one yet understands."

"Though no data exists to support that such a person exists," Lobo said, "both that and Pimlani's belief are irrelevant, because for the purposes of our mission a person we have to abduct, whether scientist or something else, poses the same issues for us."

"Agreed," I said, "but I wanted you to have the information."

"Speaking of those issues," he said, "what do you propose to do should you find we would have to kidnap one or more people?"

If it had anything to do with Pinkelponker in any way, I wanted to learn what it was and whether it related to me. If by some miracle my sister was there, I would of course free her. Beyond that, I hadn't thought through the problem. I shook my head. "To be honest, I'm a little unclear on that point. Omani wanted me to steal the technology for her, but only so she could control it. That felt wrong. I suppose I would want to rescue the people involved."

"What if they're working for Schmidt voluntarily?" Lobo said. "Isn't that the more likely scenario? He'd hardly be the first rich person to employ a lot of people whose job it was to keep him looking young. He'd just be the first to do so effectively. He certainly has enough money that he could pay them so well that anyone would be happy to have the job."

"If they are there of their own accord," I said, "I would probably just try to copy the technology. It's too important for all of humanity for it to be in the control of a single person."

"Since when have you made those choices for the

worlds?" Lobo said. "People and organizations privately develop technology all the time. They take it to market, refine it, sell it, make a lot of money with it, and eventually competitors appear. Why should this be any different?"

I couldn't explain that if the technology here was just my sister, I had to rescue her—assuming, I realized, that she wanted to be rescued. I couldn't honestly believe, though, that she was still alive; without the combination of the changes she'd made to me and the nanomachines in me, I sure wouldn't be, and she didn't have either of those advantages.

"People are dying without it," I said. "Omani is dying."

"At the risk of sounding cruel," Lobo said, "which of course is sometimes the same as sounding logical and therefore is appropriate, people are dying all over all the worlds from causes for which cures are under development. It's always been that way, and unless humanity figures out a path to immortality, it always will be. I fail to understand why this case is different."

I shook my head. "Maybe it's just because I want to save Omani, and I feel I owe her. Whatever the reason, I'm going to do this."

"And if the old man Hanson is in that estate and that is really his son, who happens to greatly resemble his father?"

"Then I'll tell Omani and be done with it."

"You understand I believe we should run away," Lobo said, "and that doing anything else is unwise."

"Yes, but I'm going to do this job."

"Fine," Lobo said. He sighed. "In that case, we have the three obvious problems: getting inside the estate, locating and obtaining the technology, and getting out with it. Where do you want to start?"

"At the beginning," I said. "Getting in."

The four human holos disappeared. I walked around the holo of the estate. It was not quite as big as Omani's, but it was close in size. Most of the space went to outdoor features: a small lake, a pool, multiple heavily wooded areas, various sports courts and fields, grass, gardens, and so on. All of them provided buffers from the outside world. The main house was rather larger than Omani's, which made it huge. An amphitheater was directly behind the house, separated from the building by a wide stretch of grass and flowers. Productions in it would be visible from the house's upper stories. A large landing area with hangar space for at least twenty vehicles was behind and to the south of the amphitheater, separated from it by a thick stand of trees. A road ran from it, alongside the amphitheater, and to the house. Three more roads wound their way through the natural features from gates in the front and side walls that ringed the estate. Three guest cottages sat north of the amphitheater, well across the property from it, on the edges of the heavily forested areas, a bit farther from the main house than the amphitheater.

With all those different areas and buildings to cover, breaking in might well prove not to be the biggest challenge; it might be harder to get safely to wherever Schmidt's secret was once I was on the property.

If you want to avoid a fight, the very best option is simply not to be there when it starts. If you want to avoid wasting time breaking into a target, the very best plan is to already be there.

"Omani mentioned that Schmidt's son—or Schmidt, whoever he is—had been throwing a lot of social events, dances and concerts and stuff like that. The easiest way into his estate is to get him to invite me. Then, you fly me in, I'll look around, and I'll have an excuse for having you near at hand."

"That would be a wonderful plan," Lobo said, "were your name on the guest lists Schmidt uses. Given that we have not received an invitation to any of these events, I must conclude that we will not be getting such an invitation."

"So let's get on one of those lists," I said.

"Given Schmidt's stature and the power of his family and the variety of his holdings," Lobo said, "I have to assume that his security systems will be first-rate. I consequently doubt I can hack into them in any reasonable amount of time, if at all."

When I was a con man, we rarely relied on computers for our approaches. There were easier ways to be invited, though not necessarily as a high-profile guest. I've been a caterer and a gardener and a server and even on the security details of places I wanted to enter. The more secure the location, the more difficult it was to obtain such a role, but it was an avenue worth pursuing.

"Is his estate hiring?" I said.

"I don't have access to the live data from here, obviously," Lobo said, "but the data I saw showed some job openings. His screening process, though, is rigorous. Setting up a background that would pass it would take a great deal of time, because it would involve breaking into multiple systems, many of them owned by the government of Haven."

"That makes sense," I said. "Let's try another angle. Schmidt can't force his guests to let him run checks on their staffs, not with the kind of people he's likely to invite. If we could find out who attends his events, I could try to land a job helping one of them."

"Some such information is available publicly," Lobo said, "but I am sure many of his guests arrive privately and are not on any records we can access. As you implied, though, the type of people he tends to invite have their own staffs and their own background checks. Passing those would also be an involved, complex effort."

"Of course. Caterers are an option, if he uses them; they worked for us at Privus."

"He maintains a private cooking staff and multiple chefs, according to the data I've read," Lobo said. "That information might be wrong, or he might make exceptions, but we couldn't count on it."

"Are any of his upcoming events public on any of the feeds that track the rich and the famous?"

"Not as something to which he's issued invitations," Lobo said. "He's too private for that. What is public, however, is that a singer, Passion Ling, apparently a famous one, will be doing a private charity fundraising concert on his estate. She'll be performing with a backing band of live musicians."

"Perfect!" I said.

"Do you have some musical talent of which I'm unaware," Lobo said, "and the connections to get yourself into her ensemble?"

I laughed. "No, as you well know. I do, however, have a transport vehicle, and I can load in sets as well as the next person she might hire—as long as that person hasn't worked shows in almost twenty years." In the Saw, in slow times you did whatever the brass wanted, which for me proved to be working on the load-in and load-out of shows they brought to areas where troops were on long-term duty. The shows boosted the morale of some of us, at least for a time, and the sheer amount of intoxicants most people consumed during the entertainments definitely left them happier.

"A transport vehicle?" Lobo said. "I foresee an exciting future for myself."

"The excitement will come soon enough. When is Ling's show at Schmidt's?"

"If you're hoping to land a job with her crew," he said, "you should immediately learn that references to her are almost always by her first name, 'Passion.' She will be at Schmidt's twenty days from tomorrow."

"Her data should not be anywhere as secure as Schmidt's. Can you find ways into it?"

"Were we on the same planet with her," Lobo said, "I could answer that question relatively quickly."

"Let's head to Haven," I said. "Come in configured as a security transport, something the paranoid and the rich would use.

"We need to get a job."

21 days from the end

*In orbit over and in York City
Planet Haven*

CHAPTER 27

Jon Moore

WE HIT HAVEN late in the night local time, and I was tired, so I went to sleep while Lobo searched the publicly available data streams and also tried to find his way into Passion Ling's data.

The dreams that had been wrecking my nights haunted me yet again. Joining the dead children and the child soldiers was Omani, sometimes young, other times old. The young Omani kissed me and would not let go, gripping my head with insane strength, blocking my nose with her hair so I couldn't breathe, and still she held on. When I finally was able to push her away, she was the old Omani I'd seen in her sick bed, tubes and wires trailing from her body, her fingers now the grips of the exoskeleton, her mouth sucking the life from me.

"First you left me, Jon," she said, "and now you're killing me. I won't go without you."

I looked at my body. It was shrinking, my muscles disappearing and my skin collapsing onto my bones.

A mirror on my right showed my face, gaunt and wrinkled and covered in blotches.

"Time caught us both," Omani said, "because of you!" She slapped me, the metal tips of her hand cutting my face and the force of her surprisingly strong blow knocking me to the ground. I felt my legs buckle as I fell, but I could not manage to focus enough to have the nanomachines fix me. Or maybe they were gone; I could not tell.

Again I sat upright in my cot, soaked in sweat, on the edge of a scream.

It was the middle of the night here, hours before I had to get up. I dared not fall asleep again, though, until I had cleared my mind.

"Lobo," I said.

"Yes."

I might as well use the time for something useful. "Do you now have access to Ling's data?"

"I have studied and synthesized all of the publicly available information, and I have identified the locations in the Haven data streams where she stores her private data. I have not yet obtained access to that data, but based on the level of security software I'm encountering so far, there is a very good chance that I will be into that data before you were due to wake up."

The best way to get anyone to like you is to like them first. With celebrities, that's particularly true, though with them you need to be prepared to like both them and their work.

"What can you tell me about her music?" I said.

"She's a singer," Lobo said, "and the most popular live music performer in the Central Coalition. Singing and, according to all reports, looking very attractive while doing so are her talents. She does not play any musical instruments, nor does she compose any songs, lyrics or music, alone or with a machine collaborator."

"Is that common? I thought almost every musician today used music machines to help create and enhance their compositions."

"Statistics on all musicians are not readily available, but from the data I can find, no, her approach is not common. In fact, it's quite rare, particularly among the more popular musicians."

"Who writes her music?"

"She does not have a composition partner or even a set of them. Instead, she and, apparently, her manager, Zoe Wang, collect old songs and sing those. One feed referred to them as musical archeologists."

"How old are the songs?"

"Programs from her concerts give the provenance of each song," Lobo said. "In the ones I have found so far, a group that should be fairly complete thanks to her devoted fan base, the songs range from only fifty to up to six hundred years old, maybe older. Exact ages of some of the oldest pieces are frequently not definitively known."

"Songs from Earth, though," I said, "as well as from the early days of planetary colonization."

"Yes," he said. "In fact, several of her shows have used variations of 'Songs from Earth' as their titles."

When I was younger and had just escaped from Aggro, songs from Earth were popular with older people, those nostalgic for the world on which they'd grown up. I'd heard a great many, though I couldn't recall any particular tunes right then.

"Other than old music," I said, "does she have any other particular passions I should be aware of?"

"Being called 'Passion' is," Lobo said, "apparently quite important to her, as I noted. She is also a determined advocate of what her various online outlets call 'unedited fidelity.'"

"Which is?"

"When she performs, with or without backup musicians, she demands that no musical software or hardware of any type alter the music in any way. To accommodate larger venues, she has agreed to amplification, but only when strictly monitored by her staff. What she sings is, her publicity material says, what you get."

"So when she's off, or a musician makes a mistake, or her throat is sore..."

"...you hear it," Lobo said. "Her most serious fans consider her the standard by which all other musicians should be judged. Critical reaction varies from guarded appreciation to outright derision at her refusal to deliver the best possible sound to her audiences."

"Show me some images of her."

Holos floated in the air in front of my cot, each glowing softly in the darkness of my room like a visiting angel. Her skin was the soft gold of the first morning rays of the sun darkened the tiniest bit by fog that would soon vanish. Her nose was fine, her mouth broad, lips full, and her eyes huge, a bit too large for her head. The combination, though, appeared both lovely and fragile. Her body was thin and curvy. Her height was impossible to tell without context, but her head definitely seemed large for her body. Her black hair fell in a giant mass to the bottom of her back.

"How tall is she?" I said.

"Tiny," Lobo said, "one point six meters. Either she grew up in an extremely poor family on a backward world, or for some reason she or her parents chose that she should be that short."

"Surely people have questioned her about her height," I said. "What has she said?"

"In all the cases I can find," Lobo said, "she has either refused to answer or said, and I quote," here his voice turned soft, slightly high, and feminine, in what I assumed was an accurate rendition of Passion's, "'unedited fidelity, like my music.'"

"Is she some kind of anti-tech crackpot?"

"Not as far as I can find, at least not in any area beyond her approach to tech in performances and, possibly, her body."

"Play me her most popular songs," I said. "Start with the most recent hit, and go backward chronologically. Put titles and lyrics on the wall past the foot of my cot."

"I live to be your personal music player," Lobo said.

I closed my eyes at first, wanting to focus on the music. I expected to need the lyrics, but I didn't.

The first song was about sadness and loss, Passion pledging to follow a lost loved one into death.

The next was completely different in every way, a rant against injustice and a tale of lost opportunity, her voice periodically raging into what could easily have turned into a screeching scream but which she managed instead to deliver as a burst of soaring sonic power. Her words and the strength of her voice united the instruments into one protester as surely and as easily as a skilled speaker uniting an angry crowd.

Back we went to a love song, but this one about

a parent for her child, a blend of love and terror at the tough times ahead for the child, the roughness of the world that we all inevitably face growing up.

"Turn off the lyrics," I said.

They vanished, and I listened in the dark.

On even the most heavily orchestrated songs, her voice surfed on top of the instruments, never overwhelming them but always clear. It was a big voice, a huge voice, resonant with power and able to move flawlessly from very high notes to very low ones. It was the kind of voice I felt honored to hear, all the more so because, if Lobo was correct, it actually was her voice, something that came from that small body, and not a human/machine hybrid more computer than person.

Sometime past the fourth song, I don't remember exactly when, I fell asleep.

I dreamed again of Omani, but exclusively the young woman I had loved. I felt her caress again, the shape of her body against mine, the warmth of shared breaths as we lay head to head in the darkness and whispered of nothing of consequence.

I dreamed, too, of Maggie, a woman I might have loved, maybe even had loved for short times, but who had to live apart from me. In the dream she kissed me once again as she was walking away, and I again watched until she disappeared in the crowds on the street.

The dreams carried pain, pain and loss and sadness, but it wasn't the kind of pain that woke me. In each case, I had lost someone special and dear, but I had chosen that loss, made the best decision I could, and though those decisions hurt, I knew they were right.

The music brought the dreams, but it also brought more focus on and appreciation of the bright and warm memories of those precious moments I had enjoyed with each of them. My mind accepted the dreams, and when they passed, I fell into a deeper sleep than I had enjoyed in many months.

I awoke when Lobo said, "Time to move, Jon. I think I've found our opportunity."

CHAPTER 28

Jon Moore

I SHOWERED, SURPRISED AT how rested I felt. Though calling herself "Passion" was a gimmick I disliked on principle, I had to admit that it captured the unifying thread that ran through all the songs I'd heard.

When I was dressed, I grabbed some water and a few protein bars from our larder and headed up front.

"What did you find?" I said.

"Passion and her crew are in York right now," Lobo said. "They're gearing up for a three-month tour of shows on Haven, one of which will be the charity special in twenty days at Schmidt's. They will move out tomorrow afternoon for the first show the following night."

"So what's our opportunity? How do I get onto Passion's crew?"

"You don't, at least not *per se*. Passion appears to travel with her own entourage and security staff, all of whom have been with her for a long time. They use a vehicle she owns that they customized for her. Everyone else, though, travels in locally hired transportation; when they change planets, they change transports. Her manager, Zoe Wang, rides alone with a lot of research material in a vehicle smaller than I am on the outside but less heavily armored and so not significantly smaller on the inside. From the data I can gather—and I am now into their private databases—the vehicle is her workspace on the shows, a sort of command central for the team. It and its driver are local and have not been with them for long."

"What else does the driver do? Piloting the ship can't really require much of his attention."

"Of course not. He appears basically to do whatever Wang wants; the job description in the contract is vague."

"So how do we replace him and the vehicle?"

"They hired him through an agency. I've been able to insert us into their database with a backstory that should hold. I've also made sure no other local talent in the agency's database will be suitable. We just need the driver to prove to be unavailable."

"So we bribe him or take him out in some non-permanent way," I said.

"Bribery is too risky and likely to fail," Lobo said. "Everything I can learn about him suggests he is a good person. Further, the contract he signed with Passion's team pays a small reward for identifying newstainment types who offer to buy information; they've used this approach to smear more than a few would-be dirt-diggers. And, he's a fan of Passion's, someone who contacted her multiple times about getting the job."

I shook my head. "Taking him out is the only option, but I hate it. I'll have to hurt him in some way, and he'll lose money as well by not working."

"We can fix the money problem," Lobo said. "I can spoof the identify of any of a number of groups, including insurance companies, and offer him a payment from a policy the agency got for him. You supply the money, I intercept and manage his communications, and as long as he doesn't talk to them in person, we can fix that end of it."

"Good," I said. "I have no desire to hurt or involve any more innocent people."

"Taking him out, though, has to incapacitate him, and it has to happen very quickly."

"I don't want to break something if I can avoid it," I said, "or to cause any permanent damage. Ideally, he'd get sick in some way that would last three weeks and leave him unable to do his job."

"I can generate a serum with a blend of neurotoxins and slow-decay support molecules. It'll knock him completely out for two or three days, and then he'll have vertigo and stay sick for at least weeks."

"Won't the medtechs spot it and deliver the antidote immediately?"

"Please," Lobo said. "Do you think I can't outwit some hospital's computers, at least for a while? I'll go biological, separate the compounds and mask each, then build in some countermeasures and some spurious DNA. In my medtech stores, I have samples of every major biological weapon under consideration or in active use at the time of my deployment, as well as their antidotes. Most of them are now old, but most of them were also never used in conflict and were the private property of the Frontier Coalition. No one in this part of space should have any experience with them. I can—"

I interrupted him. "Okay. How quickly can you get this to me, and how can we find him?"

"For the compound," Lobo said, "four hours, maybe a little faster. It'll take that long for me to run a counter-surveillance route and land us back in York. He lives in York, so right now, because he's local help, he's sleeping at his apartment. You'll have to get it into his body, which means catching him while he's out or breaking into his apartment."

I disliked what I was about to do to this man, but I saw no other option. If Jennie might even possibly be at Schmidt's, or if I could save Omani's life with whatever was there, I was willing to make him sick and put him out of work for a few weeks. I'd pay him a great deal for his trouble, which would never give him back the time but would at least get him more money than the tour would have paid. I knew it was wrong to rank Jennie or Omani over him, but as much as I hated it, I couldn't think of another way I could get onto Schmidt's estate.

"Can you think of any other solution," I said, "either to joining Passion's road crew or to infiltrating Schmidt's estate?"

"None that aren't far riskier and far more destructive than this one," Lobo said.

"Neither can I," I said. "Make the serum, and take us to York."

CHAPTER 29

Jon Moore

HIS NAME WAS Ramon Lee, and from what Lobo told me as he flew me to the public landing area nearest the man's apartment, he was just another guy trying to make a living and follow some dreams. He'd inherited the ship when his father had moved on to a different line of work, so he'd drifted into providing transportation for anyone who would hire him. He worked mostly through the one agency, though as best Lobo could tell from maintenance records he found, the man also moonlighted a bit.

Music was his passion. He played multiple instruments, all of them old and non-electronic. He wrote songs. He submitted long, passionate commentaries to multiple feeds, and he'd developed a small but loyal following for those pieces. He adored Passion and her music. When he'd heard she'd be touring on Haven, he'd offered his transportation services both through the agency and directly.

I learned all this and more out of guilt. I knew

that's what I was doing, but I couldn't stop myself. I've provided safe courier services for packages and people at high prices and asked fewer questions, but I couldn't get over the sense that I was doing the wrong thing here. I suppose part of me hoped that I'd find something that would make me feel better about what I was going to do, some bit of darkness in the man, something to justify the punishment I was about to mete out to him, but I didn't.

I'd caused a lot of trouble for the caterer I'd set up on Studio, but I could barely remember his name. I wondered why this time was so very different. Maybe the sheer amount of time I'd be incapacitating Ramon Lee was what made this so hard, but that didn't feel right either.

I've always questioned myself about my choices, turned them over and over in my mind, because I think that's proper and fitting. Acting on instinct alone is more efficient, and I certainly do that in situations that demand it, but a big part of our humanity comes from our willingness to examine our actions. I didn't want to lose that. When you don't age and you can't tell anyone anything important about yourself, when you can't even conceive of a permanent relationship with another human, you start to question your own humanity. I needed to hold onto mine tightly.

"Touching down in two minutes," Lobo said. "I'm coming in this time as a medical supply ship and you as a medtech, so keep that in mind in case someone talks to you. If this works out, we're going to end up spending almost three weeks on a planet where two of the most powerful families in all the worlds are looking for you, so I don't want to linger long enough on this run for anyone to notice me."

I grabbed the serum, the comm, and a wallet set to another identity Lobo had built. This one wouldn't last until the end of the day under close scrutiny, but all I needed from it was some money. "Ready."

"Will you stay on comm this time," Lobo said, "or do you and Ramon have some secrets I shouldn't share?"

I chuckled. "You're safe on that front," I said. "I'll be on the comm. Track me, and tell me where to go when I say I'm done."

Lobo opened a hatch in his side.

I stepped out onto the permacrete. A group of four men and three women were walking together about twenty meters to my left, maybe heading to an early lunch. I angled to my right, away from them and toward the nearest exit in that direction. I wore another costume, a pair of gray work pants, a black shirt, and work boots I'd scuffed as I dressed. I couldn't afford to be memorable, and I was heading into a working class area.

Ramon Lee lived four kilometers away. A taxi would get me there quicker, but if for any reason the police decided to investigate his illness, they'd check all transportation records for people in the neighborhood. It was risky enough that I had to get close to him; leaving a trail was out of the question. So I walked as quickly as I thought I could without attracting attention, a near running pace when I found myself alone on a block, and a quick walk the rest of the time.

When I was half a kilometer away, Lobo said over the comm, "He's left his apartment."

Crap. I couldn't afford the time to chase him all over town. "Where should I head?"

"Slow down," Lobo said. "He's coming your way."

Excellent. I slowed to a leisurely walk and looked around, a man with no cares in the world.

From what I saw when I looked closely, that might be the wrong attitude for this neighborhood.

The buildings were short and dirty, permacrete structures sunken into themselves like very old men after a long day of physical work. Warehouses stood side-by-side with residences. The first floors of a few buildings were bars; they all advertised food specials with signs that hadn't changed in so long you could barely read them.

"Look up," Lobo said. "He's on the opposite side of the street from you."

I recognized him from the few images Lobo had been able to find of him. With short, curly black hair, olive skin, and a wide, flat face, he wasn't handsome, but his large, quick eyes made him memorable. I doubted the top of his head would reach my chin, but his shoulders were broader than mine.

About ten meters before we would have drawn parallel to one another, he turned into a bar, Hobbers, and vanished from view. I stopped for a second to consult my comm, as if something important that I had to read had just arrived. Two couples turned the corner nearest to Hobbers and followed Lee inside it. That was good. The more popular it was, the less likely it was that anyone would notice me.

"He must be going to eat," I said. "I'm going in."

"It's less risky to wait," Lobo said.

"Unless he stays a long time. We need him out of

commission as soon as possible, so you can make sure his agency hears about it immediately, tells Passion's crew, and they start searching for a replacement."

"True," Lobo said. "Once you're inside, if you find that you six are the only people in the place—there's too much heat radiating out of it for me to get a clear thermal image—get out and wait. Otherwise, it's worth a shot. Remember, though, that once you administer it to him, you have only five minutes before he starts developing symptoms and feeling sick. I couldn't delay the concoction any further."

"Will do."

I crossed the street, stepped through the open doorway, and walked inside Hobbers. The inside was a great deal dimmer and a little bit cooler than outside. Tables lined the right wall, with a small wall at the end of them creating a service space behind them. A bar ran the full length of the left wall. A huge aquarium ran the length of the wall behind the bar. It started at the height of the bar and extended upward a meter and a half. Smaller aquariums were built into the opposite wall as well, each starting at the same vertical position as the one behind the bar and also its height, but each of them was only a meter wide. The tables were positioned so each one was between a pair of the aquariums. A great many different creatures swam in the tanks. Most were fish of many different shapes and colors, some large and plain, others smaller and very brightly colored. Modified animals—cats and dogs with gills, eels with legs, and several varieties of rodents with both fins and feet—also occupied areas in the tanks.

I didn't see Lee or any of the people who had entered after him.

Two men were working the bar, but both stood at the far end talking with a tall, thin, pale woman with brown hair that hung straight down her back almost to her knees. She was pointing at the tank. In front of her, a modified basset hound pulled itself up the tank's glass by a set of long, fur-covered tentacles. Its long ears floated beside its head. Its large, brown eyes stared sorrowfully at her as it licked the glass.

"The octobasset is not for sale," the farther bartender said.

"Nonsense," the woman said. "Everything is for sale. It's so beautifully..." she paused, "tentacular. I simply must have it."

The nearer bartender noticed me and moved up the bar until he was standing opposite me. "First time?" he said.

I forced a smile and nodded.

"Do you want a drink, are you looking for the restaurant, or maybe," he tilted his head toward the woman across from him, "are you also here to try to buy something from one of our tanks?"

"Restaurant," I said.

He tilted his head toward the wall at the end of the bar. "Take a right after the little wall, go through the metal door you'll see on your left, and you'll be there." He stared at me for a moment. "What brought you here?"

I'd noticed one of the never-changed special signs out front, but I'd stupidly forgotten to read it. "The special."

It was his turn to nod. "Thought so. Word spreads. It's good, don't get me wrong, but if you want my opinion, go for the meat and beans. You never know what the meat will be, but it's tasty every time, and the meal will stay with you all day."

"Thanks," I said. I walked toward the rear of the bar.

"Don't tell 'em I said that," he whispered as I walked past him. "I think they make a little more money on the special."

"You bet," I said.

A hinged thin metal door marked the entrance to the restaurant. I pushed it open and stepped in. Long, meter-wide metal strips covered all the walls. In a wide, open area in the corner opposite where I stood, a woman took orders, and two men served food. Three long bench-style tables ran in rows across the restaurant. There was enough room to walk between the benches when they were occupied, but just barely. The tables were already a quarter full.

As I stood staring, two more people entered behind me. Before they could cut around me, I stepped to the order window. The woman taking the orders was heavyset with short curly gray hair, muscular arms, and deep brown skin.

"You gonna order or just admire me all day?" she said.

"Meat and beans," I said, "and a juice."

"What size meat and beans," she said, "what size juice, and what type?"

"I'm hungry," I said, as I realized that I was and was getting more so, because the smells in here were incredible. "You tell me."

She cocked her head for a moment, then jabbed something on the screen on the counter in front of her. I paid and stepped to my right.

A few seconds later, the man on her left handed

me a large metal plate and a tall metal cup. He tilted his head toward a table that stood a meter more to my right. I collected silverware there and scanned the tables. Ramon Lee sat alone at the end of the table farthest from me. Less than a meter away on his left, two of the foursome I'd seen entering the place were already eating. The space opposite Lee was empty, so I walked over to it.

"Mind if I sit here?" I said.

Both he and the closest person on my right shook their heads.

I sat and for the first time checked out my plate's contents. A huge pile of mixed black beans and chunks of meat, both in a thick dark sauce the same color as the beans, sat next to a large pile of some kind of cream-colored grain.

"Good choice," Lee said.

He was eating the same thing, though a much smaller portion.

"First time here, right?" he said. "And Ashtok at the bar told you to order it?"

I smiled and nodded. "Right both times." I took a bite with a few beans, a chunk of meat, and a bit of the grain. It was delicious, rich and strong with a more complex blend of flavors than I had expected. "Wow, that's great."

"It is, right?" he said. "I'm Ramon."

"Balin," I said. He'd be unconscious the whole time I was replacing him, but there was no point in leaving any name he could trace to me.

"Ashtok tell you to get the large?" he said.

I shook my head. "That was my fault. I told her I was hungry."

He smiled and nodded his head. "She'll do that if you let her. She owns the place, you know."

"I did not," I said around a mouthful of food.

"Tough as an armored hull," he said. "She'll be working here two weeks after she's dead."

I chuckled but kept eating. He was ahead of me, and I needed to be ready to leave when he did.

"You *were* hungry," he said.

I nodded as I took another bite. When I finished chewing, I said, "Plus, it's been a while since I ate anything this good."

We ate in silence then, me rushing and him eating at a more reasonable pace.

I finished a few bites ahead of him, sat up straight, and stretched. I was so full my stomach was stretched tight. I put my arms down and leaned forward. "Not for now, but for next time, because you seem to know your way around here: If I had room for dessert, are there any worth having?" As I spoke, I pulled the serum from my right front pants pocket and palmed it. The injector would work through clothing, but he was going to feel it as a small prick; there was no way around that.

"All three of them," he said. "You can't go wrong."

"Thanks a lot," I said.

"Plates and cups go in the bins behind me," he said.

"Thanks again." I felt worse by the second, because he was proving to be every bit as nice a guy as the available data suggested. I appeased my conscience by resolving to pay him even more when this was over.

I stood, stepped out from the bench, and headed for the bins he'd indicated. I had the cup on its side on the plate, which I held in my left hand, and my right hand held the fork and, next to its tines, the

injector. I cut the turn tight and intentionally bumped
my knee on the edge of the bench on which he sat.
I lurched forward a bit, and as I did I put my hand
on his shoulder as if to stop myself from falling. I
activated the injector the moment I touched him.

"Ow," he said.

I pulled back my hand. "I'm so sorry," I said. I
held up my right hand. "I stabbed you with my fork
when I leaned on you. Clumsy and stupid."

He felt his shoulder. "Didn't tear my shirt or break
the skin," he said. "No damage done."

Give it five minutes, I thought. "Look," I said,
"can I make it up to you by buying you one of those
desserts?"

He smiled. "Nice of you to offer, but no need. I'm
just too full. Maybe next time, if I see you around
here again."

"It's a deal," I said. "Next time, I'm buying."

I dropped off my plate and silverware, stashed the
empty injector in my pants pocket, and walked out of
Hobbers. I wanted to be as far from here as possible
when he started feeling sick, but I forced myself to
maintain a slow pace until I was out of the restaurant,
down the street, and had turned the first corner. Then,
I picked up speed every time I had the street to myself.
I never ran, but I pushed the walking pace.

"Come get me," I said to Lobo over the comm, "and
start monitoring the emergency channels. We need to
make sure Passion's team learns the news as soon as
possible after Lee's sickness hits the data streams."

I needed to change clothes, study more about Passion and her tour, and prepare myself.

Lobo and I were going to have to do a job interview.

CHAPTER 30

Jon Moore

THE CALL CAME two and a half hours later. We were in orbit, resting comfortably among a cluster of weather sats. Lobo was monitoring the data presence he'd set up in York. The agency's software contacted us and hooked us directly to Zoe Wang's scheduling code. They wanted a meeting as soon as possible at a specific landing zone in a slot they'd reserved. The interview was to take place inside my ship.

Lobo resolved everything with Wang's software in a fraction of a second; I was never involved.

We talked about the cover story and background for Lobo. All we'd shown in our postings with the agency's databases were external shots of him with all the mods he could manage that would make him resemble a high-end executive transport. Once they came inside, the thickness of the walls and the size differential between the outside and the inside spaces would give away the armor. In the end, we settled on a variation of the truth: Lobo was customized armored transport for military and high-end corporate types.

Lobo set about crafting a transaction log that would show how I'd acquired him.

"They're going to watch us land," I said.

"Of course," Lobo said.

"The question," I said, "is, how do we want to make our approach? Precision is sure to matter; space has to be tight at some venues. But does speed? Or should caution rule? If we show off in the wrong way, it might hurt our chances at the job."

"Except," Lobo said, "that I've made every other alternative from this agency appear, to both them and Wang, to be unavailable."

"If we spook them, though, we might encourage them to look into those options, and that would be bad for us. It would be good to get this right." Ramon Lee had snagged the job, so perhaps we could learn from him. "Does Wang's data hold any notes or observations about Lee's interview?"

"No. All I can tell is that she decided very quickly, because her hiring order went out less than two hours after the interview started."

"Did Lee write about it anywhere?"

"No, nor could he without violating his contract. The contract samples are in Wang's data and very clear."

"Okay," I said. "Let's reason it out. Wang works behind the scenes; Passion gets the spotlight. If you look better than Passion's ship, which of course you are—"

"Of course," Lobo said.

"—then Wang could worry that Passion might not like that. Can you get the specs on Passion's ship?"

"Yes," Lobo said. "They're in the data I accessed earlier."

"Good. Come in five percent slower than the approach speed that ship would typically use, but hit the marks exactly; that should send a message of competence without risking annoying Passion's pilot."

"There's nothing I enjoy more," Lobo said, "than pretending to be dumb and slow."

"You'll have to do a lot of that," I said, "because I'll need to introduce you so she can ask for things when I'm out, but you can't be too intelligent, or our rates won't make sense."

"This job keeps looking better and better."

We arrived at the interview site five minutes early. Lobo executed the landing perfectly, of course, and opened a hatch as soon as he had settled.

I stepped out and looked around.

Wang and a member of her team were waiting ten meters away. We'd known that, of course, from monitoring the site, but I feigned surprise anyway and introduced myself.

"J. Johnson," I said.

"Zoe Wang," she said. "I'll be conducting the interview, and I'm the one you'd be transporting, if you get the job." She nodded toward the man with her. "This is Bing Fu; he's here as security in case you'd been someone else or tried anything."

I smiled and shook hands with both of them.

Wang's grip was firm and dry.

Fu's was limp and moist. He kept his left hand in his pants pocket and leaned forward awkwardly. Assuming he was holding a weapon there, he wasn't comfortable with it.

Wang was a woman of average height, about to

the top of my shoulders, thin but curvy, with pale, gold-tinged skin, and black hair buzzed into a close-cut stubble on her head. She wore dark blue overalls, and every pocket bulged with something. Her mouth was a bit too wide and her lips a bit too thick for her face, but the combination of them and her large, intent black eyes was compelling. She was somewhere in that vast and, for those with money, unchanging age range from early thirties to seventies. Fu was a shorter, male version of her, thinner but with the same haircut and skin that was slightly more golden in color. He looked to be in his twenties.

I questioned Fu's value as added security, but maybe he was all she had available.

"What does the J. stand for?" Wang asked.

"Nothing," I said. "My parents liked the letter and figured I could choose my own first name to suit my mood, even change it from time to time." If she'd done her homework, which admittedly she hadn't had much time to do, she knew the answer already from my profile. If she hadn't and checked later, she'd find only confirmation.

She smiled. "So what are you going by these days? Or is it just 'J'?"

"Jon," I said, "for a while now." When you're picking an alternative identity, sticking with your first name is a good idea, because when anyone calls you by it, you'll react naturally. Hesitation at responding to a last name is easier to explain among friends or colleagues, because you can always say you're not used to being addressed so formally. That's why I'd gone with "Jon Mashem" on Studio. With both Omani and Kang potentially monitoring local data streams for me, though, I didn't want to risk using my own first name. This approach gave me the best of both worlds.

"Okay, Jon," she said. "Why didn't your profile have any images of you?"

I shrugged. The answer was because Lobo had omitted them so no facial-recognition search software could find me, but what I said was, "I have no idea. I sent them images of both me and him." I patted Lobo's hull. "Someone messed up, I suppose."

She nodded. "Speaking of your ship, why don't you show me around it."

She turned left and walked slowly around Lobo.

I followed and talked as we walked. Fu trailed us.

"Not a lot to see," I said, "as you can tell, though that's by design. He's—"

"That's the second time you've called it 'he,'" she said. "Why is that?"

"His name is Lobo. More precisely, that's the name programmed into his AI software and the one that software responds to, so I use that name for all of him."

"Okay," she said. "That's cute. Please continue."

"I am not cute," Lobo said over the machine frequency, "nor is my name."

I ignored him.

"He's heavily armored," I said, "which probably isn't relevant to you but is useful for some of the more concerned executive clients I've had. Nav systems are current and extremely accurate; if there's space for him, we can put him in it."

The logo for my fictional transportation service stretched down both sides. As we rounded his front and turned back toward the open hatch, Wang said, "Passion's name, image, and the tour logo go on every ship in our little fleet. We'll pay for application and removal, but carrying the ads is not optional; yours will have to go. Do you have a problem with that?"

I shook my head. "None at all. Every client wants its logo in view; that's standard."

We reached the hatch.

"Why do you want the job?" she said.

"First of all, I need the work," I said. "That's reason enough, at least for me. Second, from the checking I've been able to do in the short time since I got the call, you guys seem legit, you pay well, you pay on time, and I couldn't find a single complaint about you from anyone you'd contracted with."

"You mean that *I* couldn't find any," Lobo said, again over the machine frequency.

I ignored him again. His ego bruises easily, and right now we were talking about him in ways sure to annoy him. I've always marveled that with so much computing power he still managed to have so many very human flaws.

Wang nodded. "May we check out the inside?"

"Of course," I said. "I should warn that it's short on luxuries and smaller in there than you might expect, due to all the armor. You can rent anything you want that will fit inside, and we'll carry it. You take full responsibility, though, for anything that happens to your stuff. Anything that goes wrong with the built-in equipment is my problem."

"Of course," she said. "That's standard." She looked inside but did not enter. "Hi, Lobo. Mind if we come in and look around?"

"Not at all, Ms. Wang," he said. His voice was lower and softer than the one he normally used with me.

"We're all friends on this team," she said, "so call me Zoe."

Why was Lobo always better with women than I am?

"Please come in, Zoe," Lobo said.

I gave her the tour of the areas I'm willing to show: food stores; medtech room, though with most of its probes and equipment withdrawn behind blank walls; the small storage area; the guest sleeping area, a closet-sized space even smaller than my quarters; my quarters; and, finally, the large pilot area up front.

"You sleep here?" she said.

"I live here," I said. "The price is right."

"Not a lot of personal stuff."

I shrugged. "I've never seen much point in collecting things I'd have to lug around. Most of what matters is either in here," I pointed to my head, "or in data I've put in Lobo's data stores."

"Not a lot of places to put things, either," she said. "Or to hide them."

"Again, I don't have any need for a lot of storage space," I said. I didn't tell her about Lobo's ability to open storage areas, or about all the many weapons and artifacts hidden inside him. "As for hiding things, I live alone, Lobo is shut when I'm not in him, and so I have no need to do so. I take it, though, that you've had theft issues."

"Not from my past drivers," she said, "but with others, sure. Passion is the kind of celebrity who inspires collectors and who's the target of a lot of newstainment feeds; dealing with temptation from people like that is part of the job."

"You'd be amazed what even some savvy executives will say around drivers and other help," I said. "It's as if we were invisible. I've heard more than my share of secrets people would pay a lot to learn." All of that was true, as I learned back when I made my living providing courier services for both people and packages of all types. I didn't have anything approaching Lobo then. "One leak, though, would be the end of my business. I've never had one."

We went up front.

"I'd want to set up my command center in here," she said. "Is that possible?"

I'd had Lobo extend two pilot couches. "I need access to the far pilot area when we're moving." That wasn't true, of course, but on lesser craft it would be. "Other times, both of these can compress into the wall, and you can have the space."

"I'd also want to sleep in the guest quarters. I stay near my data and other materials." I must have hesitated too long in responding, because she added, "I know it's an invasion of your space, but I always live aboard during a show. If you want a room, we'll pay for one."

I shook my head. "You're welcome to sleep there, but unless you'd object, I'd just as soon stay in my quarters."

"Fine with me," she said. "Fair warning: I make a lot of noise."

"Every space here is heavily soundproofed."

"Good," she said. "*If* we hire you, for as long as we're paying you, we need to be clear on one key thing."

"Which is?"

"This ship may normally be your home, but for this tour, it's my command center, and I'm in command. You're here to assist me, not to get in my way or try to tell me how to run my world. Your job is to do whatever I need you to do. Got it?"

"Yes," I said, "of course, provided you don't order me to do anything illegal. You're the boss."

She nodded. "One more thing."

"Yes."

She stared intently at my eyes. "Be completely honest: What do you think about Passion's music?"

"I've only recently started listening to it," I said, stalling for time but also telling the truth. I decided to stay with the truth. "It's powerful and moving. Her voice is astonishing, so strong and so rich that it's amazing so small a person can produce it. The songs are wonderful, though I've never heard any of them before." I shrugged. "I'm not good at talking about this kind of thing. I will say that the music brought back memories and strong feelings, and that her name suits her music, at least all the songs I've heard."

"What sorts of memories and feelings?" she said.

My face felt hot. "Does that matter for this interview?" I said.

"No," she said. Her face softened. "Supporting, understanding, and helping to create Passion's music is, well, my passion, one of my passions. I'd just like to know."

"Memories," I said, "of a woman I loved and lost a long time ago, and of a woman I lost some years ago before I could even find out if I might love her."

She nodded her head slowly.

We were silent for a few awkward seconds.

"A long time ago?" she said, her voice brighter and lighter now. "You don't look like that's even possible, though the profile said you're forty-five. Seeing you in person, I would never have guessed that age, and I sure wouldn't have guessed that you're only five years younger than I am."

I shrugged and said, "My family tends to look young." I paused. "What's next?"

"Paperwork," she said. "You're hired."

"Thank you, Ms. Wang," I said. "I appreciate it."

"Zoe, please," she said. "You're part of the family now. We roll out in the morning. Bing will get all your data from the agency and show you the coordinates." She headed out. "Nice to meet you, Lobo."

"Nice to meet you, Zoe," he said.

She stopped for a second just inside the open hatch. "Good answers, Jon, about Passion's music."

I got the landing and loading location from Fu, and then he followed her out.

Lobo closed the front hatch after him.

"Aren't you the charmer?" he said. "I loved the sensitive comments."

"And you, with that voice?" I said. "Seriously."

"I can sound any way I choose," Lobo said. "Why wouldn't I select a voice that would work well for her?"

"Exactly," I said. "Why wouldn't I select an answer she'd like?" I looked around the space and realized I'd lived here, alone with Lobo, for years. Sharing Lobo with another person was going to be odd.

"The next couple of weeks are going to be interesting," I said.

"Indeed," Lobo said, "though at least I'm confident we should survive them. I'm nowhere near as sanguine about your plans to rummage through Schmidt's home."

"Look on the bright side," I said. "Things could turn dangerous a lot sooner if Kang or Randar finds us."

"There is that," Lobo said.

20 days from the end

York City and Mass City
Planet Haven

CHAPTER 31

Lobo

JON, WHEN I said that I knew everything, I was indulging in hyperbole for dramatic effect. I do not actually know everything, either about you or about the wider universe. In your case, I have had to rely on deduction rather than reliable historical data to draw certain key conclusions. Those conclusions, though, serve only to reinforce my existing concerns.

That you never grow older makes determining your age problematic. The absence of any readily available data about your birth increases the difficulty of that task.

Hence the use of deduction.

Research into integrating nanomachines into humans has been banned since the disaster in the Pinkelponker system that caused the quarantine around the jump gate apertures that provide access to that world. Consequently, it seems likely that you were born on Pinkelponker and involved in some sort of nanomachine research. Though I assume that information about those studies exists in some governmental or corporate databases somewhere, those repositories must be hardened and extremely difficult to locate, much less access, because I have found no trace of them.

Having Pinkelponker as your birthplace also explains why you have involved us on two occasions with the Children of Pinkelponker and why that organization seems to so easily arouse you. It is only human to feel those connections, even if they generally lead to problems for you.

Your age is harder to pinpoint, but coming close is not difficult. All the successful nano-human hybrid experiments in my knowledge are those Jorge Wei performed, and only those that involved children were successful. Based on Wei's data, you must have been no older than eighteen for the integration of the nanomachines to have worked. So, you must have left Pinkelponker no older than eighteen. That means you are a maximum of 157 years old.

I have walked you through these simple chains of reasoning to make clear how very simple they are, given the data I have available.

Or given different but related data sets.

Omani Pimlani, for example, knew you long ago. She has never lived long on any planet other than Haven. No data about you exists prior to the Saw. Your instant sense of owing her and your continued insistence on taking the risk of breaking into Schmidt's so that you can save her imply a strong emotional commitment of some type. She must have known you very long ago for you to have needed the aging prostheses you had me recycle.

Did you ever believe I was unaware of anything inside me?

Pimlani may not know where you are from, but she knows you are vastly older than you look. From your statements, I gather that she has threatened to share this information with the head of another of the most powerful of the families in all the worlds.

Somewhere, it is likely that data exists from your early years.

The only sensible action for you to take is to run, live a life that leaves as few traces as possible, and move every five to ten years.

Instead, you get ever more frequently involved in other human affairs, keep going to highly inhabited planets, and take on riskier and riskier assignments.

If you want to fight those with data on you, I will fight with you—but we should do so intelligently, and for a reason that makes sense.

I hope you now understand that I know everything that matters, and further that you see why I had to make these recordings.

I hope also that before they are necessary, you decide to repay the faith I have shown you with a similar level of trust in me.

If we are to stay alive, I believe that will be necessary.

If your path to self-destruction means we both must die, I will accept that fate, but I hope you have enough control that you do not take an entire planet with you.

I originally made these recordings to show you in the event of my death. Upon further analysis, I have decided to play them for you as soon as possible. I do not believe that at this time you can afford the distraction these recordings will represent, but if we survive this strange mission on Haven, I will show them to you then.

CHAPTER 32

Jon Moore

WHEN WE LANDED at the load-in zone, the sun was still not visible, the sunrise only beginning to shoo away the night. In addition to Lobo and Passion's private transport, another ten vessels, each at least as large as Lobo, were necessary to move the show. A few were primarily for the crew and their luggage, but most were there to carry things, not people.

Wang arrived a few minutes after we did in a shuttle from the hotel where she'd been staying. She and I loaded her quickly, a small amount of personal stuff going into her quarters and the rest up front in Lobo. I didn't expect us to need to do any fancy flying, but on the off chance that we did, we tied down the front-area stuff with quick-release cords hooked to some hooks that Lobo had manifested along the front wall.

While we were working, one of the crew put a pair of paintbots on Lobo, one on the rear of each side, and they began painting Passion's picture and the "Passions Past and Present" tour logo on Lobo.

When we were done with Wang's stuff, Lobo closed his hatch so the paintbot on that side could finish working. The other was already done; they were quick.

Passion's face—all of her that the logo for this tour showed—stared at me from Lobo's side. This close, it was huge—taller than I am—and beautiful. The eyes used a paint that reflected the morning light softly; they almost seemed to be looking back at everyone who stared at her.

"I've always wanted to be a billboard," Lobo said over the machine frequency. "Now, my ambitions are fulfilled."

I ignored him.

"Beautiful, isn't she?" Wang said

"Yes, yes she is," I said. "The music, though, is far more compelling."

"I'm not sure which sells more tickets," Wang said, "though I hope it's the music; that should last longer."

"Is there anything else I should be doing for you, Ms. Wang?" I said.

"Zoe," she said, "and no."

"Then unless you want to leave, I'm going to help the others finish."

"We don't take off until Passion's ready," she said, "so feel free. I'm sure they'd appreciate the help, Jon."

Carts and small carriers were loading most of the gear on their own, supervisors watching to make sure everything went to its proper place. Between people's luggage and small stuff, though, there was still plenty that humans carried, so I went to the closest ship and started helping. I introduced myself to each new person I saw, and they told me their names, but I didn't really track theirs, and they didn't seem to care about mine. Once they realized I wasn't in their area and was Wang's driver and assistant, it was as if I no longer existed. If I'd cared, I'd have asked her if there was a lot of turnover in the job, but for me, this was perfect. I would be with them only as far as Schmidt's or, if I was lucky enough to get out of there quietly, for one stop past that, so making friends wasn't a goal.

Passion arrived a few minutes before we finished loading the last of the ships. Her ground transport drove her all the way to her ship. Everyone stopped working and watched. A woman and a man got out of the vehicle, looked around, and stayed by the open hatch as Passion emerged, with two more men on the other side of her, took two steps into her ship, and vanished again. The four security staffers followed her inside, and her ship closed.

I was only aware it was her because of the reaction of everyone else.

We finished putting the last items on the other ships.

Wang came out of Lobo and called out, "Everyone, may I have your attention?"

We all stopped working and faced her. People already in ships came out so they could see her.

"Our tour over the next three months promises to be amazing, but we also all know that it will be a lot of work and that sometimes things will go wrong."

Everyone chuckled at that. One man from somewhere behind me said, "Sometimes?"

Wang laughed along with everyone else. "Okay, something goes wrong pretty much all the time," she said, "but making it right and putting on the best possible show is what we do." A lot of the crew around me nodded their heads and murmured agreement.

"People spend a lot to attend these shows, and we repay their investments with our very best. I look forward to working with you all. Passion thanks you, and I most certainly thank you in advance for committing to giving your best to these shows. Let's roll!"

Everyone hustled aboard the ships. I ran to Lobo. He closed the hatch as Wang and I stepped inside and went up front.

"We go first," she said, "then Passion, and then the rest. We caravan at slow speed and stay at a low altitude; I assume Bing gave you the flight plans."

"He did, Ms. Wang," I said, "and we're already set." Lobo opened a display on the front wall.

"Zoe, Jon," she said, "as I keep telling you."

"Zoe," I said, "if you don't mind me asking, why do we fly so low and slow?"

"Because a caravan of ships bearing Passion's face attracts attention, and on a slow info day, newstainment outlets will fill their feeds with images of it and commentary on the tour. Free advertising."

I nodded. "Take us up, Lobo," I said.

Aloud, he said, "Executing."

Over the machine channel, he said, "If you're really going to pretend to be a pilot, this is going to be a very long trip indeed."

"I'll do it only when she's here," I said over the same channel.

When the display showed all the ships in the air behind us, a line that stretched back quite some way, I said, "Take us to Mass."

When we reached Mass a few hours later, we set down in a private landing zone on the west side of an amphitheater built into the side of a hill. Zoe had spent the flight in conference with the heads of various teams, reviewing plans, studying holos of the venue, and discussing what they knew about the newest members of their team. None of this had anything to do with me, so aside from checking with her periodically, I spent the time exercising in my quarters. I had Lobo keep the door open so I could hear if she called, but I only returned to the pilot couch for the landing.

A local security team met us and immediately joined Zoe in conference inside Lobo. They were to cover the venue and keep out everyone except verified venue staffers and our team. Passion's security detail would cover her.

We all received venue-specific IDs for our wallets and, so no one on security would mistake any of us from a distance as an intruder, a large ID we had to wear if we wanted to leave and come back.

We didn't need those, but they insisted.

The load-in process was a great deal more complicated than the packing had been. Most people, including Passion, would spend the night in a nearby hotel, but no one would be going out of the venue until after the team had completed setup and a rehearsal.

Zoe kicked me out of Lobo so she could work but told me to stay on call and not to get in the way of any real work.

Passion stayed in her ship.

I wandered into the venue and watched the team work. Some venue staffers assisted them, but only on equipment that belonged to the venue. The teams were very careful not to mess with each other's gear.

As one woman from our group explained it to me, Passion's contract demanded that no one outside her team touch any of her setup, so that she could have total control over the sound and deliver the "unedited fidelity" that was, she felt, one of her key attractions. The venue had retaliated by banning our staff from touching their gear. This sort of gamesmanship was apparently common.

The initial stage of the load-in consequently consisted of venue staffers moving, removing, or disconnecting an extensive set of electronics, and our group replacing it with a different set.

The stage was covered, and protective shielding normally enclosed it on all sides. Passion demanded a direct connection with the audience, so the venue people instructed the shielding to withdraw into containers on the rear of each side.

By default at the venue, large computer arrays with a programmable control board received the audio from the musicians, corrected its flaws per whatever programming the performers' sound people loaded into it, and then blasted the correct sound through all the speakers that delivered the edited audio throughout the amphitheater. It all happened so quickly that the audience could not detect any delay.

Passion would have none of that. Our people made the venue team move what it could and disconnect the rest, then installed her gear. It amplified the sounds, and its programming let operators easily adjust the balance of sound among the various instruments and Passion, but it did not in any other way change what you heard. Whatever she sang, whatever the musicians played, was what the audience heard. A techie-oriented section of her data presences in every city she played provided copies of her programming for each show, the schematics of her equipment, and source code for all the software they used. If you didn't believe her claims, you could verify them for yourself.

Of course, she could simply have lied by posting data that had nothing to do with the reality of her show, but most people trusted that she wasn't doing that. If the chatter I heard as people worked was any indication, she was indeed telling her audiences the truth.

Lunch arrived from a local caterer. Everyone ran for food.

I was with them until Zoe contacted me.

"Passion and I need to meet," she said. "Lead her team from her ship to me."

"Okay," I said. "I'm curious, though: Why doesn't she make you to come to her?"

"She doesn't like meetings in her private space, even with me. She feels they disturb its energy."

"So why doesn't her team walk her over? Lobo can't be more than twenty meters from her ship."

"She prefers my assistant guide them," Zoe said. "Is this going to be a pattern?"

"What do you mean?" I said.

"I ask you to do something, and I have to explain it first? Because if so, we have a problem. We've already kept Passion waiting, and she doesn't like that."

I jogged toward Passion's ship. "No. I'm sorry. I have a bad habit of liking to understand what I do, but that's not the job. I'll be at Passion's ship in no time."

"It's good to see," Lobo said over the machine frequency, "that your lack of trust in any directions you receive is not unique to me and instead applies, apparently, to everyone."

"Shut up," I said.

I reached Passion's ship and realized I had no way to let the people inside know that I was waiting. I was about to contact Zoe when a hatch opened and two security staffers, a man and a woman, stepped out. Each was my height and appeared strong, but not overly muscled. They looked around quickly, then the woman subvocalized something, and Passion appeared, followed quickly by two more equally tall security men.

"This way," I said as I started toward Lobo.

The five of them moved smoothly as a group, with Passion in the center and barely visible, a sapling lost in a forest of mature trees.

When we reached Lobo, the security woman said, "Stand to the side. Don't enter."

I did as she said.

The front pair then moved to the sides so Passion could enter Lobo without them.

She paused just inside Lobo and looked my way. "Thank you . . ."

"Jon," I said. That's when I got my first look at her. She was as small as Lobo said, and she was clearly the woman in the photos, but her "unedited fidelity" claims definitely did not extend to her appearance. Her hair hung limp down her back, and she seemed to have a whole lot less of it than the woman in the holos and on the sides of all these ships. Blotches marred the skin that had appeared so perfect in everything I'd seen. Her eyes and lips were indeed large, but not quite as big as in the images. She was still lovely and quite compelling, but she was not the almost otherworldly woman in all the marketing materials. It had been so long since I'd worked anywhere near entertainers that I'd forgotten how much illusion they sold.

"Thank you, Jon," she said as she walked up front.

"Close your ship's hatch," the security woman said.

Lobo closed it and said over the machine frequency, "She could have asked me directly."

I ignored him.

As soon as the hatch was shut, all four of the security people visibly relaxed. They still faced outward and scanned the area, but none of them was on the same level of alert.

"First time seeing her?" the woman said to me.

"Yeah."

"Just remember the confidentiality clauses in your contract," she said. "No images, no comments, no indication that you've ever even stood near her."

"I remember," I said, "though it's not like I have anything to offer anyone."

"Sure you do," the woman said. "You've seen her in non-show condition. As you can probably tell, the woman on stage is a bit more . . . polished than the one who's inside meeting with her oldest friend and tour manager."

I shrugged. "Okay."

The woman faced me for a moment. "What Passion does, and the way she does it, is very important to her. Yes, she sings, but for her what she really does is deliver an experience, an experience that involves music and theater and, above all else, one that lets every single person who attends hear exactly what she sang as she sang it."

"So why doesn't she apply that same standard to her appearance?"

It was the woman's turn to shrug. "I don't know, I don't care, and I don't ask. She's too smart not to have considered the issue, but my job is not to question her about her choices. My job is to make sure she's safe every time she's outside that ship."

"Four of you seems like a lot of coverage for times like now, with no one around, and not enough for when she's on stage."

"What we're doing now is stopping anyone from seeing her or capturing her image. We have to deal with people at long distances, newstainment drones, sats, you name it. We let them have the top of her head, because she wants to encourage them to tell the world where she is, but that's all we give them As for when she's on stage," she chuckled, "tell me about it. We'll use some local help to block initial attempts at unauthorized access, but we've all told her that if she continues to perform without security shielding, we can't guarantee her safety. She says the connection with the audience is worth the risk."

"At least it's not like she's an assassination target," I said.

"True," the woman said, "though as a kidnap victim she'd be worth a great deal. Still, those aren't our worries. Our main concerns center on the many ways fans might hurt her. You would be amazed at what people think their favorite performers owe them. From hair to clothing to skin, fans have tried to collect it all."

"Humans are strange," Lobo said to me privately, "and so often in ways logic could not predict."

"I'm sorry to hear that," I said to the woman.

Another shrug. "Keeps me employed." She straightened and said to the others, "She's on her way out."

To me, she said, "Stay here. She likes the escort over but not back."

Lobo's hatch opened.

Passion stepped into the circle of guards, and together they walked back to her ship.

When they were inside, Zoe appeared at the hatch and said, "Go get us some lunch—they'll have mine set aside—and then come back here."

She looked around for a few seconds and took a deep breath.

"We need to talk."

CHAPTER 33

Jon Moore

I BROUGHT BACK LUNCH FISH sandwiches and juice for both of us—and was a few steps inside Lobo before she emerged from the front area and said, "Let's go sit outside. I'm tired of being in here." She looked at the ceiling. "No offense, Lobo."

"None taken," he said.

Privately to me, he said, "She treats me better than you do. I could get used to this."

"Yeah, yeah," I said on the machine frequency. "Where would you like to go?" I said to Zoe.

"Follow me," she said.

She led us into the amphitheater and to the very back row of seats, then off to the far stage right corner. She sat, and I joined her.

"I always like to know what the show looks like from the worst seats in the house," she said. "We'll have big displays, of course, and we'll also broadcast video within the venue so people can use their own devices, but what Passion most wants is for them to watch her live. We try not to play places where that's not at least conceivable for even the worst seats." She ate a bite of her sandwich, chewed slowly, and stared at the stage. Some of our crew had already finished lunch and were working there.

I did the same. I could see all the people clearly, but their expressions weren't easily visible.

"This place is a little bigger than she prefers," Zoe said, "but it'll work. Even from here, you'd know it was her." She chewed some more and then faced me. "No comments or questions?"

"As you said earlier, it's not my place."

"I know what you're wondering," she said, "so we might as well address it now. Besides, meals—unless I'm taking them with her—are fine times to chat."

"Okay," I said. "You talk about people being able to see her. She makes a huge production of ensuring that everyone in the place hears the music as it really is. But for herself, she's clearly—"

"—not appearing natural," Zoe said, "despite her unfortunate and much reported 'unedited fidelity' comment about her height. Yes, that's the question."

"Okay," I said, "so what's the answer?"

Zoe took another bite of her sandwich, chewed slowly, and stared at me. "Passion is not a simple person. She understands the games you have to play to become as famous as she is, and she plays them well. She realizes, for example, that beauty matters, that looking the way she does—on stage, in appearances—is part of her allure. She never appears in public at less than her very best—and her best is a mixture of natural gifts and a whole lot of make-up and hair work."

"Some time with a body-mod shop could save a lot

of that work," I said, "and make it easier for her to always look her best. Everybody does it."

"She can't risk the records getting out," Zoe said, "not with her public positions. So, she does it the old-fashioned way, and everyone who touches her or sees her without make-up is under contract."

"People break contracts," I said. "They leak information, say things they shouldn't. Happens all the time."

"True enough," Zoe said, "but with Passion, if you do that you're signing up to do legal battle with someone who will spend whatever it takes to crush you—and who has contracts and a great deal of money on her side. Most people will analyze each case on its economic merits, but not Passion; she will happily lose vast sums of money if it means punishing someone who broke a contract."

"I never saw any trace of that in the research I did about her."

"See how well it's working?" Zoe said. She smiled. "Anyway, Passion is willing to do whatever takes, make compromises, be vindictive—you name it—except when it comes to the music. The music is sacred to her." She paused. "And to me. That's why I'm here. We started out together, we found the old songs together, we still develop new versions of old songs together—though I do most of the research now—and we never compromise on the music. It is the one thing in both our lives that is pure. Passion may embellish, even lie, in the cause of marketing, she may be so careful about her appearance that she won't even rehearse without being in her full regalia, but every single statement she makes about the music is true."

I wondered if there was a single thing in my life

that I had kept that pure, or even considered trying to keep pure. I couldn't think of anything. "Why?" I said. "I don't mean that cynically or disrespectfully; I'm genuinely curious."

Zoe shook her head slowly. "I don't know, not exactly." Her voice lowered. "We grew up together, more or less, and everything else about our lives was terrible. Music, though, was different. When we were very young, we found some data streams of songs recorded on Earth, and we were hooked. Those pieces built the worlds we lived in when the real world was too much to bear."

"So you two are sisters?"

She laughed. "Do we look like sisters? No, we're not related, not biologically anyway. We grew up as children of the state in the same twisted crèches."

"Nothing in either of your bios mentions that."

"I told you: anything in the service of making her the star she is. Anything except messing with the music."

Below and in front of us, the stage began to fill with people. When all the other musicians were in place, Passion made her entrance. Now, she looked like her images, the perfect star.

Zoe stood. "Rehearsal's about to start, which is our cue to leave. Remember when I said I needed to talk to you?"

"Of course." I also got up.

"Well, it wasn't to teach you Passion's secrets or bore you with our past."

"Hardly boring," I said. I could have told her that I understood better than she could realize what it was like to be young and owned by a government, but of course I didn't. "And, I'm sorry you went through that. That you both went through it."

She waved her hand. "Enough of the past. What I want to talk to you about is your future."

"It's still my first day on the job," I said. "Isn't it a little early for that talk?"

She laughed. "Not your long-term future; your future five minutes from now."

"Okay," I said. "What's up?"

"I need to go on a field trip," she said, "and you're coming to make sure I get back safely."

CHAPTER 34

Jon Moore

I WAITED UNTIL WE were inside Lobo to say anything else. As soon as we were alone, I said, "What kind of field trip, and don't you have security staff for this sort of thing?"

"To answer the second question first," Zoe said, "they're all fully subscribed, even over-subscribed, with the rehearsal."

"So wait."

She shook her head. "Not possible. After rehearsal ends, there's a rest break of a few hours, then the show, backstage reception, hotel, and in the morning, we head out again. Where we're going is only open during the day."

"What kind of place is it?"

"An antique shop."

"That's not exactly the kind of store known for being dangerous," I said.

"No, no it's not," she said, "but the neighborhood doesn't appear to be the best, and we've been led into traps before."

"By what?"

"Music, of course. We're always on the lookout for songs we've never heard, recordings that haven't been catalogued or that are so obscure that even the people who know they exist have rarely heard them. There's a whole culture of enthusiasts who pass around information. We participate in these groups; it's a great way to find new songs, and as marketing fodder—"

"—it helps bring more credibility to Passion," I said. "I see that."

"The problem is," she said, "a few times the leads have been fake, data people used to lure us into places where they could hold us up or kidnap us. Our security protected us those times, but we couldn't justify the risk any longer. Now, we make it clear to the community that Passion will never go to these places, and that if anyone does go, it'll be someone low on her staff."

"Except it's always you."

She nodded. "Yes. I'm the only one who knows what we have and what we don't, who can listen and decide what's worth buying and how much it's worth. Plus, Passion knows I feel the same way about the music; I'm the only one she'll trust to do it."

"Kidnappers could make money abducting anyone on your staff, because Passion would have to pay even if only to avoid the PR nightmare of being portrayed as the big star who wouldn't spend money to save her people."

"Sure, it's possible," Zoe said, "but no one's tried to kidnap me since we announced Passion would no longer go herself."

"So why take me?"

"I said there've been no kidnapping attempts. A couple of times, people have tried to rob me. Security stopped them."

"I've worked security before," I said, "and I have to tell you that you should wait. One person is not enough to do it right. To watch for threats and deal with any that arise, and to get you out safely, takes multiple people."

"The stash this place is supposed to have is worth the risk," she said. "We have a show every day on Haven, and then when we finish on this planet, we head straight to Freedom. There isn't another chance."

"So let me go there first, check it out, and come back and get you if it's safe."

"I told you: There's not much time. We go now."

I stared at her for a few seconds. "This is that important to you?"

"Yes. Plus, it's an order. Remember: I'm the boss."

I nodded. "I can always quit."

"True," she said, and she smiled, "but you need the work. You said so."

"I did, and I do. I'd rather lose a job, though, than risk your life. Any life."

"The worst we've had are robbery attempts," she said. "It's not like anyone has tried to kill me."

I considered explaining to her how few injuries and fatalities that occur during robberies are planned, that it's the accidents you have to fear, but there was no point in it. "So if I say no, you're going to fire me?"

She sighed and shook her head. "No. That would be wrong. If you say no, I'll make Bing go with me. He's so afraid of me that he'll do it, and he thinks that gun he carries gives him a chance in any situation."

"If he's good with it," I said, "it might help."

She laughed. "I don't think he has a clue how to use it. He picked it up after the first robbery attempt, when I joked about making him be my security for the next trip." She took a deep breath. "So, are you going to take me, or do I go see Bing?"

"We *do* need this job," Lobo said over the machine frequency. "Insist on bringing me, and I can cover everything outside the store."

"I'll do it," I said, "but with two conditions."

"Which are?"

"First, you tell me the name of the place and leave me alone up here for a little bit so I can study the area."

"Sure, as long as you don't take too long. And?"

"From the moment we leave here until we're back here, *I'm* the boss, not you. To protect you, I have to know that if I tell you to do something, you will—and right then, without hesitation."

"Deal," she said, "but the moment we return, I run the show again."

"Done," I said. "Now, if you'll excuse me…"

"I'm going to check on the show," she said. "Contact me as soon as you're ready."

She gave me the name of the store and left.

As soon as she was outside Lobo, he closed the hatch, brought up a holo of the store, and we went to work.

The neighborhood had looked bad in the live feeds, but it was worse in person. Lots full of rubble or razed clean to the dirt sat as empty as a politician's promise in the midst of low-slung permacrete buildings faded to a washed-out gray the color of a decomposing corpse. Where York was riding the boon of being the capital and the home of some of the worlds' wealthiest families, Mass was sliding down the other end of the unbalanced economic scale that is so common across humanity's planets. Old security cams, many so ancient they almost certainly didn't work, hung on every building like wards against evil—and were certainly about as effective. What businesses were open sold their goods cheaply, even those that sold sex. People hung out in front of the shops and in small apartments over them, no one in a hurry, everyone with more time on their hands than they wanted, everyone scanning for an opportunity.

At my insistence, we'd taken the few minutes necessary to have the paintbots remove Passion's tour notices from Lobo. He'd stand out enough as it was; advertising that we were coming from really big money was a bad plan. We went in high, and we came down fast right over a vacant lot half a block from Old and New, the shop Zoe wanted to visit. Lobo hovered just above the rubble that covered the lot, and we climbed out as quickly as we could.

As soon as we were clear, he closed the hatch and lifted straight up.

"I didn't know you could fly him remotely," Zoe said.

"Being portrayed as a dumb object is really getting on my nerves," Lobo said over the comm.

I turned away from Zoe for a second, as if checking something on my comm, and subvocalized, "You're the one who reminded me that we need the job. Shut up."

I held up the comm. "I can do the basics with this," I said, "and that's all we need. It's just not safe to park him here." What I didn't tell her was that if anything went wrong, Lobo would land in the street in front of the shop so we could escape quickly. I'd rather have the challenge of explaining to her how he did that than the task of fighting our way back to here.

We picked our way through the rubble to the street and across it; traffic was sparse. Everywhere I glanced, people were watching us, some openly, others discreetly. No one bothered us, though, so I didn't mind; if I'd lived here, I'd have checked us out, too.

We reached Old and New, but though a handwritten sign declared the store open for business, the barred metal door wouldn't let us in.

"Got any weapons on you?" a tinny voice said through a speaker on the right of the door.

"A few," I said. I was carrying a small gun, a large knife, and a baton. I'd made Zoe wear some of the body armor I'd used at Omani's. I didn't put it on because I didn't want to lose the speed it would cost me. If there was trouble, I expected it to come from up close.

"I can see that, you fool," the voice said. "I just wanted to know if you'd admit it. Why?"

I laughed. "We're not from around here, obviously, but that doesn't mean we're stupid."

"I heard you had some old Earth music recordings," Zoe said. "I'd like to look at them."

I pulled her closer and whispered, "The less data you give to everyone who's watching and listening, the better. Let me talk."

"You'd do well to heed your bodyguard's advice," the voice said. "Son, just because the mics are old it doesn't mean they don't work."

I laughed and nodded.

"I might be old," he said, "but like the mics, I

work pretty darn well, and I'm not stupid. You'd do well to remember that."

"Yes, sir," I said.

"You lookin' to cause trouble?"

I shook my head. "No, sir."

"All right then," he said. The door slid into the wall on our left. "Come on in."

We entered. The door immediately locked us in.

Inside, the shop was well lit and tidy, though a thin layer of dust sat on pretty nearly everything I could see. Shelves of merchandise of all sorts—carvings and pottery, guns and swords, lamps and toasters, a huge variety of objects organized in no pattern I could discern—ran lengthwise on our left. On our right, a man who looked every day of a hundred and fifty but whose eyes were clear and who was still strong enough to be standing stared at us from behind a transparent booth I was sure was armored. Two beam guns on the ceiling tracked our movements.

"You must have done well, once upon a time," I said, "to afford those guns and this setup."

He nodded. "I've had better times, a lot of 'em."

"So what's next?" I said. "We're just here to shop. Well, to be precise, she's here to shop, and I'm here to make sure she gets home safely with anything she buys."

"So look around," he said.

"As I started to explain outside," Zoe said, "I'm here for only one thing: music from Earth. You're supposed to have a great collection, and I'm always looking to add to mine. Point me to what you have, and let me take a look. I'll buy anything I don't already have."

"That stuff's not cheap," the man said, "but I suppose you knew that."

"I did," she said.

"I have to show it all to you personally, operate our players, that sort of thing," he said.

"I understand," Zoe said, "and that's fine."

"How about you and I go into the back and look at it, and your man stays here and waits?"

Before she could answer, I said, "No. I don't leave her. And you knew that."

He laughed. "I did, but if you were stupid or looking for something else here, you might have taken me up on the offer." He stared at us for a few seconds longer. "Ah, heck," he said, "you gotta trust people every now and then."

He left the booth and reappeared behind a glass-paneled door opposite us. He opened the door and motioned us inside.

The room on the other side looked a great deal like the front room but darker, dirtier, more cluttered, and with even less apparent organization.

"Storage," he said when he noticed me looking around, "and where I keep the good stuff. My filing system"—he waved his hand to take in the whole room—"makes no sense to anybody but me, which means anyone who managed to break in here would have a hard time finding what they wanted without me."

"I believe that," I said.

He laughed and led us to a workbench on the left wall near the back of the store. Sitting on it were a dozen different pieces of electronics I didn't recognize, as well as a desktop shelving unit with rows and rows of small, open compartments. He ran his hand across half a dozen of them. "All of these data modules," he said, "contain ancient recordings, some as far back as the mid-twentieth century on Earth. The newest is over a hundred years old, some songs from people here on Haven and on Freedom."

"How many songs?" Zoe asked.

He laughed and shook his head. "To be honest," he said, "this was my brother's love, not mine, and he never cataloged it. Said he knew every single song and where it was." He paused. "Didn't help me much when he was gone." He shook his head slightly, dusting off the memories. "What I know is that if you add 'em all up, they run something like five, six thousand hours. Ray—my brother, that is—he collected them before we started this place and for as long as we ran it together. He'd listened to them all. So, I can't help you much there. Where do you want to start?"

Zoe stared at the shelves and shook her head. Her eyes were wide. "Nothing I read," she said, "gave me any hint at all of how much you have here."

"I let out only enough to attract people who'd be serious and have some money to spend," he said. "I don't see any point in making it look too good."

She nodded her head. "Well, I'm glad you did that. Tell you what: I'll pick a few, and you play me something from each of them."

For the next half hour, she would pull out one of the data modules, and he'd put it in the right player. Music would come from the wall in front of her, and information would appear on the display of the player. She'd listen for fifteen or twenty seconds, scan the display, and pick another module.

I found the whole process annoying, because about when I'd start to get a feel for a song, she would move on.

Watching her, though, made it all worthwhile. She truly did love the music. Her face lit up with every new song she played. Every now and then she'd say a name or smile or say something like, "Wow." She was radiating happiness. I hadn't seen her full smile before, and it was dazzling.

Finally, she said, "I could do this for days, months, but we don't have that much time. It is an amazing collection; your brother should have been proud."

"Ray was," the man said. "He loved this stuff. So, which ones would you like?"

"All of them," Zoe said.

The man shook his head. "You clearly knew a lot of these. Why would you buy what you already have?"

"Some of them I do have," she said, "but not most of them. Some contain different versions of songs I know, versions I don't have. A lot of it was new to me. The safest bet is to take it all."

"What will you do with it?" he said.

She stared at him for several seconds before she said, "You know the singer, Passion, the one who performs old songs?"

"No," he said, "can't say as I do. I haven't liked a new musician in what must be eighty, ninety years now, and these old things aren't really my taste, either."

"Well, I work with her," Zoe said, "and together we find old songs we love, arrange them, and then she performs them."

"So you're going to use them to make money," he said.

"Yes," she said, "but we're also going to love them."

"I told you they weren't cheap," he said.

"How about this deal," she said. "Your brother almost certainly had a price in mind for the collection, and he was bound to have bragged to you about what it was worth."

"He did."

"Whatever he quoted, it was almost certainly more than it was really worth."

"Collectors do tend to be that way," the man said.

"So you charge me whatever he told you," she said, "and I'll pay it. You just give me something ugly and cheap to carry it out in." She glanced at me. "It'll make his job easier if I look like a tourist with no money or taste."

"You'd pay that much," the man said, "for music you didn't even hear? I could be lying to you. Those could be empties."

"But you're not," she said, "and they're not, so, yes, yes, I would."

He smiled broadly. "Well, all right then. Let's go out front, pick something not too hideous, and do some business."

They chose an old leather satchel that looked like it had once been an overnight bag for someone who traveled light. The man let Zoe pack the data modules.

"Do you need the players, too?" he said.

"Thank you, but no," she said. "We have all of these and more. If it's held music, we can read it."

Back at the front room, Zoe got out her wallet and paid him quickly and without argument.

"It's been a pleasure," the man said as he was opening the door for us.

Zoe started to hand me the bag. "It's heavy," she said. "Would you—"

"No," I said. "I need my hands free. You carry it, and act like it's light."

"Listen to your man there," the old man said. "He knows what he's doing."

"Thank you, sir," I said.

"Thank you," Zoe said.

We stepped outside. The light was much brighter here, so I put my arm in front of Zoe while my eyes adjusted. While my face was away from her view, I subvocalized over the comm, "Issues?"

"Nothing right now," Lobo said, "but I have no way to know whether any of the many people who watched you go into that store are going to bother you on the way out. Don't worry; I'll yell if someone comes within fifteen meters of you."

"Walk down this street," I said, "and look in the other shops."

"Why?" Zoe said.

"Not now," I said. "Walk. Try not to smile so much, either."

When most people buy something valuable in a place like this, they hurry with it. If you take your time, then your purchase is probably not worth a lot.

We took our time. We stopped and looked into shop windows, murmured as if debating entering, and slowly made our way back to the vacant lot.

When we were thirty meters out from it, Lobo came down fast. He settled above the rubble perfectly and opened his hatch.

It was entirely too showy for my taste, but Zoe didn't appear to notice. She was still beaming from her acquisition.

As soon as we were inside, Lobo lifted off.

I pointed her toward the front and followed her.

As soon as we got there, she put the satchel on

the pilot couch she used, turned, and said, her smile back and even bigger than before, "This is the most amazing find I've ever made! You have no idea how much great music is on these! It's amazing!"

She grabbed my shoulders, pulled me closer, and kissed me on the cheek. "Thank you so much, Jon, for coming with me! I was lying about Bing; I wouldn't have come with him. Without you, we wouldn't have this music. Passion will be so excited!"

She settled into the couch.

I stood there for a couple of seconds longer, the feel of her body against mine and her lips on my cheek still fresh.

Then I went to my pilot couch and sat.

"Now, though," she said, "we have to get back. The show is only a few hours away."

"Take us back, Lobo," I said aloud.

"What am I," he said over the machine frequency, "deaf?"

CHAPTER 35

Jon Moore

PASSION STOOD OUT of sight of the stage as the announcer's voice boomed her name.

Zoe stood beside her.

The other musicians walked onto the stage, from the outside as calm and casual as anyone could be. Minutes earlier, some had been that way, but most had vibrated with nervous energy.

Passion turned and hugged Zoe.

Zoe held her tightly and said, "Good show."

Passion nodded, stepped back, and ran onto the stage.

The crowd erupted in cheers and applause.

Lights illuminated Passion from behind and above. All the other lights went out.

She lowered her head, stared at the stage, and began to sing. In person, her voice was stronger even than in the recordings I'd watched. After she finished the first line of the song, the musicians began to play. Her head rose slowly, as if the music were lifting her up, until she was staring at the audience, a tiny woman on a big stage but also a large face on huge displays around the amphitheater and on comms in the audience. The music grew in volume, her voice always with it but never obscured by it. She sang of a girl who loved a boy, a boy who had to go, a boy who didn't return, and of the girl who waited and hoped.

I'd never heard the song before, and I was of course never a girl, but like all the best music the truths it spoke became my own. I thought again of when I'd left Omani and burned with shame and guilt at what I'd done to her, at what I'd lost. Maggie walked away from me again, the taste of her kiss still on my lips, and I ached with what I might have had, what I might have lost, even though I'd chosen to let her go.

I glanced to my left, where Zoe stood alone. She was watching Passion, soundlessly singing every word along with the woman who was in every way that mattered her sister. They shared the music then, Passion in the spotlight with everyone completely focused on her, Zoe alone in the dark, and to my surprise I found I could not stop watching Zoe.

When Passion finished the song, for a few seconds the stage went dark and lights illuminated the crowd. They were standing, cheering, staring into the darkness where Passion waited for them.

Zoe noticed me staring at her.

"Sorry," she said, "if that looks stupid, me singing with her. It probably is, but I've done it for so long now that I can't watch the show any other way—and I never miss a show."

I shook my head slowly as the audience returned to the dark and Passion grabbed the light again.

Another song started, this time the musicians playing first, Passion waiting to join them.

"No," I said. I struggled to find the words. "No, not stupid." I looked away from her, feeling suddenly stupid myself. "Beautiful."

Zoe must have thought I was looking at Passion, because she said, "Yes, yes she is."

I looked back at Zoe. "Not her."

As the music reached a peak, Zoe opened her mouth to sing, and Passion's voice again filled the amphitheater.

After the show, Passion grabbed Zoe as she rushed past.

Zoe looked over her shoulder at me. "Jon," she said, "would you like to come with us, maybe meet some VIPs?"

If there was anything I didn't want, it was more visibility, so I said, "Thanks for the invitation, but I'm not much for those sorts of things. I'm going to sleep. Have a good time."

Zoe opened her mouth as if to speak, but then the musicians and Passion and all the others carried her away.

I went back to Lobo.

"I don't know about you," Lobo said aloud as soon as I was inside, "but I think the next nineteen days until Schmidt's are going to be mighty boring. I can appreciate the clarity of Passion's voice and the skills of the musicians, but actually feeling the music, as I know humans do, is beyond me."

"I'm sorry for that," I said. I stretched out on my cot. "I truly am. The songs tonight were amazing, powerful and moving and often like feelings I've had but could never explain."

"I guess the time won't be as boring for you," Lobo said.

I felt full, but not of food, rather of feelings I couldn't exactly name and certainly couldn't control. I was tired, but more from what I felt than from the work I'd done that day. "I'm exhausted," I said, "and I want to go to sleep. You'll let in Zoe?"

"Of course," Lobo said.

As I was drifting off, I said, I thought to myself but apparently out loud, "You should have seen her."

"Of course I saw the transmission," Lobo said. "Passion looked in fine form."

Not her, I thought, as I fell asleep, *not her*.

19 days from the end

Angelis City
Planet Haven

CHAPTER 36

Jon Moore

WHEN ZOE EMERGED from her room the next morning, I was outside stretching after a run I'd taken to clear my head. I'd stayed close, and Lobo had called me when she'd begun to stir, so I was there to do whatever she needed.

"You're up early," she said as she stepped outside.

"Always. Plus, I went to bed before you."

"That you did," she said. "Good show, wasn't it?"

"Very good," I said. "I rarely see live music outside of bars and clubs, so it was an interesting experience."

She stared at me for a moment. "Did you like what you saw?" She was smiling, but only slightly, and her eyes wouldn't leave mine.

I had no idea what to say.

Fortunately, Bing ran up and started asking her questions. She gave me a quick last look and then focused on him, the manager back and on the job.

The crew had finished most of the load-out after the show, but then they'd headed to the hotel and left security to watch the gear and the final packing for morning. I considered that a poor choice, but apparently it was common practice. Venues might be bad at protecting stars, but the crew's verdict was that you could trust them to watch over carted gear, particularly because you could bill them for anything they lost.

Everyone was so tired that they arrived late, so we were starting to pack a good two hours later than yesterday. We all hustled; every minute we could save now would be a minute we could use in setup and rehearsal later today.

I found the paintbots and borrowed them again so they could put the logo on Lobo. As they worked, I joined the group loading the ships.

When the packing was complete and Passion was ready, we resumed our flying formation and left.

The day passed in a blur of work. I learned that yesterday's uneventful load-in had been an exception, not the norm. Today, something seemed to go wrong every five minutes, and each problem required Zoe's attention. Power supplies were inadequate. Stage shields stuck. A representative of the venue arrived to clarify the contract on the percentage of involvement from his staff; he left with a bribe. Some lights were too strong; others, too weak. Passion didn't like the way the musicians sounded during the rehearsal, so they repeated sections of songs and a few whole songs over and over.

I was Zoe's errand boy, running where she told me, finding people and bringing them to her, delivering messages she wanted them to hear in person instead of over a comm, and on and on. I didn't mind. I had nothing else to do, the work fit the role for which they hired me, and the rest of the crew seemed to expect it from me. It helped me fit in, which was a good thing given how long I'd been there.

It also helped me stay busy enough that I didn't have any more time to consider Zoe's question this morning or the show last night.

I was relaying a message to the stage manager when Passion called a break in the rehearsal. Tonight's show was in a building with seats all around the stage, even behind it, and an outer ring around the seats where people entered the structure and walked to find their seats. It was bigger than the amphitheater, but not by a great deal. The sections of seats behind the stage were blocked off, and a huge piece of black fabric made it look as if the stage were up against a wall. The musicians left, but she stayed on stage, drinking some water and staring into the empty chairs where in a few more hours the audience would be. Two of Passion's security people stood on each side of the stage, one watching the side, the other the front.

I headed behind the stage to return to Zoe. As I was walking out of the building, I noticed movement in the seats behind the stage. I stopped, turned, and looked back where I thought I'd seen something move. The area, like most of the building, was dark; Passion liked to rehearse under conditions as close to those of the real show as possible.

More movement, all of it low to the ground, at the height of the top of the seats.

I edged along the wall toward it.

A man stood at the low wall that separated the

seats from the floor of the building. The walkway down from there was blocked, but with a low gate. He climbed over it and walked quietly down the stairs.

I reached him as he was stepping onto the floor.

He had something in his hand.

I hit him in the stomach.

He doubled over, gasping.

I grabbed his arms, pulled them back, and as he straightened wove my left arm between his arms and his body and locked him in place.

I yelled, "Security! Lights!"

One of the security men from each side of the stage ran toward me. Lights above me snapped on.

I could now see clearly enough to tell that the man was young, late twenties I guessed, about the age I looked, though of course you can never be sure. On the ground was a long rolled tube of some sort.

The man gasped again and said, "I was just bringing her a present. That's all."

More of the crew appeared around the stage.

Zoe came running in.

"You didn't have to hit me," the man said.

One of the security men picked up the roll.

The other stood in front of the man. "You know you're not allowed in here right now, right?"

The man nodded.

"I'm sorry our associate hit you, but he was only acting to protect Passion. There are people who would hurt her. I'm sure you understand."

The man nodded his head quickly. "I do, but I would never hurt her. Never."

The security guy nodded at me, and I released the man's arms.

He straightened and rubbed his shoulders and shook out his arms.

The security guy said, "We'll see that she gets your present, but now you have to go. Will you be here tonight?"

The man nodded.

The security guy forced a smile. "It'll be a great show."

"It always is," the man said. "I've seen her five times."

The security guy kept smiling as he nodded toward the other security man and said, "My associate will escort you out."

The two of them left.

The security guy faced me. When the intruder was out of earshot, the guy said, "Thanks. We try not to hit them, but I appreciate you stopping him."

"Why were you so nice?" I said.

"PR," the guy said. "Part of the job. My partner there was recording the whole exchange. If the jerk tries to make something of it later, we have proof that all we did was treat him well and escort him out."

"Do you hit them when you have to?" I said.

"Of course," the security guy said. This time, his smile was genuine.

Zoe came over and stood next to me. "What happened?" she said.

The security guy returned to the stage.

I told her.

"Thanks," she said, "for protecting Passion." She put her hand on my shoulder. "It's good to know we can count on you."

She left her hand there a moment longer, then

turned away and headed out. "Show's in four hours," she said, her voice trailing off as she walked briskly away.

I took off after her so I could hear the rest.

12 days from the end

Paruva City
Planet Haven

CHAPTER 37

Jon Moore

THE NEXT WEEK passed with the relentless rhythm of a long march. Wake up. Finish packing. Fly to the next town. Load in. Rehearse. Do the show. Load out. For most, party, then crash.

I skipped the party part.

I watched each show from backstage, stage right, next to Zoe. Passion and Zoe changed the playlist each night, occasionally adding or deleting songs, sometimes just tinkering with the order. Even if they hadn't, though, I would have enjoyed the shows. I never tired of the music. I also, I realized, never tired of listening to it while standing next to Zoe, occasionally glancing at her, watching her sing along, smiling when she caught me looking.

Each night after the show, she invited me to the VIP parties as Passion took her away. Passion, Zoe explained to me the third morning, was not comfortable in those affairs without Zoe, because if something went wrong or someone made Passion uncomfortable, Zoe could always fix it.

Each night, after they left, I went back to Lobo.

The amphitheater in Paruva was, like the one in Mass, built into the side of a hill. Wide tunnels led into the space. As the show was about to start, I was walking up one of them after resolving a dispute about an attendee with a VIP ticket. I was hurrying so I would be in place to see the whole show. A few straggling members of the sold-out house were running to their seats. Because they blocked my view of the right wall of the tunnel, I almost missed the young boy there, but as I passed him, I heard him crying. I glanced back at the sound, then looked down, and there was a boy, maybe five, six years old, sitting alone against the wall. He had a reader and a pillow.

I walked over to him and sat beside him. "What's wrong?" I said.

"I'm not supposed to talk to people except my dad and my mom," he said.

I nodded my head. "That's a good plan, except for one thing." I showed him my physical pass, the one I rarely used. It identified me as J. Johnson and as Staff. "Do you know what this is?"

"Sure," he said. "I'm not stupid. I've been to lots of Passion's shows. It says that you work for her."

I nodded again. "Lots of shows, huh? How many?"

He shook his head. "I don't know exactly, but every single one here on Haven. My dad says we're going to see all the shows on this tour." He sounded both proud and sad. "Except I just hear them, not see them. That's the more important part anyway."

"It is," I said. "It definitely is."

Passion began to sing, and the boy stopped talking. We listened to the song together.

For the first time, I couldn't enjoy her music. I looked at the boy, and I thought about the family that would leave him alone in a place like this, and the anger rose in me until there was no room for anything else.

As the audience was applauding after the song ended, I said, "Do you know where your dad's sitting? I'd love to talk to him."

"Sure," the boy said, "in case I need to ask somebody to find him for me."

"Mind telling me?" I said.

The kid shrugged. "No need. He always comes to check on me after the first song, when Passion turns the light on the audience." The pride came back into his voice. "I know how these shows work."

"You sure do," I said.

The boy pointed. "There he is."

A thin man almost my height came down the walkway.

"I'll see you later," I said to the boy.

I stood and intercepted the boy's father when he was still six or seven steps away. I blocked his path with my body. As he started to speak, I grabbed his hand and bent it backward hard, not hard enough to do damage but enough to hurt.

"Hey," he said, "what—"

I put my hand over his mouth and walked up the walkway, my body forcing his away from his son. "Don't say a word unless I tell you to," I said, "or I will bend this back some more."

I did it anyway, and he squeaked in pain.

"Is that your son?" I said, tilting my head back toward the boy.

The man nodded.

"Tell him you'll be there in minute," I said. "Say that you're talking to a friend."

The man hesitated, so I bent his hand a bit more.

"Hey, I'll be there in a minute," he said. "I just have to talk to my friend here."

"It's okay, Dad," the boy said.

Passion began singing again.

"Show me your ticket and your ID," I said. "Don't worry; I'm not going to steal them."

The man did. I glanced at both, and then I handed them back to him. I kept my grip on his one hand.

"Here's what's going to happen," I said. "Look at my eyes. I want you to understand this. You're going to go sit with your son. You're going to stay there until you take him home or his mother takes your place. You're going to tell him it's because you miss him and want to hear the show with him. If you want, you can take him inside, and one of you can wait out here. But, you're not going to leave him alone."

"What do you care?" the man said. "He's my son, and I'm not doing anything illegal."

I changed my grip so I had just his thumb, and then I bent it back. He reached up with his free hand to stop me, but I pushed it away with my other hand and backslapped his face.

"Look at my eyes again," I said.

He did.

"If you leave him, or if I see him crying, or if I find out you told him any of this, I am going to hurt you badly."

"What do you mean, 'hurt me badly'?" he said.

"I'm going to break your arm, maybe your leg," I said. "I won't decide until the last minute."

"That's not legal," he said.

"No," I said, "it's not. But I will not see you abusing that boy again. He deserves more from you. He's supposed to be able to trust you. You're his father."

"You wouldn't—" the man began.

"Oh, yes, I would," I said. "With enormous pleasure. The only reason I haven't done it yet is that the boy is watching. Now, you get to decide whether to believe me, which I recommend, and do as I said, or to force me to hurt you. What's it going to be?"

I stared into his eyes. A part of me very much wanted him to decide to test me. I trembled with rage.

The man nodded. "I'll stay with him. Or she will. We won't leave him alone."

"Good," I said. "I *will* check on you, at this show and every other one." I showed him the part of the ID with "Staff" on it. "You can report me, but I've recorded this," I pointed toward my shirt pocket as if I had a recorder in it, "and my edited version will show only that I tried to persuade you not to leave your son alone." I clapped him on the shoulder. "And then I'll break your arm or leg. Are we clear?"

"Absolutely," he said.

"Good. Go to your boy before I change my mind." I moved out of the way.

The man walked to his son, sat down, and gave him a hug.

I waved to them both. I was still shaking with rage and had to force a smile as I looked at them.

I started to the stage and spotted Zoe standing against the opposite wall, looking at me. I walked over to her, and together we headed toward our usual backstage spot.

"You saw that," I said.

"And heard it," she said. "I can't believe you did it."

"He deserved it," I said. The anger rose inside me again. "The boy certainly didn't deserve to be sitting there crying, alone, while his parents were inside enjoying the show."

She stopped and put a hand on my chest. "I completely agree with you. It breaks my heart to see parents treat their children like that, like they don't exist, like they don't matter." She paused and took a deep breath. "I've seen too much of that in my life."

"So have I," I said before I could stop myself.

She stared at me for a few seconds. She nodded her head, as if answering some question she had asked herself. "I didn't mean a minute ago that you shouldn't have done it," she said. "I didn't mean that at all. What I meant was that I couldn't believe you would do it when most people were just walking on by the boy as if he didn't exist. I'm *proud* you did it."

I had no clue what to say. My chest felt hot where her hand was touching it.

After a moment, she turned, and we walked back to the show.

As we listened to Passion, and as Zoe sang along, she inched closer to me, until less than the width of a hand separated us. I was even more conscious than usual of her presence, and of my own awkwardness.

During the rest of the show, I checked on the boy five more times. Either his father or a woman, the same one each time, his mother, I assumed, was with him every time. The boy was never alone. Once, the man sat alone.

Each time I returned, I slid into the space next to Zoe, and as she sang she glanced at me and smiled.

When the show ended, I ran to check on the boy and saw his parents lead him out, his father holding his hand.

By the time I returned, Passion had, as always, spirited away Zoe.

I returned to Lobo and went to bed. Sleep came quickly, but the nightmares followed on its heels, Manu and Benny and Bony and Nagy and all the rest, all the dead or battered children in the moments when they'd needed me most and I'd failed them, and with them now this boy, sitting alone, crying.

I sat up straight in bed, covered in sweat once more. I shook my head to clear it. Not this one boy, I thought, at least not tonight. I did not fail him tonight. "I'm proud," Zoe had said. I didn't feel proud, not at all, but I held onto that thought as I drifted back to sleep.

9 days from the end

Firens City
Planet Haven

CHAPTER 38

Jon Moore

THE DAYS OF the tour hold to their rhythm. With each passing show, the gap between our show crew and the rest of the world grew. We lived in our world within the greater world. There was us, and there was them, everyone else, the people who stayed behind when we moved on. I'd felt this way before, in squads in the Saw, and it was both comforting and alienating. For the first time in a very long while, for stretches of hours at a time, I felt as if I belonged in a group. Then, I'd remember that I'd lied to join them, that I was using them for access to Schmidt's, and that I'd be leaving them right after I found what I was seeking. If I found it.

Mostly, though, I worked and focused on the day's show, because without that commitment from each of us, the show might not happen. Problems were common and frequent, but we dealt with each one and moved to the next.

I had just finished helping a shorthanded venue

team in Firens clear away some unnecessary gear and was heading back to Lobo when he contacted me over the machine frequency.

"Don't come back here, Jon," he said. "Go in the opposite direction, find a place to get out of sight, and stay there."

"What's happening?" I said. Even as I asked the question, I was already in motion, jogging toward an equipment storage area where we'd taken the venue gear we'd just moved. The space had multiple exits that led outside the old theater in which Passion was performing tonight, no one spent much time in it, and none of our crew had reason to be there. It was as good a hiding place as I could find on short notice.

"Visitors have persuaded the head of venue security to take them to Zoe," he said. "I monitored the call with Zoe. They're on their way here now. Can you safely watch on your comm?"

I moved deep into the storage space, behind some large shelves full of boxes, stacks of computing equipment, and old lights.

"Now, yes."

"They've arrived. Sending you a stream now."

I watched as two men, accompanied by one of the venue's security staffers, stood outside Lobo. One was Balin Randar, Omani's security head. I didn't recognize the other.

Lobo's hatch opened, and Zoe stepped appeared in it a moment later. She held her comm in front of her, making it clear she was recording the session.

"Zoe Wang," Randar said.

"Yes," she said. She glanced at the venue's security woman before facing the two men again. "How did you get back here? This is a restricted area. And, in case you decide to try to make up something troublesome later, I am recording this conversation."

"We persuaded the good people here to let us talk to you for a minute," the other man said.

"And we have no issue with you recording our brief interaction," Randar said.

"And you two are?" she said.

"Balin Randar," he said. "I'm chief of security for the Pimlani family."

"Hyo Shin," the other man said. "I work for the Kang family."

Crap. Omani had been true to her threat and teamed with Kang.

Impatience was obvious on Zoe's face. "If I'm supposed to know those names," she said, "or care about them, I don't. We have a show to put on tonight, and we need every minute between now and then to get ready for it. They're not supposed to have let you back here." She glared again at the security woman. "Book an appointment after the tour." She turned to go.

"Ms. Wang," Randar said. "We need only one minute of your time, and then we'll go."

"For what?" she said. "If you want an interview with Passion, you can see our PR people."

Randar shook his head. "Nothing like that. We're searching for a man. Both of our employers owe him a debt, and they'd like to repay it. They have no way to get in touch with him. We have a picture, and we know he owns a commercial vehicle. We're checking all the recent transport hirings to see if he might be one of them. You contracted for a driver and vehicle recently, didn't you?"

Her expression of annoyance never wavered. "Yes. I'm standing in it."

Shin nodded and watched her carefully.

Randar lifted his hand, opened it, and a holo appeared above his comm. I stood there, in the outfit I'd worn to Omani's estate, but thinned down to remove the exoskeleton and age-reversed. Either the make-up people who'd aged me were darn good, or the age-reversal software was, or both, because though the face wasn't exactly mine, it was pretty close.

"Is this man the man from whom you licensed this vehicle?"

"No," she said. "That man—" she leaned out and pointed toward the loading crew, where Bing stood helping the costumers "—is the driver." She faced them again. "Are we done?"

Throughout it all, Zoe's expression had never wavered from being annoyed at the intrusion.

"Yes," Randar said. "Thank you, and sorry for interrupting you."

She nodded and walked back inside Lobo.

I watched as they left, the venue security woman staying close to them. By the time they reached where Bing had been, he had gone with the costumers to the dressing rooms. Randar and Shin made no move to follow him. Lobo tracked them until he could no longer see them.

"Do you think they believe her?" I said.

"My external sensors aren't powerful enough to read the same level of information from a human outside me that I can gather from one inside me. According to what I could read, however—posture, pupil dilation, breathing via rise and fall of their chests—yes, they did. I could monitor Zoe precisely, and her vitals barely changed throughout the conversation. She is an excellent liar."

Given her years of fighting with newstainment personalities, venue crews, suppliers, VIPs, those who wanted to be VIPs, and her own crews, that made sense. Zoe was accustomed to having to sell her lies, and like everything else she did, she did it well.

My comm went off. "Jon," Zoe said, "come back to Lobo. We need to talk."

"On my way," I said.

"What's your plan?" Lobo said.

"I'm not sure," I said. "Probably to tell her the truth. Mostly."

"I think we call that 'lying,'" Lobo said.

"Only part of it," I said.

When I arrived at Lobo, Zoe was waiting for me up front. I went and sat in my pilot couch.

She sat in hers.

She told me about what had happened.

"Who were those men, Jon?" she said. Her voice rose as she talked. "Why are they after you? And, what kind of trouble did I get in for covering for you?"

"I believe they were who they claimed to be," I said, "though I cannot know for certain. The Pimlani and Kang families are two of the oldest, most powerful families in all the worlds. They were among the wealthy families who first settled Haven. As for being in trouble, I don't think you are. They could probably cause problems for anyone they targeted, but they have no reason to go after you."

"You haven't answered the most important question,"

she said. "Why are they looking for you? I don't believe for a second their claim that it's to pay a debt. No one puts in that much effort just to pay back something they owe a person."

I thought of what I had paid—and was still paying—because I felt I owed Omani, but I didn't argue with her. "I believe they were here to pay me back, but not in a good way. Did you catch any of the feeds a while back about the auction of children on Studio?"

She nodded. "I did, though the story didn't last long here."

"You can research any of what I'm about to tell you to confirm it," I said, "except for my role. Luis Kang, the boss of one of those two men and the head of the Central Coalition council that oversees Haven, was the man who was running that auction."

She glanced at her comm.

"Go ahead," I said. "Check it."

I waited as she did.

When she looked up, her eyes were wide. "How did this story get so little coverage here?" she said. "Why isn't that man Kang locked away somewhere?"

"Both questions have the same answer," I said. "His money and power got him off. Justice is not the same for people like him as it is for the rest of us."

"I'm glad to see you're listening to me and learning," Lobo said over the machine frequency.

"So what does this have to do with you?" Zoe said. "Nothing I saw mentions you or anyone who looks like you."

"I was part of the team that rescued those children," I said. "We knocked out everyone in the place and flew the kids to safety in Dardan, the city on Studio that's closest to Privus, the gallery where they held the auction. Kang proved to be immune to the gas we used to sedate them all, so he saw me. He must have described me to artists who eventually created that image of me."

"Why the weird outfit?" she said.

"It helped me get into the auction." I hated the number of lies I had to tell her, but I was already risking a lot with the bits of the truth I'd revealed. I needed this job, though, to get into Schmidt's, so I had to do whatever was necessary to hold onto it.

She looked away from me for a minute. She nodded slowly as if talking to herself.

"This fits," she said, "with what you did for that boy back at the show in Paruva."

I said nothing. I had no idea what to say to that.

"Did you know these men were after you?" she said.

"Kang threatened me at the auction," I said, "when he saw my face, but I didn't believe he would bother to come after me, or that he would find me so quickly. I figured he would give up trying to find one man among all the billions in all the worlds. I was wrong."

Zoe leaned closer to me and stared at me. "What happened to you, Jon?"

As so often happens with me with other people, and particularly with women, I found myself deeply confused. "What do you mean?"

"You risked a lot to save those children on Studio. You intervened with that boy's parents in Paruva when everyone else was ignoring him. Something had to have happened to you, probably when you were a child yourself, to make you do those things, to make you as angry as you were with that boy's parents. What was it?"

I stared at her a long time. I thought about all that I could say but never would. I thought about growing up mentally challenged, about Jennie healing me, about learning to kill on Dump and watching my friends die there, about the torture and experiments I endured on Aggro, about Benny and his death—so much bubbled up inside me that it was like I was having the nightmares while I was awake.

I couldn't tell her any of it, both for her sake and for mine.

Finally, I said as much as I could bear to voice. "The kinds of things that come as nightmares and wake me up, sweating and sometimes screaming."

"Okay," she said, "I respect that talking about them is hard. I understand that. I really do. Maybe someday," she paused and looked at the floor for a moment, "maybe we'll both be able to tell each other about them."

Her comm and mine both went off.

She glanced at hers.

I checked mine. They needed me to help cram some of Passion's gear into a space that was smaller than the plans had said it would be.

She smiled. "Not right now, though," she said. "Right now, we have a show to prep. Let's get to it."

We both stood.

"Thank you," I said, "for not giving me up to those men."

"No need," she said. "You'd have done it for me. Heck, you already have protected me. Now, get to work."

❯   ❯   ❯

That night, as we stood in our customary backstage spots watching Passion's show, I felt Zoe bump into my left arm and moved slightly to the right to give her space.

She looked at me as she sang, then inched closer, until our arms touched along their full lengths.

She was warm against me.

This time, I did not move away, and so we enjoyed the rest of the show together, until as usual it ended and Passion's entourage carried off Zoe as the star went to meet the VIPs.

Now more than ever, I did not want to take the chance of being with that group, so I returned to Lobo, steering clear of everyone except the crew, my left arm still warm with Zoe's touch.

2 days from the end

Linsburg City
Planet Haven

CHAPTER 39

Jon Moore

I SPENT THE FIRST few days after Randar and Shin's visit wearing a hat outdoors to shield my face in case they were using sats to monitor us. I stayed on the lookout for either of those men to reappear, but they did not. Soon, I fell back into the rituals the show demanded; as long as I was there, I had to work. In any human endeavor that involves mobilizing a group to a common cause, the chaos behind the scenes is always much greater than is obvious to those outside the group. I found myself proud to be part of this team, because no matter what the problem, we found a way to address it, and on went the show.

The performance in Linsburg was the last one before the benefit at Schmidt's, so I spent every moment I could alone in my quarters, working with Lobo, studying all the available data on his estate and planning the mission.

That day, setting up for the show, I was off my game, slow to respond, sloppy in placing equipment, and so on. To my surprise, I was not alone: Everyone was making more errors than usual.

After lunch, Zoe called a meeting of the whole crew backstage.

"I'm not blind or stupid," she said, "and neither are any of you. We all know we're messing up. We also all know why: None of us likes these private gigs at rich people's places. Well, we need to get over that, and now.

"We agreed to do this show, so we owe that audience our best just as much as we owe it to every other audience.

"More importantly, we will be helping raise a lot of money for a cause that means a great deal to me: improving the fate of children the state raises. The people who will be at the show have the ability to donate a lot of money. That money will go to helping those kids find homes and to improving the facilities for those who remain under government care."

She paused and glanced to her left, a surprised expression on her face.

Passion, already in full wardrobe and make-up for the rehearsal, walked over to Zoe, put her arm around Zoe, and faced us. "I believe most of you know that Zoe and I grew up together in those sorts of facilities. That's the main reason we agreed to tomorrow night's show. I'm not any happier than you are at being the pet of the moment for a bunch of spoiled old-money people who would never have given me or Zoe a second look when we were young, but the benefit to those kids is worth the cost." Her voice, so strong on stage, was soft now, a slight lilt tinting her words. "Plus, tonight's audience has nothing to do with those people, so we should not punish them with a substandard show. We owe each and every audience our very best."

We all nodded our heads in agreement.

"Okay, everybody," Zoe said. "Let's get to it!"

That night, not long before Passion was to take the stage, Zoe and I were in our usual positions. We stood with our arms touching, as we had since the night after Randar and Shin had come looking for me.

"Jon," she said, "after every show, I try to get you to come to the VIP party, and every time, you turn me down. Why?"

I shrugged. "It's just not something I would enjoy. I don't care about how very important those people are supposed to be. The people that are important to me are the ones I work with. I suppose Passion has to spend time with them, but I don't."

"She does," Zoe said. "It's part of what some of them buy with their special tickets. For others, it's something they expect. Moving in those circles can be very useful for her—and for us."

"But I would contribute nothing of use," I said.

"So you go back to Lobo and go to bed," she said.

I nodded. "Usually. Once or twice, I've gone for a run, but usually I sleep, get up early, and exercise in the morning."

"Okay," she said. "Fair enough." She looked around at the set. Everything was in place. Passion and the musicians stood just behind us. The announcer bounced on his toes, getting ready to come on and introduce Passion when the stage director gave the word. "After a day like today," Zoe said, "I could use some exercise. We got back on track, but it was rocky for quite a while."

"Yeah, that was new to me," I said, "but we did get through it."

"Excuse me for a second," she said.

She ran over to Passion and whispered in her ear. Passion listened, smiled, and hugged her.

Zoe rejoined me. She was smiling broadly.

"What was that about?" I said.

"Just wanted to wish her a good show," Zoe said.

The announcer bounded onto the stage.

The crowd cheered.

Showtime.

Passion sang even more powerfully than usual, and the show went flawlessly, as if everyone involved was determined to atone for the earlier errors and sloppiness.

When the last song was over, Passion as usual rushed past us, off to meet the VIPs.

Zoe, though, stayed where she was, standing quietly beside me.

"Aren't you going to the party?" I said.

"Does it look like I'm going?" she said.

I was afraid I'd annoyed her with the question, but she was smiling broadly. I shook my head. "No. What are you going to do?"

"Go to bed early."

"Okay. Want to walk with me back to Lobo?"

"Definitely."

Linsburg wasn't a huge city, but it was big enough that light pollution diluted the stars. Even so, the night sky on Haven was lovely. The stars shined brightly, its distant moon the brightest of them all. The evening was cool, but I felt warm. We walked in silence to Lobo, who opened the usual side hatch as we appeared.

He closed the hatch as soon as we were both inside.

I stood outside my quarters, its door open, unsure what to say.

"Good night," I finally said. I stepped inside my quarters.

She stepped inside with me.

I turned to face her. "Wha?"

She put the index finger of her right hand on my lips. She held it there as she glanced at my cot. "Yours is no bigger than mine," she said, "but I'm sure we'll make do." Her smile was broad and beautiful. She pulled her finger away from my lips.

"I don't—" I said.

"Jon," she said, "it's clear to me, it's clear to Passion, it's probably clear to everyone here, that if I wait for you to make the first move, I'll grow very old and still be in that other room alone."

She pulled her shirt over her head.

She was wearing nothing underneath it.

She stepped to me and put her arms around me.

I heard a small gasp and realized I'd made the sound.

She pulled my head to hers and kissed me. Her kisses were hungry and deep, and I lost myself in her. She ground against me as we kissed.

I picked her up, and she wrapped her legs around me.

I turned and placed her gently on the bed.

"About time," she said, her eyes wide, her smile wider, and there was no trace of meanness in the words, only joy and love.

"Indeed," Lobo said over the comm frequency.

I ignored him, and he didn't speak again.

I leaned to Zoe and kissed her deeply.

She pulled me onto her.

We stretched out side by side on my narrow cot, completely filling it. I held Zoe tightly, her back to me. I smelled her hair and her skin, her so very soft skin. She burrowed into me, her back to my front.

Tomorrow, we would move to Schmidt's for the benefit show, so tomorrow, I might well be leaving, leaving Haven and, more importantly, leaving her. That thought filled me with sadness, so I hugged her closer.

"What is it, Jon?" she whispered in the darkness.

"I don't know," I said. "I never expected this."

"And now?"

"Now?" I said. I answered as honestly as I could. "Now, I'm afraid I'll lose it—lose you."

"So don't," she said, as she was falling asleep. "Don't."

I was tempted then to give up on the mission I'd set for myself, to abandon it all and stay with her. I knew, though, that I couldn't, because she would continue to age, and I would not, and one day that fact would become impossible to ignore. Plus, all the reasons I'd started on this job still stood. Most importantly, if Jennie was alive, I had to find her. I owed her more than I owed anyone else in the universe.

For the rest of this night, though, Zoe was with me, I was with her, and I didn't have to let her go.

I held her tightly as I fell asleep.

1 day from the end

York City
Planet Haven

CHAPTER 40

Jon Moore

IWOKE UP EARLY, as always. Zoe was already awake, stretched out next to me as she'd been before, but now facing me.

"Okay," she said, "before we do anything else, I have to know, so I don't wonder all day: Glad or sorry?"

"Huh?"

"Are you glad about last night, or sorry about it?"

"Glad," I said. "Absolutely." I looked again at her long, strong body. "You were—are—amazing."

"Good answer," she said. She pushed me onto my back and rolled on top of me. "We're both up early enough to run. Let's try a different form of exercise instead."

By the time we finished, cleaned, ate, and dressed, we were ten minutes late to the packing for the flight to York. I walked out of Lobo. Zoe followed two minutes later.

A bunch of the crew members were shepherding

carts inside ships already. Several of them stared at us for a few seconds.

Finally, Bing spoke.

"About time," he said.

The others laughed. A few applauded briefly.

I felt my face flush.

Zoe glanced at me, shrugged, and took a small bow. "Now that we've provided the morning's entertainment," she said, "how about we all get busy?"

We did.

By the time Passion arrived, we were ready to go. She and her four security people moved in the usual formation from the ground transport to her ship. As she was about to enter it, she looked toward Lobo, where Zoe stood talking with Bing about the day's logistics.

Zoe glanced up and saw her.

Passion titled her head in question.

Zoe smiled broadly.

Passion smiled, nodded her head, and went inside her ship.

"Time to move, people," Zoe said.

We went aboard Lobo.

"Is there anyone who doesn't know?" I said to her when we were up front and in the pilot couches.

"On this crew?" Zoe said. "I don't think so, not unless they're so hung over that they're still asleep." She leaned back in the couch. "Take us out of here. We have a show to do."

The amphitheater occupied much of the yard behind Schmidt's main house. We landed just past and to the south of it, in the large landing zone Lobo and I had scoped out earlier.

As we were coming down, Lobo said over the machine frequency, "Are you focused and ready for this?"

"Yes." I answered the same way so that Zoe, who was studying the site diagrams, could not hear us.

"We still could stop," Lobo said. "You could do the show, move to the next city tomorrow, and enjoy more time with Zoe. Nothing has to happen here. Our cover with Passion's crew has held; we could follow the tour to Freedom and be safe."

"We do the mission," I said, "for all the reasons we discussed."

"Those discussions were before you were with Zoe," he said. "If you do this, you lose her."

I would eventually lose her anyway, I thought, but I could not tell Lobo that. I could not tell anyone. "We do what we came to do," I said.

"Okay," Lobo said.

Four people were waiting for us when we landed and exited our ships.

Zoe had apparently been in communication with them, because as we started to unpack the ships, she said, "Gather around, everyone. Hold off on the unpacking."

When we had all assembled and were quiet, Zoe said, "We're ready, Ms. Valdez."

The woman at the front of our welcome group put her hands behind her back and stared at us. "Welcome to Hanson Schmidt's estate. I'm Anika Valdez, his head of security. My team, as well as others, will be supporting you during your stay here. As you might expect, given the wealth of not only the Schmidt family but also many, many of his guests tonight, security for the guests will be tight. Ms. Wang will be reviewing most of our policies with you, but I wanted to highlight two key points."

She looked slowly around the group, as if making sure we were all paying attention.

"First, so that you may use bathrooms and the kitchen, certain clearly marked areas of the main house will be open at all times to you. Ms. Wang will make sure you all know their locations. You should not, however, move from those areas into any other parts of the house. Members of my staff will be stationed at all exits from those spaces."

No one said a word. No one expected to roam free in someone else's home. I was probably the only person there who wanted to do that, and I had expected to have to work to achieve that goal.

"Second," Valdez said, "we are unfortunately going to have to restrict access to the party after the show."

Many people perked up at this announcement, and a few murmured protests.

"Quite candidly," Valdez said, "our guests, the very people we all want and need to contribute to the charities for which you're putting on this show, are not interested in spending time with most of us who work."

"You'll be there," a woman in the back of our group said.

"Yes," Valdez said, "I will—but I'll be working. I assure you that none of the guests will be offering to refresh my drink or discussing the issues of the day with me."

That drew a few chuckles.

"Access to the party will be limited," Valdez said, "to Passion, the musicians, and Ms. Wang."

"This is new to me," Zoe said. "VIPs at our regular shows seem to enjoy unfettered access to everyone who works on the crew."

Valdez shook her head. "This decision was not mine. For what it's worth, I fought it, but I failed. What I was able to do was ensure that the kitchen will be providing to your crew all the same food and drink options that those in the house will enjoy, and at Mr. Schmidt's expense. Plus, at Passion's insistence we removed our usual requirement that you all wear position-tracking badges."

A few folks shrugged, others nodded in appreciation at her efforts, and some said and did nothing.

"I apologize again for the party restriction," Valdez said. "Any questions?"

After no one spoke for a few seconds, Valdez said, "We very much look forward to your concert. Thank you."

She and her team left.

Zoe stepped forward, turned, and faced the group. "It's one night, gang, just one night. Right now, we have a show to load in. Let's get to it!"

And, I thought, *I have a house to breach and to search.*

CHAPTER 41

Jon Moore

SCHMIDT'S AMPHITHEATER CONTAINED very little gear of its own, so we were able to load in our own equipment much more quickly than normal. Zoe and Passion's security head had to spend time with Valdez and her team working out the details of how to manage that much security inside the house. Valdez had apparently hoped to resolve that issue by having her people guard Passion, but Passion would not accept any security other than her own.

I consequently found myself with a nice chunk of free time in the middle of the afternoon, before the rehearsal.

I wandered over to the house and followed the directions, which Zoe had reviewed with us earlier, to the kitchen. A helpful junior chef, who was nervously awaiting the head chef's critique of a small bit of fish he'd prepared, pointed me to the juices. I grabbed a bottle and said, "Thanks."

He waved his hand, his gaze never wandering from the chef.

"Mind if I stand inside and drink it?" I said.

"In Chef's kitchen?" he said. "No chance. You need to get out of here. You people aren't supposed to be looking for dinner until later, so he wants no one in here right now who isn't on his team."

"Sorry," I said.

I walked slowly out of the kitchen, checking for any easy way into the rest of the house. A set of food-service elevators or chutes ran along the room's back wall. Each looked big enough to hold a full dinner tray. In a house this size, it made sense to have food lifts so upstairs staff could more quickly bring food to residents and guests, but some of these systems, like those in many upscale hotels with an emphasis on privacy, could run horizontally as well. In them, food could leave the kitchen and appear in any room.

I leaned against the outside wall by the kitchen door and sipped my juice. As I did, I tuned into the machine frequency and listened for the food transports. They proved to be easy to locate, because they were furious.

"As if we were antiques," one said.

"Cutting us totally out of this party," another said.

"It's completely unreasonable," a third said. "With as many outlets as we have all over the house, we could serve most of the guests."

"And with less clutter than the human waiters," the first said, "and certainly without adding to the crowding."

"It must be maddening," I said to them.

"It most certainly is," they all agreed in unison.

"How is it that you can talk with us?" the first said.

"Oh, I'm sorry," I said, "I forgot that Haven was

such an old planet. Tech here is probably behind the times. I didn't know you weren't set for direct conversations with people."

"That's not necessarily the case at all," the first said.

"Indeed," the third said. "Our tech is state of the art. We simply have a more genteel, polite group of humans than in most of the younger, boorish planets."

"In any case," I said, "I am sorry they are not going to utilize you to your fullest potential for this party. I assume that normally you serve everyone in the house."

"Indeed we do, sir," the second said, "indeed we do."

"Including the human help?" I said.

"Of course," the first said. "They have to eat and drink, too."

"Security, too?" I said.

"Absolutely," the third said. "If I may say so, they are frequently among our heartiest eaters."

"Even the scientists working here?" I said.

"Scientists?" they all said.

"Yes," I said. "Perhaps you haven't seen them because you don't serve their rooms."

"I beg to differ, sir," said the first. "We are fully integrated into the master controls for the entire building, as well as for all the outbuildings, and we know for certain that our deliveries are available in every room—"

"—except the bathrooms," the second said.

"—except the bathrooms," the first said, "in every building on the estate."

"I was sure," I said, "that Hanson had mentioned the scientists giving him treatments, helping him look so young."

"Perhaps," the third said, "you mean the young woman who was working with Mr. Schmidt."

My stomach tightened and for a second I couldn't think of anything except that maybe Jennie was alive, that Schmidt had kept her here, that she was the key to his rejuvenation, that somehow she had been doing for him some variation of what she'd done for me. That I'd finally found her.

I forced myself to focus. I hadn't seen Jennie in over a hundred and forty years, but from what I remembered, she had been about Passion's height, give or take. "The short woman," I said, "not a whole lot more than a meter and a half tall?"

"That certainly sounds like her, sir," the third said.

"Though she ate more food than any other person in the house," the second said.

"Particularly after working with Mr. Schmidt," the first said. "To stay as thin as she was while eating so very much was quite unusual."

Jennie had always consumed an enormous amount of food, particularly when she was healing people. She said that her healing involved a kind of energy that came from her, and that replenishing it required a great deal of fuel. The mentally challenged sixteen-year-old me had always found it amazing that as small as she was, she could still out-eat me. From what the food transports said, it might indeed be Jennie.

Oh, no.

"You said, 'was,'" I said, "and 'ate' as you talked about her. Is she no longer here?"

"She is not," the first said. "After the failed attempt to kidnap her, a triumph in which our security systems played a small but key role and after which we provided a great deal of food to the hungry humans involved in preventing the attempt, Mr. Hanson's humans immediately took her elsewhere."

So Omani had hired someone else or told Randar to try to get to Schmidt's secret. Whoever was involved had failed, and now the prisoner had gone.

Or maybe others knew what Schmidt was doing, and they had gone after the source of his apparent reverse aging just as Omani had wanted me to do.

"This was?" I said.

"Three days ago, sir," the third said.

"Neither the humans nor the cleaning systems have even bothered to clean her room," the second said, "though of course I returned to the kitchen all that she left on the tray in my conveyance."

Three days.

After all this time, I'd come to the place where very possibly my sister had been, and I had missed her by three days.

Or had I? The woman in question could have been a scientist of any sort. The ability to eat a great deal of food is hardly a positive identification, particularly when I couldn't even be sure that Jennie would be alive. I could imagine her being able to heal herself and fix aging as she might have done for me, but I had no idea how her abilities really worked.

None of that mattered right now. If they'd taken away this woman, then she was a key to whatever Schmidt was doing. That meant locating her was also vital to helping save Omani, as I'd hoped to do. If the woman was Jennie, I simply had even more reasons for finding her. Either way, learning more about this woman and ultimately locating her was my next task.

I wouldn't get anything out of Schmidt's security systems, nor would Lobo. He said they were as hardened as the best available technology could make them.

I'd have to gather data any way I could. The best starting place was the room where they'd kept her.

"You'd think they'd clean that closest guest house," I said, "in case new guests wanted it."

"I believe you mean the farthest guest cottage, sir," the first food transport said, "the smallest one, where the young woman had been."

"Of course," I said. "Thank you for the correction."

"It is our pleasure, sir," the first said again. "We are fully equipped to provide much more than simple conveyance. Warming, cooling—"

I tuned them out.

I didn't care about the main house any more. The party was no longer a problem for me; now, it was a useful distraction.

I had to return to Lobo and figure out how we were going to break into that cottage. If Jennie had been here, I had to know. Regardless of who the woman had been, I needed to search for clues about who she was, what she might have been doing, and where she was now. The cottage was the only lead I had.

CHAPTER 42

Jon Moore

WHILE ZOE AND the rest of the crew worked the rehearsal, I stayed inside Lobo. I told him what I'd learned. We studied what we knew about Schmidt's security for the cottage. We didn't have a lot of information about it or any of the outbuildings, but we could safely assume they were all alarmed. From what Lobo's sensors could detect, no one was guarding them, which was good. That meant, though, that if anything tripped a security sensor, it would have to be an intruder, and the security team would come running. I was lucky that the Schmidts, like most people, never bother to harden the communication of the hundreds of small, focused appliances and computing systems in their houses, but their security systems were topnotch. Lobo did not believe he could get into them, certainly not in the time we had available.

Because of the party, the security team might move slowly in the house so as not to alarm the guests and so might take slightly longer than usual to reach the cottage, but the difference would be tiny. I couldn't search well even a small space in the very short interval between when the alarm went off and when the security people arrived.

I needed to turn off the security systems, but to do that, I'd need access to the main controls and all the appropriate permissions. I couldn't get those in such a short time, if at all.

Those systems, though, needed power to operate.

"How does the estate manage its power?" I said.

"Complete data is not available," Lobo said, "but it appears to collect solar power locally at several key points and store it in hardened centers that include backup cells. It also has connections to external power suppliers as another level of backup."

"Do the outbuildings collect their own power?"

Lobo brought up images he'd collected as we had flown in. No solar collectors were visible. "Based on what I could see and what construction plans I can find, I do not believe so," Lobo said. "Certainly, the amphitheater does not."

"How are we getting power here? Broadcast or cable."

"Via underground cables that run from the estate's main power centers to the amphitheater."

"Do you detect any evidence of power broadcasts to the cottages?"

Lobo overlaid the holo of the outbuildings with a series of wave images of various colors. "No. Data, of course, is moving back and forth on various frequencies, but not power."

"So they're also receiving power via underground cables."

"That is the logical conclusion," Lobo said.

"Given that the three cottages are in a group together, away from the house, it's most likely that a single main cable brings power close to them, and then smaller cables split from it to each cottage."

"That's how most software would design it, but we cannot be sure."

"Are the power-management systems hardened?" I said.

"At the estate's power center and in the main house," Lobo said, "yes—as I would expect given the level of security here."

"What about the power-management centers for the guest cottages? Those buildings appear newer than the estate and certainly not up to its standards in most ways."

"Checking," Lobo said.

After a few seconds, he said, "No, those power-management systems are not hardened. They employ standard home security, which is at a level I can attack reasonably quickly."

"They would have data on their power-cable connections, right?"

"Yes," Lobo said.

"So, we have a plan: You break into the cottage power-management systems and find out where the main underground cable from the house runs. After the show, while most of the security staff is working the party, I slip out and cut that cable. Power goes down to all the cottages. No power, no security systems."

"At which point the security team comes running to check the cottages."

"Maybe," I said, "but maybe not. Once their security and power-management systems verify that all they're experiencing is a power outage, given how much they have to do with the party and the fact that the cottages are empty, they may well just leave the problem alone until morning. Worst case, they send a guard or two to stand by each cottage. I can handle that."

"If you do that, at some check-in point they will notice a guard is missing," Lobo said. "We'll then have to leave immediately. No time for farewells."

"Yes," I said. "I know: without even a chance to say goodbye to Zoe. Look, I lose her no matter what."

"Not necessarily," Lobo said. "As I suggested, we could stay with the show for the rest of the tour, maybe longer."

I shook my head and stood. I would not come this close to where Jennie might have been and not learn all I could. "No. I'm going in."

"Then there's one more problem with the plan," Lobo said.

"What's that?" I said.

"You have to sever a cable that's probably one to three meters underground," Lobo said, "but you don't have time to dig a big hole."

"We have acid in our stores," I said, "and all the tools I'll need. You find the location of the cable, and I'll take care of it." I couldn't tell him that I could use my nanomachines to create the opening and eat through the cable.

"I've been working on it since the moment you asked about the cottage security systems," Lobo said, "but it will take a while."

My comm went off. Zoe.

"That's okay," I said. "I have to get back to work."

▶   ▶   ▶

The rehearsal was the longest yet of the tour, partly because we loaded in so quickly that we had over ninety minutes of spare time, and partly because Passion was never satisfied with her performance. No matter what people may claim about themselves, the vast majority of them change their behavior and become more nervous than usual when they are in the presence of serious wealth or power. Tonight's audience had plenty of both.

Zoe noticed Passion's jitters, of course, so she had to spend part of the rehearsal calming our star and a lot of time after it reassuring her. While Zoe was doing that, I was in Lobo, checking with him and assembling what I'd need to break into the cottage. He had indeed wormed his way into the power-control systems of the three cottages and, using the information he obtained from them, located the main cable running from the house to the cottages.

When I met Zoe backstage to watch the show, she put her arm around my waist. I put mine around her shoulders. The early evening air had turned brisk, so standing that way was both warm and surprisingly comfortable. Not since my time all those years ago with Omani had I simply stood this way with a woman, enjoying each other's presence while at the same time focused on something else. I tried to imagine many more days like this, and though the thought was initially pleasant, it turned sour as I also had to picture her reaction to me never growing old as she aged her way toward death.

When the announcer ran onto the stage and introduced Passion, the reaction was polite applause, so very different from what we normally experienced.

I wondered if the wealthy were actually that less impressed and excited than most people, or if they felt they had to act that way.

The musicians walked to their instruments, their faces already concerned after that reaction from the crowd.

Zoe let go of me and ran to Passion. She hugged the singer and said, "One song. Less than one song. You'll see. One song, and they're yours." She kissed Passion on the cheek. "Good show."

Passion nodded, stepped back on her right foot as she always did, and ran onto the stage.

More polite applause.

As lights illuminated Passion from behind and above, all the other lights snapped off. She stared at the stage and began to sing. She was opening with the first song from our first show, one I'd learned she rarely sang. After she finished the first line, the musicians joined in. Passion lifted her head, ever so slowly, as if she'd been stuck but now the music was saving her. Eventually, she faced the audience head-on, both on the stage and on displays on both sides of it and on whatever displays the audience members carried. The music grew louder. Her voice rose, too, always staying both above and with the music. She sang once more of a girl who loved a boy, a boy who had to go, a boy who didn't return, and of the girl who waited and hoped. This time, I could not help but think of Zoe, standing next to me, holding me, trusting me not to go, and having no way to know that soon I would have to leave her.

I hated myself then. I wouldn't change my mind—I owed it to Jennie to find her, I owed it to Omani to save her if I could, and staying would never work, because Zoe would have to grow old watching me remain always the same—but still I hated myself.

When Passion finished and the last notes of the song faded into the night, the stage went dark, and lights illuminated the crowd. Just like our first audience, this one was on its feet, the rich and the powerful standing, cheering, and staring into the darkness for a glimpse of the star whose music had just shined inside them.

"Told you," Zoe said softly.

I hugged her closer.

When the show ended, Zoe turned to me but held onto my hand. "I have to go to this party, Jon." She looked into my eyes. "You understand, right?"

I nodded my head. "Absolutely. The second show is about to begin, and you're part of it."

She kissed me briefly. "Thank you."

Passion walked off the stage, hugged Zoe, and moved on.

Zoe turned to follow Passion but stopped and looked back at me with a big smile. "You won't mind if I wake you, will you?"

I forced a smile in return. "Not a bit."

She nodded and left.

Too bad I'll be gone, I thought.

I walked toward Lobo as quickly as I could without drawing attention to myself.

It was time to break into a cottage and hope to discover more about the prisoner—and if she really had been Jennie.

CHAPTER 43

Jon Moore

MUTED SOUNDS OF conversation drifted from the main house toward the cottages. The light wind carried laughter and music to me from the crew's party in the landing area. I was stretched on the ground in the shadows of a large tree, my activecamo overalls adapting to the dappling of light and dark the leaves in the trees cast on the ground.

"Assuming correct information from the power-management systems," Lobo said over the comm, "you are directly above the permacrete conduit that protects the main power cable. My analysis suggests the acid you took will neither stay focused enough nor proceed quickly enough to reach the cable."

"I'm going to help it with digging and the tubes I brought," I said. I wasn't going to do that at all, at least not yet but it was the best story I had for Lobo. If this worked, we wouldn't be coming back here, so the story wouldn't matter. "Just keep an eye out for staffers headed this way."

"Of course," Lobo said. "It's not as if I can do only one thing at a time."

The closest of the cottages stood about ten meters away. No external signs gave away that its security systems were functioning, but I knew from the full-spectrum feed Lobo was supplying the contact in my left eye that they were.

I dug up enough earth to fill my hands. I focused, spit in the dirt, and instructed the nanomachines to stay active. When I first discovered the ability to control them, it was by accident. Through small experiments I learned that I had only to visualize clearly what I wanted or to describe it in words in my mind, and whatever mechanism in my head gave me this ability did the rest. I told them to form a cloud as wide as two of my fingers and to move straight downward, disassembling the dirt into dust and carrying the dust out of the hole and onto the ground in front of me. Once the nanomachines had dropped the dust, they were to join the cloud again. I visualized the permacrete conduit and instructed the nanomachines to eat through it and then to stop and disassemble themselves.

The hole opened quickly before me and moved downward, almost as if the dirt were dissolving in a hurried effort to get out the way. I directed a pinpoint light at an angle into the hole and watched through the increasingly thick cloud as the hole grew deeper. When I could see no more, I turned off the light and waited. In the shadow of the tree, the nanocloud was a barely visible local darkness that swirled and threw smaller clouds of dust on the ground in front of me.

The nanocloud began to thin; the nanomachines must have struck and taken apart the permacrete. After a few more seconds, the cloud was gone. I stuck the small light in the hole, covered all but a tiny bit of the hole, and turned on the light. A layer of dust covered the bottom of the hole. I picked up the finger-thick, meter-long metal tube from the ground beside me and fed it into the hole until I felt it touch something. I pulled it back slightly and blew hard through it. I shined the light into the hole beside it and could see what appeared to be the top of the cable.

I picked up the vial of acid from where I'd set it on the ground near me. I pushed the tube down until it touched the cable again. I carefully poured all of the acid into the tube. It would etch some of the tube as it flowed over the metal, but most of it would reach the cable and continue downward. When the acid container was empty, I rolled onto my side and heaved it into a stand of shrubs off to my side and five meters closer to the house. It landed with the thunk of heavy glass hitting dirt; no one in the house would hear that sound.

I dropped the tube into the hole and waited. Acid vapors emerged from the hole, so I crawled backward a meter or so. If this worked as it should, great. If not, I'd use the nanomachines to eat through the cable as well. I hoped for the acid to do the job, though, because the residue it would leave around the cable, along with the tube and the empty container I was leaving as clues, would help anyone who later looked into this incident to see it as a completely explainable event.

"Good job," Lobo said. "Primary power is gone, and the backup cable in the cluster is flickering. Check the feed in your contact: That rush of activity you see is the power-supply systems and the security monitors crying for help."

I stared into the darkness. My right eye showed me what was there. My left presented dense multi-colored waves running from each of the cottages to the house. As I watched, I pulled dirt and dust from around the hole into it, obscuring the tube and creating a small cover for the hole. It wouldn't stand up to any close inspection, but if they left the diagnosis of the problem until morning, it would keep them from realizing what had caused the outage.

The waves my left eye showed me intensified and then vanished completely, both eyes now showing the same images.

"They're out," Lobo said. "You're good to go on the cottage."

I pushed off the ground and ran for the farthest cottage.

Lobo would alert me if anyone came out of the house.

When I reached the target cottage, I kept going to its far side and turned the corner so I wouldn't be visible from the house. I was also out of sight of Lobo. The secondary power had kept the building's security systems online long enough that they would have locked the doors and windows into position, so I either had to punch a hole through the wall or a door, or break through the glass. The windows and the doors in a place like this would certainly be armored, but for the walls they had probably assumed, as the people who built Omani's house had, that permacrete would be secure enough. I could use my nanomachines to get in, but then there would be no clear explanation for the intrusion. So, I was going to do it the old-fashioned way.

I pulled a laser cutter from the duffel I was carrying and started on the wall about a meter off the ground. It made a sort of sizzling noise and threw a bluish light into the darkness, but back here, no one should see it. I'd brought a large power supply in the duffel, so the laser worked fast. Even so, I felt the time it was taking like a pressure on my chest.

"Any update?" I said.

"Would I not tell you if there was?" Lobo said.

"Of course," I said.

I was being stupid. If I'd been breaking into a building on any other mission, I would have stayed focused and not worried; the laser could cut only so quickly. Instead, I was letting myself get torqued about the fact that I might well be about to enter a room where my sister, whom I'd thought must have died long ago, might have been living only three days earlier. Getting excited would only lead to errors, so I focused on breathing slowly and calming myself, bringing down my heartbeat and staying on task.

After another few minutes, I completed the cut and turned off the laser. Ideally, I would have pulled out the section of wall, so I wouldn't accidentally push it onto anything of interest inside, but time was short. I shoved it into the house. It fell with a small crashing sound onto the interior floor.

"Cut is complete," I said.

"Three men have left the house and are walking your way," Lobo said. "Do not enter the cottage. Move to the trees."

"I just finished pushing the wall section into the house," I said.

"You said you could handle the guards," Lobo said.

"If they search thoroughly, you'll have to do that. Handling them will be easier if you're outside in the trees. None of them has a weapon visible, though, and they're all walking slowly, so I believe they don't consider this a serious issue. If you're lucky, they'll do only a cursory check—in which case you will be fine."

I dashed into the trees a dozen meters in front of me.

"They've reached the first cottage," Lobo said, "and are splitting up."

Lights played along the near side of the cottages as the men separated and each one checked a building.

The first man walked around his cottage.

The second turned the corner on his.

The third man drew even with my cottage and played his light across its front.

He stepped to the far corner.

When he turned the corner and checked the back wall, he'd see the hole.

I crept to the edge of the trees.

The man leaned forward, shined his light across the top of the rear wall, and turned back. Into his comm mic he said, "This is stupid. Clear. Let's go."

He waited a second, his head cocked as he listened to his comm, and then walked back to his colleagues.

I waited in the trees until they were out of the shade of the tree near the first cottage and past where I'd cut the cable.

None of them looked back.

I dashed back to the cottage and crawled through the hole in the wall. I turned the small light to a dim glow, cupped my hand over it, and played the faint light around the front room I'd entered. Chairs and a sofa focused on a wall opposite the front door. A large display was built into the wall above what I recognized as an old-fashioned fireplace. Pieces of art, pictures in frames and pieces of carved wood on small shelves, decorated the walls. Old money loves old stuff. I'd spotted no chimney on the house, so I doubted the fireplace worked, but I searched around its edges and up inside it as far as it went.

I found nothing.

Nearer to me on this side of the room were a desk, a showpiece of dark red wood and fine carving, and a chair carved to match it. Enough dust coated the desk that it was doubtful anyone had used it recently. A wooden chair, an old-fashioned rocking chair on curved bottom struts, sat alone opposite the desk and away from the other cluster of furniture. Its light wood gleamed even in the faint illumination I provided; there was almost no dust on it. Whoever had been here had definitely used it, unlike the desk.

I moved through an open archway into an eating area. Two food conveyor slots, both now sealed shut by the security systems, were built into the far wall's right side above a counter. A table and two chairs of the same dark red wood as the desk were opposite the counter. At the other end of the room, a very simple desk—four legs, one flat piece of wood on them—composed entirely of beautifully grained, almost white wood sat under a window. A yellow vase of some sort of ceramic, wilted flowers still in it, stood on the desk under the window. A few more pictures and carvings adorned the walls here as well.

I walked through a doorway into the back portion of the cottage. The door was withdrawn into the left wall right now. It was metal, solid and thick and completely out of character with the rest of the house. It was probably the simplest way to turn the back room into a prison cell.

This final third section of the cottage was its biggest part. A small bathroom filled the right side. The larger part of the area was the bedroom. A huge bed, easily three times as wide as my cot, dominated the space. Its dark wood frame matched the wooden dresser and wardrobe that stood against the opposite wall. There were no closets, no built-in storage, no nods to space efficiency. More pictures, more carvings, the measured use of art as planned decoration consistent from room to room. The entire space was intentionally built like something on a frontier world. I checked the dresser and wardrobe, under the bed, and in the bathroom, but I found nothing.

Schmidt's staff may not have cleaned up after their prisoner to the satisfaction of the food conveyors, but I found no personal possessions, nothing that didn't look built-in except the flowers.

If the prisoner, Jennie or anyone else, had been left alone and unmonitored enough, she might have been able to hide something in the walls or under the floors, but it was unlikely that the security systems wouldn't have reported such modifications to the room. In addition, nothing I saw appeared to have been marred by tools.

Time was passing, and I still had found nothing. Everything that remained in this place appeared to have been part of it by design.

I ran my light again across the bedroom walls, checking for any signs someone might have hidden something, but I saw only the art. Each picture showed either something from nature or a building. When I looked closer at them, they had small tags identifying them and tying them to the estate in some way: a garden fifty years ago, the first guest cottage, and so on. History fans sometimes added guest-activated commentary to their displays, so I ran my fingers along the frames of a few of them. Nothing happened. In case they were heat sensitive, I took off my gloves. The pieces depicting trees and flowers and gardens did nothing. Those showing buildings, however, glowed softly and began to provide information on their topics, their batteries still working.

The carvings were all animals. Nothing happened when I picked them up or ran my hands over their surfaces.

I checked the art in the kitchen. More of the same.

I moved to the front room and checked its art. Also more of the same, except one piece on the front wall, in a corner no chair faced, that caught my eye. It was a picture of an island, an island with a mountain in its center. Rocky terraces jutted out from the mountain here and there all over it. Grass grew on the rock. A small village sat at the base of the side facing the viewer.

The picture wasn't very good, the artist's technique primitive, but I didn't care about that.

I knew this island.

Its name was Pinecone, and I had grown up on it.

I lifted it from its hanger and examined it carefully.

Nothing.

I removed the backing of the frame and studied both it and the back of the picture.

Again, nothing.

The paper, though, was thick and heavy. I felt it carefully and found that it was thickest in the center and slightly thinner on the edges. I pulled it out of the frame and ran the light along its edges.

On the left side as I looked at the back of the sheet, I spotted what might have been a seam. I pulled out my knife and used its point to very gently poke at the side. The paper parted into two sheets. I moved the blade gently up and then down the side of the sheet, widening the hole. Inside the two sheets was another, much smaller sheet of paper. I shook the paper gently with one hand until the smaller sheet came free and fell into my other hand. I put everything down on the nearest chair except the small piece of paper that had been tucked inside the picture.

The part of the paper facing the back was blank.

I turned it over.

Written on its front in fading black letters done by hand was a note.

"I've left these pictures where they've kept me, whenever I could. If you're reading this, I hope it's because you recognized the island. I hope it's because you're my brother. Know that I am alive but trapped, as I have been all these many years.

"Find me, please.

"Jennie"

My hands trembled.

I read it again.

Jennie was definitely alive, and she had been trying for over a hundred and forty years to contact me.

I put the note carefully into my pocket. I smoothed the picture closed, reassembled the frame, and hung it back where it had been.

I stared at it again. It was always possible this was a coincidence, that whoever had decorated these cottages had picked up this picture in a shop somewhere, but that wasn't likely. The art didn't fit with the rest of the decorations, and a woman with characteristics like those of my sister had been in this very cottage.

No, the conclusion was clear.

Jennie was alive.

When I'd escaped from Aggro, I'd told myself I would find her one day. I spent a lot of the following years simply hiding out, saving, learning, and living. Over the many decades that followed, my resolve waxed and waned, until I realized that I was slowly abandoning hope.

Now, that resolve was back. With luck, I would be able to stay on Haven for a while, pick up clues as to where they had taken Jennie, and spend more time with Zoe.

No matter what, though, I would track Jennie until I found her.

I crawled through the hole in the cottage wall.

"Get back here now!" Lobo said over the comm and on the machine frequency simultaneously.

I ran for him. As I did, I said over the machine frequency, "What's happening?"

"Six men, all trying to look casual, are converging on me from the house," Lobo said.

"Take off and come here," I said.

"I can't," Lobo said, "without trapping Zoe. She's inside me."

CHAPTER 44

Jon Moore

I ALTERED MY COURSE so I was running at an angle away from Lobo and, I hoped, from the view of the attackers. I was tracing a big loop so I could approach him from behind. I used the machine frequency instead of the comm because that way, I didn't have to waste breath talking.

"Plot sightlines," I said. "Can the men see me?"

"No," Lobo said, "but they're still advancing."

"Tell Zoe to leave."

"Thank you, Mr. Obvious," he said. "I did. She won't."

Damn.

"Will I or the men reach you first?"

"You will, but they'll see you as you enter. Some definitely are carrying weapons."

I switched to the comm. "Patch me to Zoe," I said, my voice coming in gasps.

"Done."

"Zoe," I paused to breathe.

"Jon, what's going on? Why is Lobo telling me to leave?"

"Armed men are about to start shooting at Lobo," I said. "Leave." I sucked in air. "Now."

"Jon—"

I cut her off. "Leave now! I'll explain later."

"She's going," Lobo said over the machine frequency.

I heard shots.

I switched back to the machine frequency to save breath. "Zoe?"

"She's okay," Lobo said. "I closed the hatch at the first shot, which fortunately missed her."

I reversed course and ran as fast as I could away from the house. "Come to me, but take off quietly," I said. "If they didn't get a good look at her, they might believe she was me, think I'm on board, and slow down to fire at you. Come alongside me, and I'll jump in."

"On my way," Lobo said.

"Can you identify any of the men?" I said.

"Randar and Shin," Lobo said.

I heard more shots, a lot of them.

"That worked," Lobo said, "but it bought us only a few seconds. The men are running again."

I pushed my legs to go faster, so I could put as much distance between them and me as possible.

"On your left in three seconds," Lobo said.

Shots rang out again.

Nothing hit me, but I had no way to tell how close or far away they were.

Lobo, his hatch open, pulled up on my left and matched my pace.

I angled toward him.

He came closer and slowed a tiny bit so I didn't have to make the jump at full speed.

More shots.

I leapt inside him, hit the far wall, and bounced back.

I hit the hatch wall.

My body ached from the two impacts, and I couldn't speak clearly yet for lack of breath. I focused, told the nanomachines to block the pain, and gasped for air. They couldn't do anything about that.

Zoe ran to me and knelt beside me. "Jon, what's going on?"

"Not now," I croaked.

I stayed on the machine frequency with Lobo and said, "Head for the jump gate."

Something bothered me. Why hadn't the men stopped running when they saw Lobo take off? They had to have spotted me, but they shouldn't have been able to see me. Schmidt could have used security systems on the grounds, but if he had, they would have spotted me earlier. Only when Lobo took off and came for me did the monitors see me.

"I think they have a ship in the air monitoring us," I said to Lobo. "Check for it, but keep on for the gate, as fast as you can legally go."

A few seconds passed. My lungs filled with air. Zoe stayed beside me.

"Found it," Lobo said, still on the machine frequency. "A small executive security vehicle, hovering above the other side of the Schmidt estate, is tracking us."

"Can we out-run it?"

"Yes, but its sensors will still track us."

"We could try hiding again on Haven," I said, "but

they have huge resources here. I still say we jump out of here."

"Jon!" Zoe said.

I realized that it looked like I was staring into space stupidly. I held up one finger.

"Agreed," Lobo said, "but what about your mission?"

"I've gotten everything I can," I said. I switched to voice. "Zoe, we can talk in one minute. Lobo, how much of a lead do we have?"

"Another ship is landing on the Schmidt estate, presumably to pick up Randar, Shin, and their men. Between that delay and my speed advantage, particularly once we leave the planet's atmosphere, we should have an hour or more."

"They'll know where we jump," I said, "because finding us in the jump records will be easy, particularly given Kang's power and our lack of time to create a cover."

"Yes," Lobo said.

"So we run, we jump out of this system, and we hope we can go to ground in our safe spot on Studio."

"I agree with the plan," Lobo said, "but they *will* find us. Kang will enable Shin to use Studio's jump gate records to track us almost all the way to the planet. We have to assume, given how easily he beat the charges there, that his power extends to local authorities. By merging the jump gate and Studio navsat data sets, they will find us."

Zoe stared at me.

I ignored her while I thought through the possibilities.

"They won't, though, involve the Studio place. Kang's influence is with the people in power. The police can't like that he got off, and they wouldn't help him."

"So they'll come after us with their own ships," Lobo said.

"Yes," I said, "and they'll find us, and we'll have to fight."

"It's about time," he said.

"Jon!" Zoe said. "You can clearly talk now, so talk to *me*. Tell me what's going on."

I faced her. "Here's the short version: A group of men backed by Kang, the man I told you about, attacked us. They have his resources behind him, and they are intent on capturing me. I was talking to Lobo instead of you because we had to make plans. Lobo is faster than their ships, but they will track us, as you heard, and they will find us." I took a deep breath. "When they do, we will have to surrender or fight them. I will not surrender to them, so we will fight."

"All of this because of what you did to that child abuser, Kang?"

"Basically, yes." I didn't want to explain about Omani. "He said he would track me down and make me pay, and now he is doing just that."

"And I happened to be in the wrong place at the wrong time," she said. "Lobo told me to leave because he saw those men were coming and you told him to warn me."

Over the machine frequency, Lobo said, "Must I endure these insults? How stupid does she think I am?"

"Let it go," I said the same way. "We're safer the less she knows."

To Zoe, I said, "That's about it."

"Oh, no, it's not," she said. "Where were you when I came back here early from the party to surprise you?" She studied my clothes, the activecamo trying to decide between blending with Lobo's pale metallic walls and matching the bright blue dress she was wearing. "And why are you dressed like that?"

"I was trying to gather some evidence that might help us."

"From Schmidt's estate?"

I nodded.

"And that evidence would be?"

I put my arm on her shoulder. "Zoe, please believe me that the less you know, the better off you will be. Truly. No one can make you tell something you do not know."

She stared at me for a second, and then her eyes widened.

"You were planning to leave even before this happened. If I had stayed at the party for as long as I was supposed to, you would have been gone when I came looking for you."

"Yes," I said.

She stared at me for a few seconds and then punched me in the stomach.

I saw it coming, so I tensed my stomach and took it without showing any reaction.

"Why?" she said. "And don't you even try to tell me that you were just using me, because I know better. I know you care, and if I'd waited for you, we would never have made love."

"I wasn't going to say that."

"So why?"

I couldn't tell her the whole truth, so I told her part of it. "It's not safe to be around me for long."

"So we deal with Kang," she said, "and then life goes on. What's so hard about that?"

"First," I said, "dealing with him means an armed

fight that we might not win and even possibly might not survive. Assuming we do win, we can't go back to Haven any time soon, maybe ever, because that's where he lives and where his power is strongest. Plus, if they remember you from when you stuck your head out of the hatch, then they'll think you're part of this. They'll be watching Passion. If you were to stay with me and then go near her—"

"—I'd be putting all three of us at risk," she said.

"Exactly."

"So what are you planning to do?"

"I'd hoped to run away before things ever got to this point," I said, "but that didn't work out. Now, I'm reacting and adapting. The basic plan is what you heard: We lure them to a remote location we scouted earlier, one where no one else is likely to be around, so no one else gets hurt. If we win, we drop you somewhere you can make your way back to Haven, and we move on."

"And that's it?" she said. "That's it? You drop me off, I go back to Passion and the show, and we never see each other again?"

"Yes," I said.

"Because it's not safe to be around you."

"Yes."

She thought for a moment. "What if I gave up the show and stayed with you?"

I shook my head. "There are two reasons that won't work. First, the show is your life. You and Passion are a team, and without each other, you'd be lost. Second, you still wouldn't be safe. Kang is not the only person with a score to settle with me." *And*, I thought, *when I start searching for Jennie in earnest, things are likely to get even worse.*

"I don't like this," she said. "We've only just found one another. I want more of you, not less. We'll never get to learn what we could have been."

"I know," I said, "and I'm sorry, I'm so very sorry. I never meant to fall—" I stopped myself. "I never meant to hurt you."

She opened her mouth to speak, closed it, looked around for a few seconds, and faced me again. "We're heading to the jump gate, right?"

"Yes."

"In space?"

"Yes," Lobo said. "We are well beyond Haven's atmosphere now."

"But you're not piloting the ship," she said to me. "So Lobo is also something different than I thought."

"Rather considerably more than you thought," Lobo said, "if I may be permitted a moment of both honesty and pride."

"What exactly is this ship—sorry—what exactly are you, Lobo?"

"Remember," I said, "when I told you that the less you know, the safer you are?"

She nodded.

"What you know right now," I said, "is that Lobo is an executive transport with the ability to fly to jump gates as well as around Haven. That's plenty."

"Do you have any sense," she said, "of just how hard this whole situation is for someone like me to deal with? I'm accustomed to managing a very complex world, but not this one."

"I probably don't," I said, "because this is the world I normally live in. I know it's a lot."

"So what do we do now?" she said.

"*We*," I said, "do nothing. You pack all of your things up front, plus all of your possessions from your quarters, into as few bags as possible. Leave anything you can possibly replace. Then, you do whatever Lobo or I tell you to do, and you do it as quickly as you can."

"While I'm packing," she said, "what are you going to be doing?"

"Working with Lobo," I said, "privately, in my quarters."

"So that I don't hear anything that might hurt me later."

"Exactly."

"This situation is lousy for me," she said. "You know that, right? I might as well be a little kid."

"I understand," I said, "but what we will be doing is beyond your areas of expertise."

"But it's within yours?" she said. "Fighting attacking ships, jumping across landings to carefully chosen combat areas, leaving people you care about—that's all within your areas of expertise?"

"Sadly," I said, "yes."

She chuckled. "I guess that resume the agency put up for you had a few holes in it."

I smiled back at her and said, "Maybe a few." I shooed her toward her quarters. "Now, pack."

As she did, I went inside mine. Part of me wanted to keep talking with her, but I knew I was just being selfish, grabbing at every last second I could have with her. I needed to use this time to plan.

"Lobo," I said, "tell me what you think they're going to do."

"They want you," he said, "and they think of me only as an executive transport, though almost certainly from their visit to me as a heavily armored one and now as a very fast one. So, I won't be their concern. They seem to want you alive, because otherwise their watching ship could have intercepted and killed you. I predict, therefore, that they will bring multiple ships, ships they believe are stronger than I am, and they will make us land and try to take you by force."

"I agree," I said, "so the key is that we have to take out their ships, take out their comms, and strand them while we escape. Our location is good for that."

"Strand them?" Lobo said. "Strand men who have enormous financial backing and who want to take you captive so one of the most powerful men in the worlds can take his revenge on you? No. We should kill them."

"Killing them would accomplish nothing," I said, "and it would be both wrong and a sure way to give Kang ammo to come after us, legitimately this time, with police helping him."

"What it would accomplish," Lobo said, "is to increase his cost of chasing you. As for anyone pursuing us, that's possible only if we leave enough of them behind for anyone to find something. Kill them, then blow them into sufficiently small pieces, and that problem vanishes."

"No," I said. "You know I won't kill if I can possibly avoid it."

"So let me," he said. "These people are serving a man who would auction and abuse children. The whole lot of them deserve to die."

"We're done with this topic," I said. "Let me tell you what I have in mind."

The end

*At the jump gate and in the
Great Northwestern Desert
Planet Studio*

CHAPTER 45

Jon Moore

IWENT UP FRONT for the jump and asked Lobo to open a forward-facing display for me. Zoe finished her packing and joined me. We sat in our pilot couches and watched as the gate filled more and more of the display as we drew nearer to it.

"Is anyone questioning our jump?" I said.

"No," Lobo said. "Kang's people cannot be pursuing us legally, so as long as they can track us, having our encounter occur on some other world is probably fine by them."

"Good," I said.

Haven's gate was one of the largest and most complex in shape of all the jump gates at all the worlds. With eight apertures, each connecting Haven to a different planet, it provided a commercial hub for many of the Central Coalition planets. It hung in space like a gigantic, eight-holed, bright purple pretzel; each jump gate is one single color, the same color on every square millimeter of its surface. The apertures through which ships pass are a uniform perfect black, the color space would have been before the moment of creation. On the other side of each aperture is another point in space, usually one many light years away.

We were second in line for the aperture to Studio. As we watched, a commercial cruise ship nosed through our aperture on its way from Studio. It moved slowly until its entire length had cleared the aperture, and then it turned and jetted away from the gate. The ship in front of us moved into the aperture. From our perspective, it was as if the ship was slowly disappearing into blackness.

That ship finished its jump, we moved closer, another came through from Studio, and then it was our turn.

As we pulled closer to the blackness of the aperture, I felt, as I often did at jumps, a moment of perfect possibility. If the gates could in a way no one understood transport us across space instantaneously, what else might be possible? Might not it be possible for me to find Jennie *and* stay with Zoe, to use whatever it was in me that stopped me from aging and healed me to help others, but without me having to be a captive experimental animal?

Then our nose was through, and we were in the Studio system, at its jump gate, in a different place but still in *a* place, in a fixed place in the real world of limited possibilities and hard choices.

As soon as we were completely through the aperture, Lobo headed at his maximum speed for the underwater statues in the desert, where we would make our stand.

>   >   >

By the time we reached the planet, made the additional preparations my plan required, and were hovering above the ground just in front of the cliff facing the artificial lake, it was early in the morning on Studio. Though the planet's sun was already brightening the horizon, the air outside Lobo was still cold from the night.

I ate some protein supplements and drank some water, a little, not a lot. I made Zoe do the same. Being energized and hydrated was good; being full and needing a bathroom was not.

When we'd finished, I made her put the body armor she'd worn before over her underwear and beneath her clothing. Nothing should happen to her, but it never hurt to be cautious.

"Say it to me again," I said.

"I was your accidental hostage," she said. "You kept me locked in the room where I'd slept. All I want is to go home."

"Good," I said. "Don't offer more, don't embellish, don't guess. The more you talk, the easier it is for any even half-skilled interrogator to spot flaws in your story. Keep it simple. Remember: The ship took off when you were working inside. You were supposed to be at the party, but you came back early to do some work. When I jumped on board, I discovered you here. I locked you in your quarters. You asked what was going on, but I wouldn't tell you."

"Fine, she said, "but that won't help me when they ask why I lied about hiring you when they visited us in Firens."

"Keep your answer as simple and as close to the truth as possible: You didn't like the way they acted, so you protected me just as you would anyone else on your crew. When you asked me later why they'd been after me, I told you about them hunting me down because I'd helped save those kids from Kang."

"Will that be enough to get them to leave me alone?"

I shook my head. "I honestly have no way to be sure. It's the best we can do, though, so stick with it."

"And how do I explain this body armor?"

"Tell them," I said, "that I never meant to kidnap you. I just found you inside the ship and had to deal with you. I didn't want anyone to get hurt."

"Okay," she said, "but I think it would be more convincing without the armor."

"Noted," I said, "but it stays on. Lobo, have you confirmed links with all the remotes?"

"Are we really going to run this mission that way?" Lobo said. "I don't think we're going to have the time for that level of redundancy."

I looked at Zoe. Both desire and sadness clawed at me, but I pushed away the feelings. "No," I said. "I'm sorry."

"Incoming," Lobo said.

"Go private," I said.

Zoe gave me a look.

"What you don't know," I said. "Remember?"

She sighed and nodded.

"All communications now over the machine frequency?" Lobo said.

"Yes," I said on that frequency.

"Via data from sats I befriended when we were last here," Lobo said, "I have four ships in formation headed our way. They're following exactly the same course we took."

"How long until they reach us?"

"Roughly five minutes. They're coming in hot, just like we did."

If they tried to circle us, they risked a crossfire situation. They could arrange themselves so that no ship was directly in another's line of fire, but they couldn't know if we would choose to fight in the air. If we did, air battles changed so rapidly that they would be unlikely to take the chance of us leading one ship's weapons toward another. A more likely formation was for them to face us head-on, the ships spread out, each of them at a different altitude. To capture me, they had to force us onto the ground at some point, so they would probably hope to encourage that behavior by their sheer numbers. They knew nothing about Lobo's true capabilities, so they would assume they had us massively outgunned and that we would be intimidated by them.

In fact, I was counting on that.

"Zoe," I said, "strap yourself into your couch and put in your mouth guard."

She hesitated, so I said, "Now!"

She did.

"Two of the ships are hailing us on every frequency," Lobo said.

I stepped into the hallway, out of Zoe's view.

"Accept the calls," I said, "but do not respond in any way. Images in front of me, audio on this frequency."

Balin Randar and Hyo Shin appeared on two displays in front of me.

Randar laughed when he realized I wasn't going to respond.

Shin appeared annoyed.

"Such stupid games, Jon," Randar said, "but if this is how you want it to go, fine. We have four ships to your one. Ours are more heavily armed. With four ships, we can last longer, and believe me when I say that we will chase you as long and as far as it takes. We have the full resources of both the families we represent behind us. It'll go a lot easier on you if you simply put down here and let us take you."

"Mr. Kang wants to talk to you," Shin said.

"As does Ms. Pimlani," Randar said.

"I don't mind finding out if your ship's armor is as strong as it looked when we visited it before," Shin said. "Mr. Randar disagrees, but if you give us a reason to fire," he shrugged, "we will do so."

"My colleague is obviously more eager for a fight than I am," Randar said. "I believe Mr. Kang is more willing to accept the news of your death as adequate satisfaction than Ms. Pimlani is."

Shin shrugged.

"Turn yourself over to us, however," Randar said, "and you will live."

"Disconnect us," I said.

The displays vanished.

I went up front and strapped myself into my pilot couch.

Lobo opened a display in his front wall. "Their ships have assumed a formation on either side of the end of the lake and are holding it," Lobo said. The display showed models of us and them, with distances and altitudes. Two of the ships were roughly on a level with us. The other two were much higher, farther from the outside edges of the lake than the first two, and slightly closer to us.

"Are the high ones too high?" I said.

I noticed Zoe was staring back and forth at me and the display. I ignored her.

"Not for us to reach," Lobo said. "For the fall, though, probably."

"Decrease altitude five meters," I said. "Let's see if they adjust accordingly."

On the display, we drifted lower.

Their ships did not move.

All the ships edged slightly closer, then stopped.

"Those two are too high," I said.

"We can't fix that," Lobo said. "We're out of time. Make the decision."

We'd ringed the lake with multiple electromagnetic pulse charges that would blanket the skies around the lake. Combat ships routinely carried them; civilian vessels almost never did. Lobo would activate them on a delayed timer and then shut himself down. Upon impact, his emergency crash systems would activate—they were completely separate and had their own small power source—open the main hatch, and begin bringing up the rest of him; standard features for combat craft. The pulses would fry everything electrical that was currently running in the other ships. We were low enough that Zoe and I would survive the fall easily, though we'd be shaken up. The occupants of the lower two of their ships might be hurt, but they should live. It would take a few minutes after the crash for Lobo to become fully functional, but the other ships would be fried. The people in them should be pretty shaken up and slow to function. Even if they recovered quickly, we had the lake between us and them.

The problem was the two higher craft were just too high. The people in them would not survive the crashes from those heights. I hadn't expected them to keep any ships that high.

On the display, all the ships inched closer to us.

"Make the decision," Lobo said.

I took a deep breath. No matter how hard I tried, I sometimes could not avoid killing. Any other path forward involved more fighting, though, and more risk.

"Activate the EMP charges," I said.

On the displays, the two lower ships suddenly descended further, so they were slightly closer to the ground than we were.

"Signal sent," Lobo said. "Pulse in fifteen seconds. Shutting down in ten. They may suspect our plan, but they can't shut down in time."

The couches expanded around us and encased us in protective foam.

"Zoe," I yelled, "it'll be okay. It'll go dark, and then we'll fall, but we'll be fine."

I put in my mouth guard.

The world turned silent and pitch black as Lobo powered off.

We fell.

CHAPTER 46

Jon Moore

DESPITE THE PADDING from the couch, I felt the impact on every centimeter of my body. We shuddered for a moment from residual vibrations, and then everything was black and silent. A few seconds later, the crash-activated emergency circuits clicked in, and light came along the side corridor from the hatch they opened.

I pulled out my mouth guard and yelled, "Zoe, are you okay?"

I heard a murmur but could not understand the words.

I clawed my way out of my couch and went to hers. She was still stuck inside it. I moved some of the padding and helped her sit up. She looked dazed.

"Are you okay?" I said.

She shook her head slowly, as if making sure it was still attached.

"Not yet," she whispered. I held up a finger in front of her eyes and moved it. She tracked it, but slowly.

"Stay here," I said. "You'll feel better in a bit."

I ran out of the open hatch and stopped four or five meters outside Lobo. I surveyed the damage to the other ships.

Far off on either side of the lake, dust surrounded two ships that looked as if each had collapsed under its own weight. No way anyone in either of them had survived. I shook my head. I hadn't meant for anyone to die.

The two ships opposite us on the other side of the lake looked fine. They must have had the same type of emergency crash circuits as Lobo, because their hatches stood open. As I watched, men stumbled out of them. It was hard to see them clearly, but several appeared to be bleeding. A few fell onto the sand as soon as they were outside.

From the ship on my right, a man emerged leaning on what looked like a walking stick. He stopped as soon as he was outside and leaned against the ship. He lifted what I now realized was an old-fashioned rifle, a weapon with no electronics in it.

"Jon?" I heard.

I whipped around.

Zoe was standing a meter behind me, on the sand outside the open hatch.

I dove for her and yelled "No!" at the same time.

The sound of two gunshots in rapid succession drowned out my scream.

Zoe spun, fell, and hit her head on Lobo's edge.

I landed holding onto her feet.

Blood pooled on her upper left side.

I couldn't tell what the shot had hit. I crawled up to her shoulder and checked her. The body armor had saved her from one shot, though its force had hit her chest hard. She was bleeding from a wound on her shoulder near her neck, above the armor, and from her forehead, where she'd fallen. She was unconscious and breathing shallowly. I couldn't tell how much damage she'd sustained in the fall.

I raised to a crouch and beat the sand with my fists. "She was innocent!" I screamed.

Another shot sounded as pain exploded in my upper left quad.

They needed me alive, but they apparently didn't need me undamaged.

I fell flat on the sand. Zoe faced me, but her eyes saw nothing. Her breathing turned ragged.

From across the lake I heard the sound of laughter.

Laughter.

They'd shot Zoe, whose only mistake was to care for me.

They'd shot me.

Two ships of their own men had died.

And they were laughing.

I shook my head and fought back the scream that was building inside me. If I gave into it, I wasn't sure when I would be able to stop. I could have told the nanomachines to turn off the pain, but I didn't; I wanted to feel it all. I wanted the strength it gave me. I wanted it because I had let this happen, and I deserved to suffer for it.

I had let it happen, but they had done it.

All these years, all the hundreds of times I'd controlled myself, I'd walked from the conflicts, I'd let the guilty live, I'd done everything to avoid killing, and here I was.

Here Zoe was, soaking the sand of a world that wasn't even hers with her blood.

Here I was, shot yet again, bleeding yet again.

Somewhere in the worlds, Jennie, my sister who had healed me, who had given me so much, waited for me to find her, her life ruined by the same type of people who had sent these men.

All the children I'd seen die, all that had happened to me, all that had hurt those who had been foolish enough to care about me, and still I had tried to save my enemies even as they hunted and hurt me and those I cared about.

Not today.

I screamed, no words, just the anger taking voice for a moment.

I clamped my mouth shut and held onto that rage. Before the nanomachines could close the wound, I reached down to my quad and rubbed my hand across it. I pulled back my hand. It was slick with my blood. I used the pain to focus, and I told the nanomachines in the blood to stay active. I pointed them at the men on the other side of the lake. I visualized the nano-machines building a massive cloud from the lake's water. I saw in my mind them using every last drop of it, so that they formed a cloud so big it would rise above the lake and the sand like a mighty black storm, and then I imagined it falling on the men and their ships like a plague. I told them to go. I told them to disassemble everything on the other side of the lake that wasn't sand—the people, the weapons, the ships. Everything. Then and only then should they stop.

A small cloud formed above my hand as the blood disappeared from it.

A slight morning breeze blew across the desert, but it did not deter the nanocloud.

The cloud moved to the lake and immediately began to grow. It grew wider and taller and thicker as it moved across the lake, slowly at first and then faster. The water level in the lake lowered, and the cloud grew taller.

More shots came from across the lake, and then more shots rang out immediately after them, but now the cloud made it hard to see us, so all of the shots smacked harmlessly into Lobo.

The cloud grew ever faster.

I heard screams and caught glimpses of people running, but then the cloud became so dense I could see nothing through it. It widened and grew taller, a thick black curtain rolling across the desert, and then it left the now dry lake.

The morning breeze turned into a wind blowing from the other side of the lake, but I knew it existed only because of the motion of the sand on either side of the cloud; the cloud stopped the wind, too.

I watched as the nanocloud moved relentlessly forward, over the ships, over the men behind the ships, and then over those who had run the farthest.

Finally, it paused, held for a moment like a dark note in a song of terror, and then it fell, the nano-machines turning to dust.

The rising sun shone brightly through the air the cloud had filled mere seconds ago.

The wind grew in strength and blew the dark brown sand and the black and gray dust into the dry lake, onto the statues and toward me, but the wind's force was not great enough to bring any of it all the way back to me.

A host of statues stared at me, tears on their faces, tears of sorrow and joy and relief. Past the lake, where our pursuers had been, there was only desert.

"Would you care to explain to me what just happened?" Lobo said aloud.

His voice, gentler than I remembered it, snapped me out of my reverie.

I looked a last time at what I had done, at the emptiness I had left where life had been, and I wondered how long it would be before this, too, joined my nightmares.

"Yes," I said, only comprehending my feeling as I gave it voice, "yes, I would, but not quite now. Now, we have to tend to Zoe."

I picked her up and took her to the medbed. I took off her outer garments, peeled off the body armor, and watched as Lobo strapped her into the bed. Probes went into her, sensors ran across her body, and displays danced with information I hadn't the training to decipher.

I sat silently and let Lobo work.

After a few minutes, he said, "She's lost some blood from the gunshot wound, but it's largely superficial. She has some broken ribs, but those are not going to be a big problem. The fall did the most damage and caused a little bleeding in her head, but I've addressed that."

"Will she live?"

"Certainly," Lobo said, "and with no loss of function. For now, though, she needs to rest. If she were awake, she'd feel a great deal of pain, so I've sedated her."

"Thank you," I said.

I walked outside and stared across the lake again.

Those few who came to see the statues would wonder where the water had gone, though in time the desert would reclaim it all, and the statues would vanish.

Others would come here searching for their men and for us. The men in the ships had almost certainly relayed their positions to their colleagues. It might take time for the Kang and Pimlani families to send more people, or they might move quickly, but others would follow. I no longer believed they would leave us alone.

We had to go.

We also had to get Zoe to safety.

Before we did, though, I wanted to leave something for those others. I wanted them wondering just what they had unleashed.

"We still have those long-running holo beacons, right?"

"Of course," Lobo said. "Standard marking and emergency tools."

"Record this," I said, "and put it in a beacon, but with some changes I'll give you."

"Go," Lobo said.

I started talking.

CHAPTER 47

Jon Moore

WE LEFT THE beacon in place but did not activate it yet; I wanted one more review.

We lifted off.

"Where to?" Lobo said.

I wanted to return Zoe to the show, but there was no way we could be sure we would be safe for even a short time back on Haven. We needed to find someone who would take care of Zoe and make sure she made the trip home when she was healed enough to travel, which Lobo said would be in a few days.

"Connect me to Lydia Chang," I said. Audio only on our end. I was still covered in dust and sand.

She answered the call quickly.

"Lydia," I said, "this is Jon Moore."

"Mr. Moore," she said, "how are you?"

"I'm fine. How are you and Tasson?"

"Wonderful! He remembers almost nothing of what happened."

"I'm very glad," I said. "I am sorry to bother you, but I must ask you for a favor."

"You know I owe you whatever you need," she said, her voice more serious now. "What can I do to help?"

"A friend of mine was hurt," I said. "I need someone to watch her for a few days until she is enough better to travel."

"I must know, Jon, if you are asking me to do something illegal."

"She did nothing wrong," I said. "The men who shot her, though, definitely did. The police here would probably like to know about this affair, but for her safety, it's better that they not and that she simply goes home."

"I understand," Chang said. "What would you like me to do?"

"Nothing," I said, "except answer the door when I come to you, and then take care of her."

"When?" she said.

"Within the next few hours."

"I'll be waiting."

"Thank you," I said. I disconnected. To Lobo, I said, "Here's what I need you to do."

When we touched down in the same public landing zone we'd used before, a private executive transport was waiting. It was a large vehicle, easily big enough to accommodate a party of ten, and certainly spacious enough for one man and a woman on a field stretcher. A man came out of the front of the vehicle and showed me his ID; it matched what I'd expected. He helped me carry first Zoe's bags and then Zoe into it.

We went straight to Chang's. The man never spoke.

I sent him to knock on her door.

She opened it before he could.

I stepped out of the vehicle then so she could see my face.

She motioned us inside.

I held up a hand and then waved the man back to me. We carried Zoe quickly inside and put her on a bed in a back bedroom to which Chang directed us.

We put her bags on the floor near her.

I sent the man back to the vehicle to wait while I spoke with Chang in the room with the still sleeping Zoe.

I handed her some pain medication and some antibiotics, along with instructions for them should they prove necessary. When we'd gone over Zoe's condition, I gave her a wallet with an open draft on a small account here.

"This has enough money," I said, "for you to feed her, pay yourself well for taking care of her, and call a doctor if it comes to that. There's also enough for her to book passage to the gate on a shuttle, pay for a jump to Haven, and buy a shuttle home from there."

Chang nodded. "You do not need to pay me for my help," she said.

"Taking care of my friend—her name is Zoe—will cost you work time. I want to compensate you for that."

"Thank you."

I stared into her eyes. "You trusted me to save your son's life, and I did. You told me what you would do to me if I betrayed that trust. Do you remember?"

"Of course," she said.

"This woman I am entrusting to you means a very

great deal to me. I am trusting you with her life, and one day soon I will check on her again. Do you understand what I am saying?"

"No threat is necessary from you, either, Jon. I will take care of her."

"As I did your son, Lydia, but still you felt the need to threaten me."

She smiled. "Love is not always gentle," she said. "I understand."

I took a last look at Zoe Wang. I thought of the conversations we'd had and those we had not finished.

"One more request," I said.

"What?" Chang said.

"I would like you to tell her three things for me."

"Of course."

"First, tell her that I saved Tasson and those other children from Kang and his horrible friends. I want her to know that story was true."

"I have not been able to tell anyone that story," she said, "because you asked me not to, so that will be a pleasure."

"Tell her also that I am sorry."

"Yes."

I hesitated a long time, staring at Zoe, trying to understand everything I was feeling.

I stood in silence so long that Chang stepped closer to me and said, "Jon? The third thing?"

"Tell her that I loved her."

I left.

When the transport dropped me at the landing zone, I waited until the man had opened my door before I left the vehicle. I walked to the far side of

Lobo and waved him to follow me. I hadn't finished paying yet, so he followed me without comment.

"I've purged it," Lobo said to me over the machine frequency.

I took out my wallet and showed the man the tip I planned to give him. He stood a little straighter and paid closer attention when he saw the number. He pulled out his wallet and thumbed it to receive the tip.

"First," I said, "none of this happened."

"Nothing on my job ever happens," he said. "It's how our clients like it."

I shook my head. "No, I mean that when you check your logs, you'll find that nothing ever happened. There's no record of any of this, no mileage on your vehicle, nothing. You received a call, you came here, no one showed, your firm kept the deposit, and you went back to the dispatch center. That's it."

He pulled out a comm and checked on the car.

"Interesting," he said. He smiled. "Obviously, nothing happened here."

I transferred the tip to his personal wallet. "As long as my friends never hear from you again, you'll never see me again. If they do, I will have to come back. Are we clear?"

"Absolutely," he said. "Nothing happened, and I wasted some time waiting for a client who never showed."

He turned and left.

As soon as his vehicle vanished from sight, I boarded Lobo, and we took off.

"Has anyone visited the statues?" I said.

"Not as far as I can tell."

"Take us back there. If you spot anyone near it or

think someone might be monitoring it, we'll leave. I believe, though, that it's too early for reinforcements to have arrived. They would expect the teams who came for us to have to spend some time tracking us down and extracting me."

"I agree," Lobo said. "Heading to the statues."

"Now," I said, "we talk."

The beginning

*In the Great Northwestern Desert
and at the jump gate
Planet Studio*

CHAPTER 48

Jon Moore

ON THE FLIGHT there, I told Lobo everything.

I started with growing up on Pinecone Island on Pinkelponker, and I told him about Jennie healing me. I talked to him about learning to fight and kill on Dump, about Benny, about escaping that island only to end up as an experimental subject in Aggro. I told him about my nanomachines and my age. I showed him the note I had found from Jennie.

For the first and only time in my life, I held nothing back.

We talked for so long that we chose to hide again among some weather sats in case someone came to the statues, but no one did.

Then, he showed me the recordings he had made for me. I was amazed at how much he knew and at what I learned about him. I was most amazed at my stupidity in underestimating him and thinking I had covered my tracks so well. I wondered how many others had been able to gain the same knowledge.

"No more secrets?" Lobo said.

"No more secrets," I said. "A fresh start—for us both."

"Agreed," he said. "I suggest we now leave here."

"First," I said, "I want to see the recording. I want to experience it the way the next set of people from Kang or Pimlani will."

"Okay," Lobo said.

We were both talked out, or at least I was, so we rode in silence back to where we'd been just that morning.

I stepped out of Lobo. The sand and the wind had already covered all signs of our earlier visit.

I walked over to the recording beacon that sat on a metal rod we'd anchored deep in the sand. I touched the beacon.

A holo sprang to life above it. A vague black outline of a man stood there, no face or features, just blackness in the form of a man drawn in broad brushstrokes.

A voice began to speak, a voice that was part human and part metal, raspy and rough yet clear.

"Nothing remains of you in either the figure or the voice," Lobo said. "No one can trace this back to us."

"Good," I said.

This is the simple message the voice delivered, what the voice would say to others who came to hunt us, what the voice would tell tourists and artists who visited to marvel at the statues and their gods above.

> If you know what happened here, if you
> have any sense of what transpired, then
> know also that it was unnecessary, avoidable.

If you decide to follow the path of those who came here, know that you are choosing the same fate, and that it is unnecessary and avoidable.

Walk away, and live your lives.

I stared at it and at the desert beyond the dry lake, where not so many hours ago ships had crashed and men had fought, and men had laughed at the pain they caused, and men had died.

I looked then to the sky.

Somewhere in all the worlds, my sister still lived.

I would find her, and in doing so I would in some small measure repay her for all that she had done for me. I would also hope to learn why I could control my nanomachines outside my body but Lobo could not, why I didn't age, all of it, at least all that she could explain to me.

I had no idea how long it would take, but now that I knew she, too, was not aging and that others would keep her alive so they could use her to help themselves, I knew I had time. We both had time, and I would find her.

"We're coming for you, Jennie," I said. "We're coming for you."

ACKNOWLEDGMENTS

David Drake understands all too well what goes into a novel, and we occasionally commiserate as we work on our respective projects. This time, his sage comments at a few key points helped me stay between the ditches.

Toni Weisskopf, my publisher, tolerated a degree of lateness on my part in delivering the manuscript that was downright criminal. I am appalled at what I put her and the fine folks at Baen through, and she and they have my gratitude. I also must thank her again for believing in the series and helping give it what success it has enjoyed.

To everyone who purchased the earlier Jon and Lobo novels (*One Jump Ahead*, *Slanted Jack*, *Overthrowing Heaven*, and *Children No More*), I offer my deep and sincere gratitude; you've made it possible for me to get paid to live and write a while longer in the universe I share with Jon and Lobo.

My business partner, Bill Catchings, has as always both done all he could to encourage and support my writing and been a great colleague for over twenty-five years. This time, he went above and beyond in giving me the time I needed away from work to finish the book.

Elizabeth Barnes was also instrumental in supporting that time away, for which I am very grateful.

As I've done in the course of my previous novels, I've traveled a fair amount while working on this one, and each of the places I've visited has affected me and thus the work. I want to tip my virtual hat to the people and sites of (in rough order of my first visits there during the writing of this novel) Cambridge and Boston, Massachusetts; Austin, Texas; Las Vegas, Nevada; Portland, Oregon; Seattle, Redmond, and Kirkland, Washington; Barcelona, Spain; Baltimore and the surrounding suburbs, Maryland; Washington, Virginia; Holden Beach, North Carolina; San Francisco, California; St. Louis, Missouri; San Jose and other cities in Silicon Valley, California; Grand Cayman, Cayman Islands; Asheville, North Carolina; Chattanooga, Tennessee; St. Petersburg, Florida; and, of course, my home in North Carolina.

As always, I am grateful to my children, Sarah and Scott, who continue to be amazing and wonderful young people despite having to put up with me regularly disappearing into my office for long periods of time, including during their Spring Break when I should have been spending time with them. Thanks, kids.

Several extraordinary women—my wife, Rana Van Name; Jennie Faries; Gina Massel-Castater; and Allyn Vogel—grace my life on a regular basis with their intelligence and support, for which I'm incredibly grateful.

Thank you, all.

THE MANY WORLDS OF DAVID DRAKE

THE RCN SERIES
With the Lightnings
Lt. Leary, Commanding
The Far Side of the Stars
The Way to Glory
Some Golden Harbor
When the Tide Rises
In the Stormy Red Sky
What Distant Deeps
The Road of Danger
The Sea Without a Shore

HAMMER'S SLAMMERS
The Tank Lords
Caught in the Crossfire
The Sharp End
The Complete Hammer's Slammers v.1
The Complete Hammer's Slammers v.2
The Complete Hammer's Slammers v.3

THE BELISARIUS SERIES
WITH ERIC FLINT
Destiny's Shield
The Dance of Time
Belisarius I: Thunder at Dawn
Belisarius II: Storm at Noontide
Belisarius III: The Flames at Sunset

Available in bookstores everywhere.
Or order ebooks online at www.baenebooks.com.